CW00429580

Paul Blakey has been a chef for over thirty years. Quickly rising to head chef and winning several AA awards for fine dining. Originally from Sunderland, he has learned his trade from the lake district to the Channel Islands but found his spiritual home in Northumberland where he lives with his wife and son. Paul is an avid reader and fervent supporter of Sunderland Football Club.

This is his first novel.

For my wife, Debra, who bullied me into pressing the send button.
For Keith Floyd, who inspired me all those years ago to take up the craft of the saucepan.

Paul Blakey

THE COMPETITION

AUSTIN MACAULEY PUBLISHERS™

LONDON * CAMBRIDGE * NEW YORK * SHARJAH

Copyright © Paul Blakey 2022

The right of Paul Blakey to be identified as author of this work has been asserted by the author in accordance with sections 77 and 78 of the Copyright, Designs and Patents Act 1988.

All rights reserved. No part of this publication may be reproduced, stored in a retrieval system, or transmitted in any form or by any means, electronic, mechanical, photocopying, recording, or otherwise, without the prior permission of the publishers.

Any person who commits any unauthorised act in relation to this publication may be liable to criminal prosecution and civil claims for damages.

This is a work of fiction. Names, characters, businesses, places, events, locales, and incidents are either the products of the author's imagination or used in a fictitious manner. Any resemblance to actual persons, living or dead, or actual events is purely coincidental.

A CIP catalogue record for this title is available from the British Library.

ISBN 9781398461819 (Paperback)
ISBN 9781398461826 (ePub e-book)

www.austinmacauley.com

First Published 2022
Austin Macauley Publishers Ltd®
1 Canada Square
Canary Wharf
London
E14 5AA

1. The Jersey Incident

I have always hated chefs! Egotistical self-righteous arseholes. When it all comes down to it its only food, isn't it? Every TV channel you happen to turn on and there they are with their condescending smiles and bullshit supposedly simple methods, "this is so easy you can all do this at home." What utter shit! Yes, you can if you have a fully stocked larder the size of a two-bedroomed bungalow.

This sentiment regarding chefs I have always carried with me—and impress upon anyone else who will have the good grace to listen—but it still amazes people having been a chef myself for almost eighteen years and I suppose at the top of my game. Although, I must also confess that this has never stopped the love I feel towards this God-awful profession.

I will never forget the mocking laughter as I opened that first pay slip and stared in disbelief at the breakdown. Seventy hours, seventy-one quid and then the complete audacity to take a live-in payment for the shithole I had the privilege of inhabiting whilst I was there. A dirty, damp dwelling, generally unfit for human existence, with the odd mouse deposited by a mangy looking cat at your door for good measure.

Feeling a complete despair at my chosen vocation, I very nearly left the trade there and then. But mam and dad took me for a pint at the local 'Slaughtered Lamb' Inn and in between several distinctly watered-down, ammonia smelling beverages, we discussed my choices.

"Either come home with me and mam now," dad said, "or try sticking it out for another week, get to know the place a bit better along with the people and see how it goes. It's not a problem for us whatever you decide what you want to do."

It was always that simple for dad, he never pushed my younger brother or myself into anything we didn't want to. A remarkable man really, he had his first heart attack at twenty-nine, plus two more before the age of forty, the fourth one killed him, but he was eighty-three then. Can't imagine the stressful sales job he had along with the sixty or seventy cigarettes a day helped but it was a different time back then.

Mam actually brought cigarettes into the hospital after his third heart attack as some doctors believed them to be good for you. Needless to say he—along with the recommendations of a "little Asian doctor" his words I believe—stopped there and then and had over forty years of good living to come.

Mam was the same, tough generation back then, home help for years, found many a colleague crying in the street and a dead client sitting on the toilet in their final repose. She would make them a cuppa—the colleague, not the deceased—and sort the recently departed ready for the emergency services and always tried to give them a little dignity in death.

So, I made a decision there and then which would shape the rest of my life which was to try and stick it out, see how it went for the foreseeable and try and carve myself some sort of career. If it all went tits up, I would simply return home to my parents' open arms and support and try something else. But as it happened, days turned into weeks and so on and so forth and before I knew it, I was an important part of the team.

Long days and longer nights were the norm for the next few years. Different hotels up and down the country—with the same shitty live-in arrangements—and with the same results. Nightclubs, booze, drugs and fighting (always enjoyed a good scrap) and pretty much all-nighters. Thankfully, most of this was after the kitchen service was over, *most* of it, but it was not unusual for a fight to happen in mid service.

Sometimes, it was a young commis being disciplined by an older more senior chef, the kitchen was run like the armed forces (it wasn't called a brigade for nothing). A young chef would be taken to a walk-in fridge and systematically taken apart by verbal and often physical violence.

Once, a chef was for something quite insignificant beaten with a frozen turbot, sounds funny now but the kid was bleeding from nose, cheek and eye by the time it was over. Looking back now I personally would have chosen something cheaper than a turbot and now running my own kitchen I'd never freeze such a beautiful and expensive product anyway.

Some of our parties would end up continuing until the daylight hours and we'd manage to get back to the kitchen and grab a couple of hours kip on the butchers' block before the breakfast chef came in and told us to fuck off out. After begging a bacon butty from the disgruntled breakfast chef (always miserable bastards) and then dashing back to our rooms for our whites, we would be back in the kitchen. Stinking of booze and fags but ready to get down to some graft, which seemed impossible at 8 *a.m.* but in no time at all we'd be in full swing and the previous night's exploits were forgotten.

Promotions for me followed quickly and I rose to Sous chef within two years. It was a huge brigade but I had an uncanny capacity to cope with, on the one hand being a raging drunk—which I'd become by now and I was still early twenties—and on the other a quick witted, calculating and competent cook. I could tear down any other chef's perceived confidence effortlessly while at the same time benefitting my own progress.

Because of this ruthless streak, chefs that had recently been drinking partners with me began to steer clear which suited me just fine (a little act of violence would reinforce this notion if someone became over familiar). I had had enough of their bullshit as they just weren't on or, in fact, anywhere near my level.

They couldn't compete with me professionally and began to fear me personally, so it was only to be expected I'd be ostracised from the usual crowd that I'd partied with. That was fine by me and came as a blessed relief. I knew I'd always had this dark side from a very young age and not being particularly empathetic or sympathetic to my peers meant that now I frequently worked alone. Rarely did I need help or advice.

What came out of this situation was that I became interested—(and probably pushed towards by the head chef to try and regain some kind of control over his brigade, as he too was scared shitless of me)—in competition work. It was me out there on my own with no one else to rely on. I became proficient, ruthless and successful.

I loved travelling the lengths of the country to compete with every kind of chef you can imagine. The French boys had the confidence but weren't as good as they liked to think. It seemed I'd found my niche and from here I'd thrive, I believed it, fuck them all! That was all I wanted or needed. I racked up win after win and my CV looked increasingly impressive.

Live competitions gave me the buzz but there is only so many of these per year and every hotel's budget for competitions is finite. It was always with a heavy heart that I'd return to the drudgery of normal working life after a competition had ended and have to face the incompetence of the brigade.

I found I also had one other problem as I clocked up the competition wins; promotions had dried up in the hotel and as my reputation for being a no nonsense and obnoxious cunt increased over the years; other hotels would not employ me either. The risk was too much for them even though the reputation for the hotel for your regular punter would increase with highfalutin competition wins plastered all over the reception walls.

But because I wasn't likeable, I wasn't likely to be put forward or snapped up for the real prizes that I had so deeply coveted, the prizes I felt I'd always been heading towards, the TV shows.

As much as I hated those TV chefs, that's where the money and fame was but I just wasn't quirky enough, wasn't witty, not what the public wanted *they* said. No more was the raging Pierre White character idolised, the bullying Ramsey was laughable.

I was shunned for the likes of *Great British menu*, *MasterChef: the professionals*, no one would touch me on that score. I couldn't have it all as I'd wanted and I envied and begrudged all those guys who had the appeal and presence to stand in front of the camera.

Because of this conundrum I found myself in (the complete lack of promotions and TV work), I sank into a deep depression and gradually lost all faith in the industry. Eventually the competitions became farcical for me, the people unbearable and the restaurant customers ridiculous in their expectations.

I was never going to change, didn't want to change as I was such a stubborn bastard, so I decided a rethink was needed. I felt I needed to get out and away from the constraints of England and my notorious reputation. Nothing stupid like shelling oysters for pennies in some shithole shack in Alabama, I wasn't that far gone, I still had *some* self-respect.

My colleagues could see I was dangerously unhappy. As well as keeping their distance from me which was a blessed relief, I could see they were hoping and praying I'd leave and ply my misery on some other kitchen or better still in some other country.

So, what should I do? I finally took the plunge and decided to leave for a little while and regroup, not too far but far enough to start over. I'd work up a new style of CV in somewhere such as Ireland, Northern France or possibly even Jersey? I'd known a couple of guys who'd gone out to Jersey and thrived and I didn't think after competing with them that I could stomach the French on their home turf.

It was supposed to be a nice place Jersey, old folk's heaven was what I had always imagined. An easy way of life and a little bit continental, perhaps even a bit of sun? I didn't stop to think too long, I had no ties, so off I went. It was easy to get a job and with a wonderful reference from my chef—(funny that)—I left for the island haven. Never had I seen a team of chefs so relieved to be rid of me.

The new job was in a busy little hotel in a picturesque, secluded bay in the north east corner of the island called Rozel. An old Napoleonic fort that had been converted, the tide would reach and touch the hotel walls twice a year as we were literally on the beach.

Around the bay there were a couple of bars and café's, also a local pub and one other hotel set back up in the hillside. It was finally a head chefs' position and at the age of thirty-two it was not before time, it was good money, good tips and also a percentage of the restaurant takings, happy days. This was my chance to start over and I hoped I could keep my demons at bay and make it work.

***

And that's how it went for the first two years. Work was hard, fourteen-hour days, six days a week but satisfying nonetheless. St Helier was quite a party town and on my one day off a week I was able to get suitably pissed in some quirky bars while also enjoying the mild climate and good food.

Some nights I could sit on the beach at Rozel and see fireworks off the coast of France as a celebration of some kind was taking place. The pompous local or the 'Jersey Bean' was to be avoided but could be tolerated as there was another much more irritating 'local' to steer clear of, the Portuguese.

They had their own bars—(to be avoided at all costs)—clubs and food and would turn their nose up at anything else that wasn't *their* way. Slowly but surely, over what were generally enjoyable years, those opinionated, self-absorbed fuckers began to grind me down. It was always about self-preservation with that lot, nothing was ever their fault and they had the biggest chip on their shoulders you could ever imagine.

I'd always thought that Jersey would have been full of French seeing how you could see the French coastline from Rozel, I couldn't have been more wrong. Portuguese were everywhere, they had come to Jersey in the middle of the twentieth-century to aid the tourism and farming industry on the island and there they had settled. Obnoxious to say the least with their seventies taste in clothes, mullet hair styles and ridiculously outdated political views.

One lunchtime just before our usual busy service of coffin dodgers and their freshly picked crab sandwiches, we caught one of our Portuguese kitchen porters beating the shit out of his wife in the staff canteen while the other waiters and barmen (also Portuguese) just sat and looked on in mild amusement. And why? Because she couldn't carry the tray with *his* lunch on it!

I am not particularly endeared to anybody, but I took him outside—with my Sous chef trying to stop me as we had an audience—and beat the crap out of him. He was a big bastard which made me even more infuriated as his wife was this tiny snip of a thing. It felt good, the crunch of bone beneath my fists, the blood and the anger. He deserved it I have no doubt, was I wrong to do it? Perhaps, did I care? No, not at all, I revelled in it.

It was the first time the rage had got the better of me and I'd let the beast from the cage in such a long time. The problem was, as is usually the case the wife went straight back to him, probably out of fear no doubt and the owners of the hotel were even less impressed.

I could see the wife of the owner secretly agreed with what I'd done and had sympathy with what they had to do, but they couldn't condone that sort of behaviour and that was it. I was shown the door, no reference, no severance, kiss my arse, nothing. Nearly twenty-six months of hard profitable work with nothing to show for it as the sole reason for going to Jersey in the first place had been the building of a new CV, a new life.

I had cash, I'd worked so long and didn't spend much except for the odd bottle of whisky, so I decided to linger on the island for a while, getting drunk and fucking whatever I could. I lived in a shitty bed and breakfast just on the outskirts of St Helier, the owner was a repellent rat of a man and didn't much care what you got up to as long as you paid the rent. You would regularly see him in a dirty string vest, almost a parody of Rab C Nesbitt, cigarette hanging from the corner of his mouth and stinking of stale sweat and booze.

Not the impression you would ever have of Jersey and somewhere the tourists wouldn't think existed in a beautiful tax haven such as this. The rooms were filthy, infested with mice and there was even a vending machine with porn videos to rent right next door to the little hatch that served as his reception.

Thankfully, after a few beers in the local shithole bar, it was possible to get a warm female body for the night, people had needs and the island was not exempt from this. This became the way of things for me for several quite content months, but I should have realised that things didn't always work out like that

12

and that Jersey being such a small island I'd run into a certain kitchen porter at some point.

It happened as I left the local piss head bar that every town seems to have, same faces every night, bit smelly, sticky floor, the tourists never went in, furiously avoided the place like the plague. I had a feeling someone was following me as I stepped out into a typical sultry Jersey evening, I could taste the salt of the sea, mixed in with the fugue that lingered round the door of the bar from the cloud of smokers squinting into their own cigarettes.

I purposely walked on for a while into the backstreets then into an even more secluded spot amongst the discarded kebab wrappers and used condoms, fuck it I thought as I'm sure every drunk does and believes that he can fight the world. I threaded my keys between my knuckles and pretended to piss in the corner behind a particularly rank smelling wheelie bin and waited for the confrontation.

And when it came, I was ever so slightly disappointed in the fact that he was drunker than me. Silly bastard didn't even connect with his first swing and screamed—which was like a warning to me so any surprise he thought he had dissipated immediately—as he hit the wall behind me and squealed like a child as his knuckles smashed into brick. I spun round as quick as any drunk spins and laid an assault upon his face and head with repeated vicious blows, his face pretty much came apart with such a satisfaction that I found myself grinning as I rained blow after blow upon him, he crumpled in a heap, but I didn't stop there.

I just kept going until I realised that his face wasn't really much of a face anymore but a bloody pulp. He just lay there, was he breathing? Jesus, was he dead? Possibly, did I hang around and make sure? No. Did I laugh maniacally as I ran down back lanes and alleyways? I certainly did. Having had a quick reccy for cameras as I departed, I assumed (and was later proved correct) that there was nothing to worry about on that score.

I found a muddy puddle to wash some of the grime and gore from my hands and face then quickly headed back to my rooms, thankfully as I entered the building the landlord was face down on his desk, an empty bottle of Jack Daniels still clutched in his hand. I raced up the stairs and fumbled my keys into the lock, fell into the room then drew the curtains closed and collapsed onto the bed as the adrenaline started to abate.

I looked down at myself and realised that I was splattered with blood; thankfully once I had calmed myself, I'd passed very few people and they hadn't so much as offered me a second glance. I stripped naked and bagged up my clothes in a bin liner, I'd dispose of them later after I'd showered. I had to scrub my fingernails as they had blood and skin lodged beneath.

Once clean, I dressed in the darkest clothes I had and took the bin bag with me back out into the night. After walking for a mile or two in the opposite direction from where the incident had happened and then finding a building site, I deposited the clothes individually between skips and buried them deep beneath all kinds of the site's detritus.

They would not be found I was quite sure as they didn't exactly stand out as they were now covered in cement dust and grime and were, therefore, almost unrecognisable as clothing. Jersey had umpteen building sites at the time as there was always a mass of projects ongoing and there were many sites much closer to the scene of the crime than the one I'd chosen.

Walking back to my room, again I passed very few people, the ones I did were pissed and barely glanced my way. I therefore, attracted no undue attention whatsoever and arriving back at my digs the landlord was thankfully still passed out dribbling saliva down his chin and onto his desk. Back in my room and sitting on my bed, I mulled over what I'd done.

It wasn't that I felt any kind of guilt towards the mess I'd left behind and most certainly no remorse or regret, the problem I had was whether or not I'd been recognised. Or whether he'd been seen following me, I could only hope and pray that I could remain unidentified. I decided to keep my head down and stay in my rooms, I'd keep an eye on the headline news, make sure the local police (laughable really, some of them were farmers for God's sake) had no clear leads to follow.

The body was found by the bin men the next day, "*Badly beaten and left to die*" was the tag line, with a picture of the victim and one of the refuse workers—(desperately trying not to look proud at his discovery)—who'd found him. An investigation was ongoing, but they had no description of the assailant and no idea how he came to be there.

The police presence would be increased on the streets, but they seemed to think it was a random unmotivated attack—possibly within the Portuguese community—and probably drink or drugs induced and most *definitely* an isolated case as this sort of thing didn't happen in the Channel Islands.

After a month of barely leaving my accommodation and living like a hermit, scrutinising the news and becoming increasingly and dangerously relaxed and nonchalant about what I'd done, I decided Jersey wasn't an option anymore. The investigation into the murder seemed to have got nowhere, at least the papers barely mentioned it now and I couldn't go on living like this. Although the derelict wreck of a landlord was increasingly looking at me strangely, although that was probably just my paranoia.

I'd have to start earning again at some point and there seemed little or no reason for me to stay here, so I thought I would get out while I could and maybe it was time to head back to the mainland and contact my old agency. Hopefully, they had something for me and the two and a half years had been enough of a hiatus, who knows maybe I could literally get away with murder?

This invigorated me to think that it was that easy, I hadn't even been careful, I had no previous, so even if DNA etc was picked up I wasn't on file anywhere. I packed light throwing my remaining clothes into a case and the room key at the landlord. He tried to extract a little extra cash from me for giving up the room without notice but he soon gave up when he realised that I had no intention of giving him a bean and the intimidating pose I had adopted obviously reinforced that.

I flagged down a taxi for the airport; there were no flights for a few hours but that was fine, I bought the ticket and headed off to the lounge for a beer.

Amazingly, the police were everywhere. Shit, I hadn't expected this, I thought the bumbling Jersey authorities had been completely incompetent but clearly I'd been wrong. I felt my pulse increase and my heartbeat pounded in my ears as I ordered a beer next to a rozzer getting a coffee.

The lounge wasn't particularly busy, so I felt scrutinised at every turn, at one point the policeman turned to me and asked, "where are you heading today and what's the purpose for your journey, sir? Passport please?"

With the sweat rolling down my back and what I hoped was casual I said, "Just off home for a holiday, visit the folks, then back here to graft in a week or two."

Hopefully, I would not have to explain that both my folks were actually dead. With what seemed like an eternity he held onto my passport and looked firstly at me then down at the passport photo several times without saying a word. I was just about to try and run for it (God only knows where, as Jersey was only nine miles by five miles long!) when he handed me my passport and with a cheery voice said, "have a pleasant journey, sir."

15

Smiling I said, "thank you, officer, I shall try my very best" as I raised my pint in mock salute and wandered off to quietly shit myself in the corner of the bar.

When we landed in Newcastle it was hardly surprising that it was pissing down, dark clouds as far as the eye could see and it looked like there wasn't going to be any let up for a while. I checked into the Holiday Inn, a soulless place if ever there was one and phoned my agent. After the false platitudes and bullshit, he offered me several job opportunities all in the North of the country and all decent money—(my self-imposed Jersey exile obviously forgotten)—and something I could work with and improve.

He got to work, setting up the interviews asap and I sat in the bar working my way through a couple of beers and an inedible burger. It felt good to be back in the north and I felt good about my prospects back on home turf, I'd be back in a kitchen, head down, graft hard and then get back on the competition scene. Who knows maybe I could try and be a little more accommodating with the other competitors or maybe not?

2. Home Again

I'd been in a job for over six months when the rumours of a new format of TV competition started to circulate, this was going to be bigger, better and combine more than just the usual studio-based TV crap and all applicants were welcome. The hotel I had been working in for these past few months was an up and coming newly refurbished country house in Northumberland with stunning views of the Northumberland coast along with bespoke rooms, fine dining restaurant, funky bistro, pool, golf course and state of the art gym.

The owner was some software genius and had made his billions and retired at thirty-eight (lucky bastard). We had the best of equipment, great local suppliers and some competent staff, things were good, I felt content and even more optimistic when the owner expressed an interest in me entering the competition.

"You've got to keep cool Jack; remember, you're representing not just the hotel but me also, these things aren't cheap to fund."

Jesus what did he think I was, a fuckin amateur? What a bell-end and tight bastard to boot, but if it meant getting an opportunity at this new style of competition then I'd keep my council and crack on. I gently reminded him of my competition track record and that nobody else competing at the moment was as successful as I'd been.

This new competition would be something never tried before, ten chefs, a remote Northumbrian location, living on your own in a basic cabin with basic amenities, foraging, deer stalking, fishing and all done on your lonesome. No outside interference whatsoever, each chef would be miles apart, maps and basic orienteering gear would be provided.

Not only having to live day by day but also thinking on your feet, fending for yourself, who knows maybe I'd track down the other chefs and torment the shit out of them, one month alone, bliss! It would be one month in the wild to gather what was needed and to prepare the final dishes—four in total—balance, taste and textures would be judged by four top industry chefs (wankers), along with resourcefulness.

The judges would be revealed at a later date once you had completed a preliminary round which was a CV and an essay on why you felt you could cope and overcome the harsh parameters of the competition. I'd been shooting several times, I was a decent enough shot and always fished as a kid with dad, as a chef the foraging had become part of the daily routine for a remote hotel so none of these things were particularly daunting for me.

There would be a gamekeeper, a survivalist and several other *experts* who would be in charge of the rifles and shotguns and these could only be used for the first two days when they were present and only under their strict safety regulations. Apart from the first two days with the experts, there would be no actual persons monitoring or checking up on us, once we were out there, we were to be on our own.

A system of getting in touch would be made available to us on the day of arrival at our destination but these were not to be used unless you wanted to exit the competition. Once you got in touch through injury or illness, or you had just had enough then that was it and you defaulted the competition.

I felt this was going to be the one for me, I was the most exhilarated I'd been since my exploits in Jersey and the thought of going up against chefs in the wild sounded great, the competition would start in two months' time, so I'd get myself in the best physical shape in the time I had, already fit it wouldn't take much to be ready. The list of competitors would be released within a couple of weeks and I'd be interested to see who had the balls for it.

The date was set for a mid-October start, game season well under way, plenty of bounty to be had from early pheasant to Roe deer. Depending on where I was to be housed for the month, there could be mussels to gather if close to the coast, rivers to fish for brown trout, herbs and mushrooms in abundance, Northumberland was massive. I was becoming more and more excited by the prospect of being out on my own, plus it was the added bonus of getting out of the kitchen for a month, thrilling stuff.

Mid October would also mean the weather could be very changeable, tough conditions, at times a bleak barren landscape, but also heavily forested. Beautiful in the early summer but could be incredibly inhospitable from October onwards, perfect for a northerner, not sure how the southern shandy drinkers would adapt to it.

The winnings would be an added incentive to stick it out, fifty-grand to the winner, not just for producing the dishes at the end but also for the whole endurance side of things, the Duke of Northumberland—well known for his charity work—would be footing the bill, as it was seen as a showcase for Northumberland and all its rural and rugged beauty.

***

The competitors have just been made public and there have been some interesting characters popped up, most of them are known to me, the boss seemed quietly confident about my chances.

"So, Jack, how are you feeling since the list was released, confident?" he said.

"Yeah," I replied, "quite a mixed bag by the looks of it. I've worked with a couple of them over the years, I don't feel there's too much to worry about."

"This is different from anything else you've done in the past; I hope complacency isn't an issue?"

"Not at all and let's remember it's different for all of us, none of these guys have done anything like this before either."

"True, Jack, true. You going to play nice when you're out there?" he asked.

"Not at all, boss, I'll do everything within my means to win, the money is a great incentive but if this is the first of many of these competitions then this is the one to triumph in. Everyone remembers the first winner, no one remembers the second."

"Ha-ha, very good and I'm glad to hear it, I didn't get to retire at thirty-eight by playing nice!"

I thought yeah we know just fuck off you smug cunt, but replied enthusiastically, "Absolutely boss!"

He liked to tell us on a weekly basis how young he was when he retired.

I could tell he was as excited as I was but whereas I had no worries or fears, seeing past his bravado he was troubled with stories of my past and how far I was willing to take things, I as well as some of the other staff had confided certain things to him over the odd beer but not to the extent of what had actually happened. I liked the thrill of someone knowing what I may be capable of but I'm not a complete muppet to tell them the truth.

"At least we're up in Northumberland Jack, and you have some knowledge of the weather and terrain up here, some of them won't know what's hit them, that north east wind is a fucker!" he said.

"It is indeed," I replied, "I've been in and amongst this county all my life, I'm running four and five times a week and I'm in the gym after work most nights, so I'll be ready."

I wanted to be the fittest I'd ever been, I wasn't going to take any chances with my personal ability to survive if the conditions were as tough as I hoped they would be.

With that and a brief nod of his head he left me to my devices, I still had service to prep for and a wedding tomorrow. Most of the chefs were enjoying that I was going to the competition but more for the fact I'd be out of their hair for a month, which is unheard of. Let's hope they don't fuck it up while I'm away.

When I arrived home after the gym I showered and had a bite to eat, my flat was small but new, I had some home comforts, laptop, PlayStation, fifty-inch TV and a quality Bang and Olufsen stereo which was all I really needed. The flat was situated in the small village of Longshorseley, which was pleasant enough, reasonably quiet but as always had the obligatory council estate and undesirable element.

I had no significant other, no one to rely on me so I could be as selfish as I liked, I was always alone but never lonely. I'd cut back on the booze while I got myself ready for the competition, but I'd be sure to take several decent bottles of single malt with me when it began. I settled in with a coffee to do a little research and make some notes on the competitors and film crew.

There was to be a presenter named Phillip Schroder who would be hosting the competition for the TV, he'd be bivouacked somewhere with all the comforts we wouldn't have and pretend to be slumming it with the rest of us. He was well past his prime and if I remember correctly, there was some scandal involving underage girls and the BBC, but the evidence was not substantiated and the lucky bastard walked free.

It had hung about him ever since though like a bad smell, he was obviously guilty but unproven, he'd been shunned for years and from what I could gather this was his big chance for redemption and getting back into the limelight. Recent photos of him showed how much he'd aged and how out of shape he was; fuck me what a mess; I think he's only mid-fifties, obviously been hitting more than just the Pringles in the mini bar.

3. The Competitors

Joseph Pritchard

Standing at least six five there was no doubting Joe's presence, a monster of a fella, at about thirty-eight years old; he's only a couple of years older than me and hails from some shithole in Dorset and has a sordid history of bullying. But that's it with Joe, a bully.

He has very rarely come to blows as his size put people off, while obviously one to watch as he would think he was suited to the conditions (because of his self-professed prowess), but he's just a big unfit fucker. Bluster won't cut it with this competition, he has to back it up and I just don't think he will cut the mustard when it comes down to it.

He'd done well in his cooking career, gained three rosettes at several places and even a Michelin quite early on when he was only twenty-eight and still hungry for recognition, but he seemed to be a journey man, which told me he got bored quickly and a month in the wilds of Northumberland might be just the thing to get that cut and run gene in motion.

He had a family, two feral kids, ten and thirteen and an estranged wife; wouldn't surprise me if he were beating the shit out of her, he was obviously signed up for this for the money, naive and stupid. I'd met Joe on a couple of occasions previously, never worked with him but had spoken to him briefly at the *Salon Culinaire live theatre,* while he was picking up a bronze medal to my gold.

The other time we had bumped into each other was in *The Nags Head* in Covent Garden, I'd been in London on a scouting mission to try out a couple of restaurants whose chefs would be competing against me and I was enjoying a quiet pint. I'd tried to ignore him when he approached me to blather on about some such shite, but he was pissed up and wouldn't take the hint.

In the end I'd threatened to stick my beer glass in his head and he'd slunk away suitably chastised like the child he was to his equally drunk pals, he'll be one not to turn my back on if our paths cross in the competition.

William Cohen (Fatty)

Not a great deal I can say about this useless fat slob, he's got to be twenty-five stone (obviously single) enters every competition going, fails every time to even get placed but for some reason still perseveres. You could say he had heart to keep going like he does but why bother when you're so shit?

Strange thing is he actually thinks he's good at what he does and then looks perplexed when he fucks it up again. He is the most unkempt chef I've ever had the displeasure to meet, he smells like a pig pen and yet he still finds employment. I have absolutely no fears of meeting him in the competition as he'll probably not last a week!

Think he's of eastern European heritage but has been in England for most of his life, now lives somewhere in the home counties, so he'll probably have a nosebleed when he has to come so far north. He's quite tight with Pritchard as they've frequently worked together and are roughly the same age.

Alex Simmons

A Yorkshire girl, Alex could be the one to watch, thirty years old, excellent cook, super fit, tough cookie and ruthless. I look forward to going up against her, she has a reputation in the trade for a no-nonsense approach to food, life and everything else in between. Her wife is Asian and also a chef, the pair don't work together as they'd probably kill each other but out of work they're the perfect couple.

A little cliched what with the blue hair, sleeve tattoos and nose piercings but still the one too watch. Alex rose quickly through the ranks to the position of head chef and from there, she has gained two AA rosettes everywhere she's been, meticulous in her planning and always makes her employers money, she has the same hardcore crew everywhere she goes and runs an incredibly tight ship, promotes from within and protects her team.

I truly admire her, but once the game begins, she's just another one I need to defeat or destroy, whichever comes first. Yes, I shall relish this challenge, may have to sabotage whatever progress she makes if she is in striking distance and the threat is genuine.

Sohaib Kahn (Subi)

Know very little about this guy, he's of Pakistani origin, very quiet but from what I can gather a good cook, small wiry fella, about twenty-five years old. Been in England most of his life, although born in Pakistan; runs a funky bistro in central London and I can't for the life of me understand why he'd do a competition like this, he's never so much as stepped foot out of the capital and has never entered a competition of any kind before, very strange. I shall endeavour to find out more but for the most part this guy is an enigma.

Charlie Dickens (Bos)

His parents must have been pissed when they named this arsehole, he's the biggest gobshite I've met and I'm sure he thinks pretty much the same of me. He's a pretty boy, the girls love him until they realise what a cunt he is; his self-professed shagging antics are well known in the trade but how much of it is true is anyone's guess.

I worked with 'Bos'—that's what he likes to be called, I'm sure he gave himself the nickname as very few people who we work with would know the significance of it—briefly in the nineties at a small hotel in Kendal, lake district. A fractious few month ensued until it was deemed necessary for me to put him on his arse outside of a local pub, I left Kendal soon after and we've met only briefly on a couple of occasions since.

He is disliked as much as me but mostly for being so far up his own arse, a good cook I'll grant you but such a dick with it. I'm almost convinced he's only in this comp to try and get to me somehow, this could be interesting and an opportunity to cause some real discomfort to him. I will relish this encounter and hopefully his overconfidence will be his downfall. He's worked all over the UK and currently runs a restaurant in Derby, where he has an excellent reputation for quality English food with a modern take, fresh local produce and a passion for foraging in the local area.

According to a magazine article he is thirty-two, married and with a kid, two years old. Hard to believe someone could put up with him enough to actually have a child with him and what's even more exasperating is to think that he could actually father a child. Another one to watch but talent wise not as troublesome as Alex, he won't even consider her a threat as his self-confidence is so high.

Orry Jones

Bit of a shock here but I actually quite like this kid, he's twenty-four, good cook, decent lad. Worked with him for several months in a small Bistro when I was younger, he's conscientious, clean, tidy and there's no bullshit with him. If he doesn't know something, he asks otherwise he can be left to his own devices and very rarely let's anyone down. This lad will go all the way to the top I have no doubt but there'll be no sentiment on my part once we're in the thick of it, another one to watch but maybe a bit too soon for him.

He's working down in the midlands in a nice-looking place, few accolades and a good reputation, he's single—probably gay but hasn't come out yet—so no baggage to worry about, therefore he should be wholly committed to winning. Pretty sure he told me once his name came from a Patrick Swayze character as his mum was in love with dear old Patrick; fuck me, we had all thought it was made up or some kind of ridiculous nickname. I heard once that an old head chef of his had called him *Roy* for the whole time he was there as he wouldn't acknowledge that Orry was even a legitimate name.

Harry Celestine

If there was ever going to be a wildcard then this fella is it, why in god's name a fifty-four-year-old would enter this kind of competition is beyond my reckoning. He's not exactly sane, sober or fit, he's unemployed again (because of the booze) and absolutely unhinged. If our paths cross out there in the sticks then it's not going to be pretty, he's quite a big fella and he's one scary bastard.

Thankfully, I've never had the pleasure of working in one of his kitchens, but I understand they're not for the faint hearted. He has a number of assault charges to his name, mostly against aggrieved chefs and most of the assaults have taken place within the kitchen. He's had regular drunk and disorderly charges, has no driving license (obviously) and has been married more times than I care to know, four kids that he knows of and from what I can gather it's no surprise he lives on his own now in some shithole in Middlesbrough.

Can't understand why he's entered this competition, he'll probably wind-up dead in his bunk having drank himself into a stupor and died in his sleep. It'll not be a great loss to humanity if this scenario plays out, an absolute bum.

***

There was only going to be eight of us now, one place hadn't been filled—strange I thought—and one guy had dropped out after the line-up was revealed. That could have been my fault but probably it'd been Harry's name on the list, which either scared the shit out of them or brought back previously thought forgotten disturbing trauma caused by said Harry.

It was an interesting list of names, some fearsome competitors but I felt quietly confident that I could definitely outlast them physically and I was confident in my ability to cook with whatever I could lay my hands on. The one thing that does bother me is the idea that I could go too far. Extremes and breaking down any barrier, whatever it may be holds very little fear for me and I know I enjoy—in the words of *Alex and his Droogs, "a bit of the old ultra-violence!"*

I always felt empathy was a possibility, albeit a distant one or at least I could empathise with a certain demographic. But I don't know if this is real, conditioned (from my schooling and good upbringing) or just me, kidding myself and that when it comes down to it, I can be the most heartless, ruthless cunt there is. Time will tell and I must remain focussed on the job at hand, I want to win and win, no matter what it takes, I can feel this is it, this competition is going to put me on the map.

4. Postponement

I have just received an email to say the competition has been postponed for a month, this is excellent news. Sunday, 15th November will now be the start date, the email claimed, "that's so we can have you back to your families for Christmas". *Ha,* like I give a fuck about that, more like we can have you back in your respective kitchens for Christmas.

The weather will most definitely be deteriorating by then and it'll give me a bit more time to train, I'm feeling great now, so by then I should be in peak physical shape. I will not even have had a beer for months never mind anything stronger, no one with the exception of Alex will be able to compete with me physically, but I feel mentally, no one will.

Apparently, the reason behind the postponement is Phillip bastard Schroder, the dirty old fucker has supposedly sprained an ankle in a fall whilst out on a run, a run? What a crock of shit, he's obviously taken a tumble while pissed up and it's too late to replace him, so much for his big chance at redemption, obviously cares more about his drink and drugs addiction.

In his recent photographs he has the distinctive look of an ageing Oliver Reed, those drawn red haunted eyes desperately trying to mask it with his beguiling smile (and another whiskey), what an utter prick, has a man ever looked more guilty or desperate. He's going to be an easy target, not just for me but the likes of Harry, Joe and especially Bos (the self-proclaimed silver-tongued git) will have his life, even if it's only a brief skirmish with the fool.

Suppose I should be thanking him as I truly feel the later in the year we get the better I'll be able to adapt, can you imagine if it snows? Not unheard of in November, I shall have to pack accordingly.

Most of my kit is complete, amazing to think you can still purchase hunting knives as long as you have *a good reason for it.* Posters and adverts are everywhere in the local area and beyond advertising the competition, so very little explanation was needed as to why I'd need such a large *Bowie* style knife.

I've tried to cover every possible weather scenario even down to an old set of snowshoes—I purchased at an old army and navy store—climbing ropes (not that there'd be much climbing involved but you never know), plenty of winter clothing, extra skins and a few sets of thermal underwear.

I also have a robust sleeping bag, headlamp, torch (extra batteries), matches and a lighter (extra fuel), first aid kit, compass, a self-erecting tent, fishing gear, chocolate bars (lots, always an essential in case stranded as they can sustain energy levels), a journal and pencils to keep a record of day-to-day happenings.

The email also gave us details of the lodges provided which are basically elevated wooden huts (Hagrid's cottage from the Harry Potter series springs immediately to mind). Basic but will give us running water, a wood stove and fire (along with a woodpile to build a fire but then "*wood will have to be procured for oneself*", their words not mine), an axe for firewood, elevated bed (just in case of rats), candles, pots and pans. It really is going to be basic living, more of an existence really although there is a hammock at the front of the property, nice in the summer, not so sure about mid-November.

***

With the announcement of the postponement normal life has resumed, the running is progressing well, ten miles in about an hour and a quarter and the recovery time is pretty much nothing at all, feeling good. Gym sessions at the hotel are also going to plan and I feel I'm getting stronger from one day to the next. I'm becoming quite excited at the prospect of living in the wild, I'm also a little apprehensive but that's a good thing, don't want to get too complacent, I must remain focussed.

The kitchen and hotel are doing well, it's such a busy place, weddings are becoming more and more popular right through the year not just July and August anymore. The team I've put together is a strong one and will have little trouble coping in my forthcoming absence, although we did have an incident where a commis chef neglected his basic duties and a fire almost broke out.

He'd asked the kitchen porter to 'drop' the fryer—basically to empty and clean it—in a satellite kitchen after service was over, but the dipshit porter did it there and then whilst the oil was at about a hundred and eighty degrees, unbelievably he also failed to actually turn the fucking gas off first.

We were busy next door when the said porter came through and asked quite innocently "is the fryer off by the way?" While he was choking on black smoke billowing out of the fryer compartment. Needless to say I ran through, turned the gas off, bailed the hot oil back into the fryer and thankfully disaster was averted.

I collared the young commis and frogmarched him out of the kitchen, the rest of the team carried on with their jobs in hand while I, once outside proceeded to slap the commis about the head and then threw him into the rubbish barrow.

I screamed at him, "do you understand what just happened you absolute dipshit? Do you even realise what could have happened?"

He mumbled something about having told the kitchen porter to do it after service, but this just didn't cut it.

I said, "you make sure it gets done, you are responsible, no one else, don't throw it back in that inbred's face, it's your fault, don't let it ever happen again!"

With that I marched back into service (with a look from the KP as if to say 'inbred?' Me?) and carried on, no one looked at me or even spoke unless it was work related. If nothing else, chef's do have the capacity to understand the gravity of a situation and when best to shut up, get your head down and bash on.

The next day the owner had caught wind of the incident and stormed into my office red faced and full of hell, "what the fuck Jack, are you slapping the young'uns about now?"

"Come on, boss," I said, "the kid is a liability, your precious little hotel was this close," here I held up my fingers almost pinched together, "to going up in smoke; what do you want me to do, give him a rub down then buy him a beer?"

"What, it was that close, the hotel could have gone up?" he said.

"Yep," I said, "then where would we all be, Boss? That's right, out of a job!"

"That infernal little bastard, just wait till I get my hands on him!"

And off he went even angrier than when he came in, while I had a little chuckle to myself. Needless to say, I was now looking for another commis chef, I didn't feel bad about it, it's tough shit in this game.

That night, exhilarated, I thought I'd go for a run, it was late, about 11 pm but it's a good time as there are very few people out on the streets. Where I live is quiet anyway, although there is a local pub full of hairy arsed farmers and the like. It's not the most reputable of places and the meagre food offering is deplorable, the usual fare of soggy scampi, pies or steaks cooked beyond edible. When not working I'd never consider myself a food snob, but my expectations are normally well met.

I was about four miles into the run and feeling good when I noticed a bit of a scuffle up ahead, it looked like two lads battling, but as I got closer, it was a guy trying to get a young girl of about seventeen into a nearby alley. He was obviously very pissed as he wasn't doing a particularly good job of it. The girl as I approached wriggled free and shouted to me for help.

I slowed down then stopped and assessed the situation, then happily obliged and punched the lad once in the nose. He dropped to the ground and started mewling like a child and threatening to kill me. I gave him a hefty kick to the ribs, just to be on the safe side and told the girl to phone the police and not to worry as I'd happily wait with her.

I told her to sit on a nearby wall while we waited and then asked her what had happened, apparently the guy was her cousin and didn't seem to understand that that sort of thing is most definitely frowned upon.

The police were quick to respond and were there within what felt like minutes asking all kinds of questions whilst eyeing me suspiciously.

One officer turned to me and asked, "where were you going this evening, sir?"

As I looked down at my running attire, leggings, trainers and running top, not to mention I was sweating like a pig, I simply looked at him with eyebrows raised.

"Well, obviously, I'm out for a run officer when I saw this piece of shit trying to drag her into the alley," I said.

"And did he fall and sustain these injuries, sir?"

"Well, no officer," I said, "I battered him one, was this the wrong thing to do considering what was happening, should I have spoken to him gently and asked him to refrain from his nightly exertions?"

"Now, sir, there's no need for the sarcasm, I'm only trying to ascertain the facts," he said.

"The facts officer was this girl was on the verge of being raped and if I hadn't to have happened by—well, I'm sure you can imagine. How about if you to speak to—?" at this point I turned to the girl.

"Sophie," she mumbled between sobs.

"Sophie," I repeated, "I'm sure she can let you know exactly what was going on officer and fortunately for Sophie here I came along."

As he took my details and assured me that they would be in touch, an ambulance arrived to check Sophie over and I stood feeling a little unappreciated for my gallantry. She did turn to me and mouth thank you, which lifted my spirits somewhat, although I didn't feel my actions needed vindicating or approval. The police did seem to know the culprit who was now in handcuffs and proceeding to throw up all over the officers' feet, which lifted my spirits even higher.

Once the ambulance left, the police gave me a knowing look, which I couldn't work out if it were approval or disapproval of my actions; fuck them, I thought and resumed my run. It was 1 *a.m.* by the time I got in, I had a shower and proceeded straight to bed happy in the thought that I'd had the chance to twat someone and again without hopefully any repercussions.

It was a while before I realised I didn't actually care much about young Sophie, the violence was as always the ultimate euphoria and I was really enjoying the buzz.

The next day I had a phone call from the local constabulary, while I was in the middle of lunch service. I explained to them I'd phone them back at a more convenient time, which was met with fervent protestations, so I happily hung up.

Two hours later I contacted them and was told to come to the local station asap. When I arrived, they left me sitting for ninety minutes before some jumped up office boy took a brief statement, which was no more in-depth than the one I had given them the previous evening. I had to make sure that I was available if any other information came to light, but I would probably not be needed again.

Obviously, the small matter of me giving the guy a bit of a kicking had been brushed under the carpet. Coming down to the station had been an utter waste of time as the guy accused of committing the assault had already admitted the charge. Sophie was fine if I was interested to know (not particularly if I'm honest) and she commended my bravery and her good fortune in my arrival to the officers in charge, too fucking right!

5. Northumberland

Even though I'm from Northumberland, I thought I'd research a little more about where we were going to be encamped. We'd been told we'd be dropped at our individual cabins somewhere between Otterburn and Wooler and that it'd be too far a distance on foot for us to communicate with each other as competitors and it was strictly forbidden anyway. Rules were rules and had to be adhered too or face instant disqualification.

I had no intention of communicating with any of them except in the pursuit of possible disruption and sabotage, I felt confident that within the first week or two I could reduce the numbers significantly with a few gentle nudges in the right place. I appreciate that Northumberland is big and the area they had chosen was pretty damn remote, but there were still farms and hamlets and the like dotted all over this barren landscape. I'm sure some of the, shall we say, lesser competitors will be hoping to pick these out for a little charity as the days get harder and the nights get colder.

The area they had chosen had been picked by the survivalist and the gamekeepers that were on the competition staff. Remote as it was it could be reached via helicopter if one of the contestants suffered an accident or became ill or simply just wanted to get the fuck out of the north.

We were going to be in and around Kielder Forest, which I'd been to umpteen times as a kid and slap bang in the middle of the national park. I hoped and was quietly confident that we'd all be positioned near the River Coquet. Our built for the occasion huts would be scattered along the length of the river which could then supply water for drinking (although there was running water in each cabin, probably from the Coquet anyway) bathing and fishing.

Although the fishing season would be officially over, I'm sure there would still be fish to catch and that the organisers had gained the requisite authority for us to catch what we could. I had a plan that If I could catch a decent size salmon or sea trout early on then I could cure it for gravadlax, I must remember to pack sea salt and sugar. I had to remember that the food and the survival were the main goals and hopefully, I could remain focussed on not just scaring the shit out of the others.

I was quietly confident that I could bag a deer, butcher it, hang it and use pretty much all of it for the main course. I'm thinking, slow braised haunch, stuffed saddle (with what I hadn't decided as I'd have to wait and see what could be found, but probably use the offal for this). I'd salt the other haunch and preserve it for later personal use, I wouldn't need a whole deer for four prissy judges, so the rest could help to sustain me.

I'm sure that all the competitors would be thinking the same way (or should be), so I'd have to create something special. The gamekeeper had to be involved with the rifles which was understandable—safety would always remain key—and it had been organised that each person should they choose to would have a deerstalking day put aside within the first week of the month. (No help would be forthcoming with the carcass once it had been delivered form the kill site to within at least hauling distance of the individual's cabin.)

This basically meant that they'd leave you to your own devices from their drop off point, it was time to get dirty. I also knew from past experience that certain species of wild mushrooms could be foraged in this particular part of Northumberland. Hen of the Wood for example with its earthy and yet, mildly spiced flavour and the sheer size of it could be used to create all kinds from broth to sauces.

I hoped also to find the Liberty Cap which has hallucinogenic properties, which I fully intended for personnel use and if my games progressed, I could possibly slip some of these into my 'neighbours' tea.

With just a week to go to the start of the competition I was becoming more and more convinced that I could have some real fun with the selection of utter fuck-ups that had been gathered together for this little excursion into the countryside—except for the odd exception like Alex and possibly Orry. My fitness, diet and daily life was perfect, I had even taken to having early nights to bed in order to get the rest I needed for forthcoming event.

***

I awoke suddenly to someone screaming and leapt from the bed and desperately tried to gather my senses, I could feel something was wrong but couldn't quite orientate myself with my surroundings. The room was in darkness except for a lone streetlight burning through the blinds. I could hear the rain battering the window but couldn't remember that being forecast as it had been a crisp autumn evening when I'd gone to bed. I then suddenly realised that it'd been me the screaming had come from.

I sat on the edge of the bed but had a distinct clawing feeling at my brain that something was amiss, the sweat ran down my skin and I had tears in my eyes, what in God's name was happening to me? It was then I heard breathing, slow and rasping coming from the darkest recess of the room, fear hit me as a hulking figure slowly and what ultimately looked painful emerged from the darkness.

It was hard to make any discerning features out as the face was horribly disfigured, a mass of blood and gore was all that remained, part of its scalp was nothing more than a flap of skin exposing skull beneath. My throat felt raw as I screamed again at the sight of this nightmarish ghoul staggering towards me; it was then I recognised the clothing. The seventies attire was unmistakeable and I realised then that it was the kitchen porter I'd battered and left for dead in Jersey.

How on earth was this possible? How could this possibly be happening? I tried getting to my feet and clambering for the door, but my movements were slow, cumbersome, almost dreamlike. He shambled ever closer and I remained where I was paralysed with fear and pinned to the bedroom wall. He painstakingly pulled himself up inch by inch onto the bed, his hands grabbing for me tearing at my face and arms.

It was then that I woke up.

Reminiscence: The Helmet

When I was young maybe only nine or ten years old, I like most that age had a close group of friends, six of us who were pretty much inseparable. We did everything together, 'Knocky Nine Doors', 'Kick the Can', 'the grand national'—which was running and jumping over everyone's hedges in their front gardens trying to clear the top of the bush but more often than not, ploughing through it—then getting chased from the garden owners for what felt like miles. But what we really liked to do was to wind up the local farmer, who was a miserable old bastard.

We'd gather up his freshly harvested hay and pile it together for hay jumps, we'd make dens, start fires all using his precious hay, not thinking we were doing

34

much harm, but what must have been an absolute ball ache for him. Sometimes, he'd chase us in his pickup and we'd escape him by running deep into the woods nearby.

Amongst my friends we had one lad who was particularly slow (we'll call him Billy), we called him a nutter, a divvy, a retard, pretty much anything back then that you could get away with. Thinking back now, the kid was on the spectrum and probably had a form of autism or Asperger's or some other undiagnosed illness, but back then he was plain and simply nuts.

He always seemed to go further, take more risks, seldom would he not be the one out front leading us into God only knew what. He had taken of late to wearing an old second-hand motorcycle crash helmet—complete with dirty brown stains amongst the dog tooth pattern inside it—whenever we went into the hay fields, we didn't know why but he just said he felt invincible in it.

By now the hay fields had had the baler in and the nice, neat squares of hay were just itching to be turned into a den. It was mid-way through the summer holidays and we had been allowed to camp out in my parents' back garden with the sole intention of running amok in the wee hours of the morning.

We were armed with torch, pen knife and matches—just in case—and at the stroke of 2 a.m., we headed out to the field to build the greatest shelter yet, we had great plans to build it as high as we could by stacking the bales like LEGO bricks. We crouch ran along the streets pretending we were in the SAS or some such force. Billy naturally took 'point' crash helmet wedged firmly in place and we'd theatrically leap over garden hedges whenever a solitary car came by shouting "police", even though we knew full well it wasn't.

We had the streetlights to navigate by, but we knew these silent streets better than we knew ourselves, no one was about at this time. The odd drunk would come stumbling along and we'd hide like we were about to be rumbled. Eventually, we reached the fields and started to gather bales, two of us to a bale until we had quite a gathering piled together then we went to work building.

It was quite an engineering achievement when we were finished, standing probably fifteen-feet high and maybe ten-feet wide. We'd constructed it so it was hollow inside like a hay igloo and big enough to get us all in, albeit quite a squeeze. Billy was outside taking in the stars in that way he liked to do, whereby he seemed to disappear inside himself for a while.

I had climbed to the top of the den and was starting to pitch the bales from the top laughing as I did so, this roused Billy and he told me to throw one at him.

He wanted to header it like a footy and with his helmet on he'd be absolutely fine.

To my child's brain this seemed like an excellent idea and with all my might I heaved one from the top as Billy stuck out his head jumping up to meet it. As the bale connected with him, he gave a yelp, there was a sickening crunch and Billy collapsed to the ground unconscious. The other guys came dashing out of the den to see what the noise was and I scrambled down the wall of bales.

Billy didn't look so good, his neck was at a funny angle and blood came from his nose, we panicked and just as we were about to make a run for it, the farmer's headlights turned on us and we were rooted to the spot. He ran to us full of hell and cursing but when he saw Billy he stopped, considered for a split second then scooped him up and put him in his truck. He swore to us to get back home and then he sped off with hay and soil spraying out behind.

Next day we all went to Billy's house to check on him, no one was in and we found out from a neighbour that Billy was in hospital with fractures to his neck and skull. So much for that bastard helmet protecting him, I thought. In the days to follow it had been deemed a terrible accident and no one was to blame.

Billy made a full recovery—well, as full as possible for the retard that he was—but didn't hang out with us anymore and my other friends seemed to drift away from that day onwards, always having another excuse as to why we weren't playing together. Billy refused to speak to me, full stop; at school he'd ignore me if I tried to speak. I couldn't understand this as he'd wanted me to throw the bale in the first place.

One day after school I ventured to one of our old haunts a few months later to find all my old friends laughing and joking together, Billy included and they made it perfectly clear I wasn't welcome. Confused and upset I'd headed home shamefaced but full of anger; I later found out why they had all been avoiding me.

Billy had told the guys that I'd thrown the bale without giving him any warning and that it had been all my idea and his parents had called me a psychopath and one they had to avoid. Not the way I remembered it, no matter how hard I tried to recall the events of that evening.

Friends, who needs them, pity the bale hadn't killed him!

***

Jesus, what the hell was that? I sat up in bed and untangled myself from the sweat soaked sheets, it was streaming down my face, my bowels clenched and unclenched several times then finally the feeling started to subside. Crossing to the bathroom and flicking the light on, the face that stared back at me in the mirror was etched in fear, I'd never had such a vivid dream like that before.

Was it the stress of the competition? I can't ever remember being even remotely bothered by competing before. It was strange as I'd not given Jersey much thought of late and I'm convinced it wasn't my conscience as I didn't believe I had one.

I returned to my bed and tried to relax, but every time I closed my eyes, the image of the nightmare returned, so I got up, showered and dressed. After two coffees and some mundane breakfast TV I started to feel something of my old self and packed myself off to work.

When I got to work, the boss was waiting for me hopping around like an excitable puppy and it was only six-thirty, oh God what did he want at this time in the morning?

"So, Jack, have you by any chance seen the latest?" he asked.

"No, but I'm sure you're going to tell me," I replied uninterested, it was such an ungodly hour of the morning for fucks sake.

"The judges names have finally been released, a couple you'll be interested in I think, your old head chef for one!" he smirked with glee.

Fuck, I thought, as I knew who it would be, I asked innocently, "oh, really and which one might that be?"

"Chef Clements and if memory serves me well, he sacked you when you were just a kid," he said.

"Yep, he certainly did, the old bastard. I kind of hoped he'd be dead by now."

I knew full well he wasn't dead, but one can hope.

"Tell me again why he sacked you, Jack?"

"Because I threatened him with a beating and he ran away like the bullying child he was, he locked himself in the changing rooms until I'd left the building!"

This was only half the story, I had caught him trying to get into the pants of a young housekeeper as I walked into the linen store to get my whites for the day. He didn't take too kindly to me taking the piss out of his feeble efforts as the girl told him to fuck off and kneed him in the bollocks. He must have been twice her age not to mention he was married with three kids.

When he had got to his feet, he had tried to threaten me with the sack if I mentioned the incident to anyone, which I called him out on immediately. An argument ensued and I ran for him, at which point he legged it and terrified, locked himself away in the locker room. I kicked the door a couple of times as he screamed from the safety of the other side that I was sacked with immediate effect.

I then thought what the hell, I was fed up here anyway. Maybe it was time I looked for something else and I was packed and gone within the hour, helping myself to a couple of that wankers' knives before I left. Being a young chef could be a nomadic existence, but life was that easy back then, jobs were aplenty, so I had no hesitation whatsoever in jacking it in.

Laughing the boss said, "well, that kind of thing will get you sacked, Jack. Here's the list of the other judges, only three now, looks like this competition isn't going to be as all-encompassing as we had first envisioned."

With my most radiant smile I thanked him as he handed me the list and with that brief conversation over, he was gone. I began to feel that for the first time he maybe had a few nagging doubts about me as he had glanced over his shoulder as he left with a puzzling look on his face.

As well as Clements there was a "celebrity" chef who'd spent the first ten years of his career choosing red tomatoes or green fucking peppers called Peter Sansom; another utter fool who once probably had the skill and enthusiasm to succeed but now, he was just another jobbing TV chef with no real feeling for the industry. (Then again did I really care that much anymore? Plus, he had the money so who's the mug?)

Also, on the judging panel was a well-respected local Michelin star chef called Jayson Ryan. He had done really well and was an excellent cook with a superb restaurant in the heart of Newcastle. I hoped that he would appreciate the food I produced and ignored the fact that I was a vicious bastard with a propensity for violence.

The judges would be making fleeting appearances on a panel as well as in the wilds with the rest of us, we'd see very little of them if anything at all as the *spirit* of the competition was not to be disrupted. Drones were to be used—weather permitting—mostly to monitor our progress and make sure we adhered to the rules and that we could also signal if we were struggling or in need of immediate rescue. (There would also still be certain call points we could use).

With the judge's names released that was it, all I was waiting for now was Sunday the fifteenth and the commencement of the competition.

6. Showtime

I had the car packed and I was dressed as I meant to go on, thermals, quilted jacket and hiking boots. My gators and waterproofs were at hand as it was pissing down and had been for days. The journey would only take me an hour or so to our rendezvous point at Kielder and there we would be shipped out to our various cabins, once we had been given our debriefing and final instructions.

It was a pleasant drive considering the atrocious weather. The sheer vastness of the forest loomed around me and some might feel its claustrophobic grip as the narrow road meandered through the trees. But I always felt quite comforted by its enormity, it felt like a homecoming of sorts as I'd spent so much time as a child here.

The sights and smells of the forest pine overpowered the senses, it felt completely untouched in places until eventually you happened upon the car parks and attractions of the sympathetically done in-keeping visitor centre. I'd past the observatory on the way as this was one of Britain's Dark Sky areas; officially the darkest area in the UK, perfect for looking at the night sky.

Kielder was an excellent set up, a perfect amalgamation of nature at its best with tastefully built structures, even the reservoir dam looked in-keeping with its surroundings. A stunning place and always a pleasure to visit.

I was directed to a small conference room and given coffee and pastries by some flunky mincing around us. I was the first competitor to arrive and I found out from said flunky that the others would be joining us soon as they had all been put up for the night in separate hotels and are being ferried in imminently. I settled into a comfy chair and just as I tucked into my Danish, I was greeted with an overpowering aroma of cheap aftershave and stale alcohol.

"Jack, you're the first here, how are you? Feeling nervous?"

"Mr Schroder," I responded offering my hand but not getting out of my seat, while at the same time spraying his already crumpled jacket with pastry crumbs. "Nervous? No, rather looking forward to it, are you?"

"Am I nervous? Why, whatever do you mean, Jack?" he replied with an anxious grin, eyes flittering in all directions.

I thought just because you over familiarise with my name doesn't mean I know you; I'd never met the guy before.

"You just look a little flustered, Mr Schroder, is it hot in here? You look to be sweating," I replied, he obviously hadn't had his prescribed morning intake of alcohol.

"Nonsense, I'm tip-top this morning and please do call me Phillip, we're all friends here."

"Are we, Mr Schroder? Think I'd prefer to keep it professional if it's all the same to you."

As I watched his smile faltered for a split second and then he regained his composure and wandered off with an apologetic nod, as thankfully for him some more newbies were arriving. That will keep the useless drunk twat on his toes; I thought, he'll be wary of me from now on.

As I was finishing my coffee and more competitors were wandering in, I suddenly felt cold and I had the feeling of an uncanny presence. When I looked again, more closely this time, I thought I caught a glimpse of someone or something in the far corner staring at me and slowly coming my way, meandering unseen through the small crowd.

I had to do a doubletake and rubbed at my eyes but there he was in all his Portuguese finery, the ragged flares, paisley shirt, dirt, gore and blood and he slowly and painfully made his shuffling way towards me. What the fuck was this? I must be dreaming again. I closed my eyes tightly and when I opened them, he was still there closing the space between us, almost nonchalantly and somehow, I'm convinced he was grinning at me.

How I could possibly know this as most of his face was unrecognisable; Jesus Christ, I really must be losing it? I looked away panicking, then desperately regaining some sort of composure I turned back towards this monstrosity and rose to my feet to confront him. But just as suddenly as he had appeared, he was gone; there was no one there, just the bustling flunky and the new recruits.

It was one thing to have had a nightmare whilst tucked up in bed but not while I was fully conscious, mid-morning in the middle of a busy room. I could feel a trickle of sweat running down my back and face—who was feeling the heat now, I thought without any mirth whatsoever—as the flunky returned to fill my coffee cup, which I welcomed with—for once—a genuine smile.

He looked somewhat concerned having seen me leap to my feet to accost my invisible unwanted pursuer. I must have looked like I'd seen a ghost, which I felt somewhere deep down that maybe I had, was I being haunted? This was for me the craziest of thoughts, I felt I was of rational mind.

I wasn't particularly overtaxed, so why in the last week was I now suddenly seeing this guy, why appear to me now? It'd been nearly a year since the altercation in Jersey happened and I'd felt nothing towards it, either consciously or as far as I was aware subconsciously. Plus, now that I thought about it, what was there to be frightened of?

Settling back into my seat, I looked over the ever increasingly busy room to see who had just arrived as I fervently needed a distraction and to see who would be next for Schroder's sycophantic foolishness. I saw to my utter delight that it was my favourite pair of wankers. Fat Billy Cohen and that other big bastard Joe Pritchard, they both looked my way and reluctantly ambled over, not even trying to hide their distaste of me.

I appraised the pair of them as they came closer. Fuck me, unbelievable! As well as his ludicrous beach attire, "Fatty" actually had flip flops on, *flip flops*! He obviously thought he was off on holiday somewhere, maybe he thought we were being flown directly to the Algarve this morning and fuck me, did he smell, wow! No soap and water had seen that putrid body in a while, no way would he possibly survive what was coming his way, he'd be gone within the week.

The other big fucker was no better as he was dressed in some scruffy t-shirt, shorts and trainers; I think, he too had gained a few pounds since I had last seen him, probably down to the fact that he had taken his foot off the gas and expected his team to do all the heavy lifting.

"Jesus, lads, did you not get the brief?" I asked of the pair, whilst trying and failing to keep hold of my laughter which had bubbled to the surface.

"Yeah-yeah, fuck right off, '*Cunt-ingham*', we got the brief, what do you think this is *Lone Survivor*?" he replied with a conspiratorial wink to fatty Cohen—admiring his own supposed wit—whilst eyeing my choice of clothes.

Fatty Cohen, the arse licker that he was, found this hilarious as he gazed reverently at his dipshit friend. I despised being called by my surname and he knew how much it riled me when they found it amusing to replace one of the letters, this was like being back in the school yard, for fucks sake.

"You do realise that you're going to be left to your own devices for a month with no home comforts whatsoever, mummy won't be there to wipe your arses gay boys. It's only eight fucking degrees out there at the moment and it's going to get colder, you absolute pair of muppets."

This got the response from Pritchard I had hoped as he made to lunge at me, I quickly got to my feet to better defend myself against his laboured attack. As expected with Pritchard, he was all bluster and bullshit and tried desperately to make it seem as though fatty Cohen got between us by his own volition.

"Woah, lads, for fucks sake, we've only just got here, the competition hasn't even begun yet!" Fatty exclaimed, panic etched on his enormous quivering moon face, another absolute fanny as I correctly remembered.

"You watch your back out there, Jack, any chance I get and I'll fucking have you!" Joe half-heartedly said as I watched him slump off to fill his face on pastries and coffee with Cohen trudging behind him like some huge foul-smelling lap dog, desperately trying to console him as he knew he'd been bettered without so much as a single punch being thrown.

This was exactly what I wanted, get them on the back foot, make sure they knew that I hadn't mellowed in the intervening years since we'd last been acquainted. All this kind of confrontation did was enhance my own feelings of superiority and confidence. What was there to worry about I thought to myself, but I still hesitantly scanned the room for what seemed my new Portuguese companion, albeit an unwanted one.

I knew he had to be in my head, I didn't believe in anything otherworldly, but I couldn't as yet understand why now and what he wanted with me. For what purpose was he *haunting* my thoughts, my waking thoughts at that. I must try to concentrate on the present and dismiss any thoughts of Jersey and what I had done. Was this my penance, forever to be followed by this *spectre*, albeit one that must be in my head?

More people were arriving and I thankfully became distracted from my macabre thoughts, though not all that unwelcome I had to admit to myself as it seemed to give me focus for the coming adventure. A small Asian lad almost seemed to sneak in and I recognised him from a previous photograph as Subi. He looked even smaller than I'd thought he was going to be and his demeaner was of someone who didn't want to be here, he looked frightened of his own shadow. Maybe he was trying to escape his own demons.

I watched him as he made for the nearest seat and almost seemed to disappear into the very upholstery. His eyes were cagey and he appeared to be scrutinising everyone, then his eyes came upon me staring straight back at him. He tried for an embarrassed smile and when none was returned, he dropped his gaze and began fumbling with his small rucksack, which he'd taken from his back as he sat down. I hope you have more provisions than that little backpack can hold, I thought.

No one was taking this as serious as me, well no one I'd encountered so far; Christ, those other fat fuckers couldn't even wear the correct footwear. The other competitors filed in, obviously from the same coach, Orry looking resplendent in full army fatigues and shades on even though it was still pissing down outside. The kid looked well, the trade hadn't taken its toll on him as yet and I'm not sure if he'd needed to find solace in the booze either, for his sake hopefully not.

He nodded to me as he approached with hand outstretched, "Chef," he said.

I replied with a smile and even a little warmth and shook his proffered hand, "Orry, how goes it pal?"

Looking a little uncertain as he always did and not sure as to how welcoming I would be, he answered, "not too bad, Chef, same old shit but you know how it is, the restaurants going well, busy place, good team, so that's all that matters."

"It does indeed matey, you seen some of the total fuckwits assembled here today?" I said with a slightly raised voice as I looked towards Joe and fatty Cohen, the pair of them scowling at me like some comedy villains.

"It certainly is a mixed bunch, Chef," he said hesitantly as he wasn't sure whether to rock the boat any further. "We'll hopefully catch up later, I'm gasping for a coffee," he said a little embarrassed.

"Will do, Orry, you take care out there, yeah?" And with another nod he wandered off for a brew glancing repeatedly between me and the other two, trying to judge what had gone down previous to his arrival.

He needed to toughen up that lad if he were to survive out there and I didn't just mean this competition. The industry was brutal and it could take you in and spit you out at any given moment.

As we had been talking Alex had entered the conference room in a very confident and self-assured way and sat down opened legged—very unladylike—drinking her coffee. Shit, she was lean, muscled and dressed for the part, at least someone was going to try to make a fist of it. She looked good, shame she was married and to a woman at that.

Her blue hair was tucked away under a beanie hat but her sleeve tattoos were on show, which now seemed obligatory for firstly a chef and secondly, a dyke. Couldn't help but admire her self-confidence, she seemed unphased by it all.

She nodded my way but didn't engage in any conversation with me or anybody else. The only person she spoke with was the flunky and that seemed relaxed and light-hearted. I noticed the flunky looked relieved to be speaking to someone who didn't look like they were itching to kill some of the other competitors.

Suddenly a gust of cold air swept into the room and following it was Bos, decked out in brand new hiking gear and a beautiful set of boots which had quite clearly come out of the box this morning. He arrived like he was in some kind of hair product commercial. He still looked like a twat, the years hadn't changed him since our last encounter.

To be fair he looked in good nick, it would be all front I knew as he was just one of these lucky guys who didn't have to work hard to stay lean, he just didn't get fat. He cared more about his hair than his food, I'd heard recently, which was understandable from everyone who knew him. He made a beeline for the coffee and pastries, desperately avoiding my glare. He passed a few pleasantries with everyone, even dumb and dumber (Cohen and Joe), although I knew he thought these guys were beneath him, what a prick.

The flunky stopped what he was doing mid-sentence and headed for Bos, leaving Alex a little peeved at being dumped for this wanker. As the flunky and he were talking, Bos risked a cheeky glance my way. My eyes hadn't left him since his dramatic entrance and he met my gaze for a split second then with an almost knowing smirk he turned back to his new friend, the coffee bringer. As I had previously thought he was planning something, if it were going to be anyone it would be this overconfident fool.

I could feel it, well bring it on fuck-stick, I'm ready for you. Once out there and settled into our humble lodgings I'd seek this bastard out, I'd make sure his stay would be as uncomfortable as possible.

Just as my thoughts and plotting were gathering momentum, Harry 'the bastard' Celestine staggered in. Fuck me, time had not been kind to this guy, whilst granted he hadn't got fat like some others we could mention, he'd actually gone the other way; his emaciated frame and utterly dishevelled appearance shocked me and belied his fifty-four years. I'd never worked with this guy before, but his fearsome reputation did not match this vision in front of me.

Just as I was thinking this, the smell of booze hit me, wow this guy was totally smashed. How was he ever going to make it out there? Surely, he would have had to have had some kind of fitness check? Granted the competition officials had a duty of care to all participants, but we also had a responsibility to be able to prove or at least appear to be of reasonable health, physically *and* mentally (We'd all had to sign an insurance waiver to this effect).

Initially this guy had been thought of as a threat but now, he didn't look like he'd make it a day never mind a month out there. I watched him stagger to a chair and almost collapse into it while the whole room gazed in his direction, obviously thinking the same as me. The flunky didn't even ask, just appeared at his side with coffee and helped him raise it to his lips. I hasten to add no one looked concerned, they couldn't give two fucks about the guy, just shocked and amazed.

Some had unfortunately had the pleasure of working with this guy and been subjected to relentless bullying and violence over the course of their tenure with him, no one cared what a mess he'd become. He even made Schroder look good and that was pushing it. I couldn't take my eyes from him, even when his eyes met mine there didn't seem any animosity or hatred there, there didn't seem much of anything, he just looked vacant.

If this were what became of the old guard chefs then fuck me when this competition was over, maybe I'd look to get out. Too many times you heard of this kind of downfall with chefs, the stress, the long unsociable hours, the inevitable breakdown of marriages. Seeing him made the prize money all the more important, whilst not life changing, it could be a steppingstone to a new vocation.

***

Whilst Celestine snoozed and drooled into his coffee the Judges arrived along with the competition officials, game keeper and survival expert. I was happy to notice the distaste on the *Survival Man's* face as he took in the utterly farcical dress of Cohen and Pritchard, they noticed his look and hung their heads in something resembling shame or possibly despair at what they'd signed up for.

The judges seemed more concerned with waking up Celestine, why not let him sleep it off I thought. He can't have packed that much booze, so a period of cold turkey would do him the world of good.

On entering Clements spotted me instantly, obviously he had been looking out for me (probably hoping I wouldn't turn up) but to give him his dues he walked directly over. Looking at him and the way he presented himself, he was another chef that appeared to have had it rough recently.

His sunken eyes, prominent cheek bones and a shirt collar that was two sizes too big all pointed to weight loss and it didn't look intentional. Trying and failing to express a confidence that belied his appearance and with a slight quiver in his voice he said, "Hi, Jack, been a long time?"

"It has indeed, still trying to finger young girls in housekeeping, are we?"

I couldn't help myself; I wasn't going to start or try to keep up any pretence that it was all water under the bridge. I didn't like the cunt, didn't even want to be in the same county as this fool, never mind the same room. His skeletal like face went puce with rage, he looked like he was going to explode and make a fool of himself when thankfully for Clements, the flunky magically appeared out of nowhere.

Obviously, he had been monitoring the situation and must have been briefed on all the possible skirmishes. And with the offer of coffee and pastries Clements was forced to offer his thanks through gritted teeth to the kid. He turned back to me, but I simply turned my head away and gazed at the picturesque landscape and forest through the huge bi-fold doors which would offer wonderful alfresco meetings and dining in the summer (Just a shame about the midges though).

I could sense him simmering away next to me, staring at the back of my head, deciding what best course of action to take, then with his mind made up he finally stomped off to engage with someone else. What was he going to do to me, punch one of the contestants in front of everyone before we'd even started? I think not, as apart from the fact he'd be kicked straight off the judging panel, I knew for a fact he didn't have the balls.

The atmosphere in the room was now quite tense and it wasn't all just down to me, everyone looked apprehensive, fidgety, maybe even a little scared at what was ahead. We all had one eye on the weather, which hadn't let up for days now and from what I could gather was going to deteriorate over the next few days. It was too late to call it off now as it had already been postponed once, so this was it, we'd have to make the most of it.

A briefing was about to begin with a talk from *Survival Man* and the gamekeeper, who looked like he'd rather be anywhere else than here. Gamekeeping must be tough, working for all these posh wankers with huge country estates but without a pot to piss in when it came down to actual cash.

This was ultimately why most of these stately homes organised shoots as a way to make money for the estate. Then once you'd hopefully *bagged* a few brace of pheasant, you'd be treated to the hospitality of the gentry. Which was usually in some drafty old castle with some piss poor meal, cheap whisky and stunted conversation as the said gentry would rather be anywhere else in the world than slumming it with the great unwashed!

While the three judges and several officials took their seats, I noticed the judges Sansom and Ryan almost wrestled with the chair over who had to sit next to Clements. So, it wasn't just me who deeply disliked him and in the end poor Jayson Ryan with a Michelin to his name and umpteen other accolades lost the fight and conceded politely taking his seat next to one of the biggest frauds in the business.

No sooner had they sat down than Clements was waffling on to Ryan who looked like he'd rather be anywhere else, but every now and then smiled his way then tried to engage with Sansom on any other topic possible.

The gamekeeper got everyone's attention by taking a shotgun from its bag and breaking it.

"When carrying a shotgun, you must at all times carry it broken and over your arm, you will do as I say to the letter; anyone who doesn't will be disqualified, anyone who thinks it's a game will be disqualified; I will not tolerate people fucking around or again you'll be disqualified. You will all be allocated a time slot this first week, so if you are lucky enough to bag a deer, you'll have time to dress it.

You will be with me or one of my lads, whether it's me or one of the others, you will treat these lads with the utmost respect. Again, I emphasise the point, fuck around with any one of us and you're out, no ifs or buts, out!"

This guy meant business, he let this sink in and then added.

"We'll go up into the hills, it's too late for Roe Bucks but we should see some Roe deer, I'm not here to do the shooting, which will be a rifle, not a shotgun like this."

Here he held the gun aloft again and then continued, "I'll help you stalk it; I'll get you into position and I'll tell you when to shoot but you will pull the trigger, that's if you can. Many people freeze, don't worry as it can happen, if so then it's going to be fish on your menu. We'll also have the chance at pheasant and partridge if that's something you wish, which will be with the shotgun."

Again, he held the weapon aloft.

"You'll have a full day of practice with the rifle and shotgun tomorrow, this will be your last interaction with the rest of the competitors, anyone here shoot?"

I raised my hand, "I shot frequently as a kid, but I've not been out for a few years."

"Good," he said, "it'll come straight back to you, anyone else?"

At this point Harry Celestine had woken and raised a shaky hand. "I've shot a few times but not for a while," he slurred, as the entire room stared at him in disbelief.

At this point an obviously distressed *Survival Man* with his face bright red with anger interjected, "There's no fucking way you are pulling a trigger unless you can prove to me that you are completely sober and straight, which by tomorrow I very much doubt!"

Harry didn't even have the good grace to look shamefaced, he didn't care, just smirked to himself and went back to sleep. Schroder was quick on the scene to try and calm things down in his usual slippery manor, he also wanted every competitor to be able to take part and have a fair crack at the competition.

"Now, I'm sure we can get Harry into some kind of shape for tomorrow, he'll be as right as the rain, won't you Harry?" he said while encouraging Celestine to drink from a water jug.

I very much doubted that but kept my council for once, there was no way that fucker would sober up within the next week, never mind tomorrow.

The gamekeeper continued, "as well as shooting practice tomorrow, we'll endeavour to get you all mentally ready for the next month, some of you do not appear to be taking it too seriously judging by your attire. This will be to your detriment as this competition and especially Northumberland at this time of year is not to be taken lightly.

These forests can be devilishly hard to navigate even by seasoned professionals such as myself, you will all have only the bare minimum of equipment as well as whatever you thought to bring yourselves. You were all given initial documentation highlighting the level of fitness and determination needed. It's going to be tough out there on your own, this isn't just a cooking competition gentlemen."

He then noticed Alex sitting with a resigned expression on her face, "Sorry, Miss?"

"Alex and it's Mrs," Alex replied.

"Alex," the gamekeeper said, "You look like you read the brief so that last statement was on all counts not directed at you. I hope no offence was taken."

"None at all," Alex said, "But appreciate the sentiment."

She was completely nonplussed by anything he had said.

Unperturbed the gamekeeper continued all the while *Survival Man* stood at his side glowering at everyone, *what the fuck was this guy's problem?*

"You'll all be given a map and compass if you haven't already got one and on the map there will be various points highlighted, such as ideal fishing spots, places to avoid and also the communication area, where you will be able to contact either me or my compatriot here."

He pointed at *Survival Man.* I had noticed at this point and found it strange that he had not introduced himself or *Survival Man* by name at all and that he had led the talk when we were expecting most of it to come from happiness himself. I wondered whether they were trying to distance themselves from us, in case some tried to take advantage of their positions.

Again, he continued, "whilst for the most part you will be completely alone, we will be using drones for certain elements of filming and monitoring. This will be limited and weather dependant, so if you do see a drone above you, the powers that be have asked us to relate to you to try and ignore it, as it makes for better television."

At this there was a cocksure groan from that cunt Schroder as if he were some kind of superstar always in the limelight.

"I'm sure gentlemen that we'll all be able to cope with that sort of attention with the utmost decorum and reserve," he said coyly, whilst flicking his hair from his forehead. Supposedly, he was going to be within the forest at certain points to do his *action* reports, silly fucker thought he was Bear Grylls.

"Yes, well, that's all very good for you, Phillip, but you won't be in the same predicament as these guys when you're shacked up in your five-star trailer with all the mod cons," the *Survival Man* retorted. That raised a laugh from everyone, myself included, great to see that pathetic excuse of a man squirm.

We were then guided to a large map at the back of the room, where all the positions of the cabins were located, each had a name attached to it. As well as my own, I took special notice of that pair of arseholes Pritchard and his sidekick Cohen's cabins but didn't get a chance to absorb where the rest of the competitors were to be housed as we were shepherded away.

There was a good few mile between each plot and if you so wished you could avoid all other competitors completely. If you so wished that is, a plan was forming in my head as to how I could sabotage the other competitor's chances, whilst strengthening my own.

I was quite some distance from Alex and Subi but still reachable if need be; Celestine would probably be asleep for most of his tenure, so I'd nothing to worry about there, hopefully he'd manage to keep a fire going or he'd be toast. Bos and all his bullshit I hoped was not too far out, as for those other two utter deadbeats, they were within range, still some distance but nevertheless in range.

It did dawn on me at that moment that since his Hollywood entrance Bos had been decidedly quiet, I noticed him at the back of the little huddle gathered round the map. He was shitting it now that he was here, you could see it in his eyes and his apparent bluster when he spoke to the others didn't cut it with me.

I moved closer to him and whispered in his ear, "whatever scheme you've got planned out there, you pathetic little cunt, it had better be good, do you not think I'm planning the same?" And with that I wandered off for another coffee smiling to myself, he looked like he'd just shit himself! Well at least I hoped so.

The officials then ran through the insurance side of things, explaining that we'd hitherto signed a document and we should all have read the pack that was sent to us. Also the plants that we should avoid—for the non-foragers out there—the out of bounds signs that have to be adhered too.

If we come across a farm then we have to respect the owner's property at all costs, stealing would be deemed an instant disqualification. The toilet situation was also explained and that the cesspit attached to the loo located at the rear of each cabin had been readied beforehand and could last the month easily. Thankfully, toilet paper would also be provided and there should be enough stacked in each privy to last the month. At least for most normal sized individuals, not sure how Cohen and his huge arse would get on.

At the very mention of this Fatty Cohen piped up, "Do you mean to say that the cabin has an outside loo?"

"Yes, Billy and it doesn't have a flush either," one of the officials stated with a distinct hint of glee in his voice.

"Jesus, this is going to be like a prison, I was expecting at least some relative comforts; is a flushing toilet too much to ask for?" he replied.

"Billy," answered the official really starting to enjoy himself. "The whole point of this competition is to be able to survive first and foremost in the wilds

51

of Northumberland, that means *survive* Billy, if you are staying in a five-star cabin then that's not exactly wild and not exactly surviving, is it?

I mean that's the idea anyway, secondly is that you can create some dishes with the products you can find, forage and hunt while you're out there. You do realise that there isn't a Marks and Spencer's out in the woods, don't you?"

This brought a snigger from all of us.

"But you should know all this because you've already been vetted by us and you've signed all kinds of paperwork to reiterate this fact. Now, if you want to bitch and moan about the toilet situation then maybe this competition isn't for you."

"I'm ready for this, I can assure you," replied Cohen with just a hint of indignation and then he added, "just thought we might have had a flushing toilet that's all." He said like the petulant child he was.

"I'm sure the toilet situation here is still a damned site better than whatever Eastern European shithole of a country you managed to crawl out of," I stated matter-of-factly as the whole room turned my way as one and collectively held its breath.

Again, Schroder came to the rescue as he almost ran (in his over-the-top camp shuffle) to put his arm around Cohen and smother him in false platitudes. The official wandered over to me and said, "as much of a wanker as that fat fucker is please don't ever speak like that of any of the competitors, that was bang out of order. You've got one more day and then you won't have to see any of them for a month."

Yeah right that's what he thought.

I replied, "sometimes these things need to be said, he's completely unprepared for what he's about to do, the guy's a joke and you fucking well know it."

"Well, it's one less for you to worry about then, isn't it!" he said with just a bit too much venom I felt, as he stomped off to confer with the other officials and judges.

I looked around at the rest of the competitors and saw complete astonishment on most of their faces and utter hatred on Pritchard's. But when I glanced at Alex, she was smiling at me, obviously agreeing with everything I'd said.

I'd noticed now that whenever I turned, I would catch a glimpse of someone in my periphery shambling through the crowd of officials and competitors. But then if I turned fully, they would be gone, I took a large swig of coffee and tried to slow my heartrate down. I again had the awful creeping sensation that my KP friend wasn't going to leave me in a hurry and that he fully intended to stay awhile.

Maybe this was something that I had to get used to, I wondered if that was even possible? Was this my penance for all the shitty things I'd done, culminating in murder? Catching another glance of him I began to feel that my fear of *it* was possibly subsiding, earlier in the day the utter dread was all encapsulating, but now when I looked around I almost expected to see him. Could this *spectre* even hurt me? *Spectre*? Jesus, I sounded like a loon, of course it was in my head. It had to be.

***

We were next informed that we'd be having lunch and then heading off to our respective cabins afterwards. We could acclimatise ourselves with our surroundings and then four of us would be picked up again to go with the gamekeeper and *Survival Man* for some practice shooting.

I was on the first afternoon excursion to the shooting range as I was considered to not need a great deal of practice, I was confident that this was the case. There was most of the afternoon left, although it seemed increasingly dark outside, the rain still persisted, in fact if anything it had actually worsened.

Thankfully, lunch was outstanding and plentiful. There was everything from blue-cheese burgers to Keralan lamb curry, poached halibut with baby fennel and truffle, roast cod with herb and bone marrow crust, rib-eye steaks, hand cut chips and even a veggie bean cassoulet. They were obviously fattening us up as it would be slim pickings from here on in, everyone ate heartedly but the mood was sombre.

Fuck me, it was like the last supper, except for Cohen and Pritchard, who thought they were at the inclusive buffet in some shitty Tenerife resort. No one bothered me as I sat at the end of a buffet style bench with Orry to my left and Subi opposite, cautiously glancing over at me from time to time.

Orry looked at me trying to gauge my mood and said with a cheeky smile, "Do you know what the *Survival Man's* name is?" Without waiting for an answer, he said, "Fucking Cecil! Can you believe it, all that tough guy bluster and the cunt is called Cecil. I nearly fell off my chair when I found out, I overheard that official talking to him earlier, what a muppet!"

53

I had to admit it was funny and I allowed myself a chuckle, which Orry seemed relieved with, I also thought it was a name to remember.

Pritchard and Cohen tried to engage Alex in some kind of outdated sexist banter, but she was having none of it and told them firstly to fuck off then she just ignored them completely. Celestine gingerly picked at his food, pushing most of it around his plate. I couldn't help thinking that it was probably the most he'd eaten in quite a while, although he didn't seem to be enjoying it and trying desperately to keep it down.

Bos was attempting to sound confident and was as usual full of bluster, but his hands still had a slight tremor and for all the food he had on his plate not a great deal had actually been eaten. I wondered again to myself how many would last the month, it seemed more and more likely that the numbers would dwindle to the remaining hardcore quite rapidly.

The judges ate their lunch on a separate table huddled together conspiring it seemed, now and then exchanging furtive glances between us and themselves.

When they had finished their meal, they made their way to the door and had a brief exchange with the other officials, who marched over almost immediately and then apologetically said, "we almost forgot troops, we need your mobile phones, all of them. You all read the rules and brief, no phones or electronic devices to be taken into the competition whatsoever, anyone found with one will be instantly disqualified."

Cohen started to protest but even his bosom buddy Pritchard said hand it over and he eventually acquiesced. All the phones and one or two tablets were handed in and stored somewhere out of sight, to me it meant nothing. There was no one I wanted to chit—chat with, I was relishing the idea of absolute solitude.

"They'll all be handed back on completion of the competition or if you are required to leave earlier by your own means or by ours."

With this we went back to our food, some not with the same gusto they'd had when they started it.

***

After lunch we were herded into our respective Land Rovers and driven to our would-be homes for the next month. I was third to be dropped off after a frosty journey with Cohen and Pritchard and I made a mental note where they were to be encamped. Once these two had been safely ensconced into their respective cabins, myself and the so far mute driver had an uncomfortable disorientating thirty-minute journey to mine.

It was difficult to get any kind of bearing whilst travelling on dirt tracks and then literally off road through some dense forest to what opened up to a what would be quite serene romantic setting on the edge of the river Coquet in any other circumstances. It appeared we were all approximately thirty minutes apart by car, on foot it would be a hike and would deter most from trying to reach each other. Except for the fact that the river was flowing rapidly past, the first impressions of the cabin were positive.

Thankfully, it was actually raised from the ground on three-foot stilts which would help to prevent flooding while also a deterrent for rats. The immediate area was cleared of long grass, bushes and reeds but apart from this, there were no paths or tracks to speak of, these I would have to trample down myself over time. Outside the cabin was a well-built grill made of slate and stone, a log store—third full—with axe and chopping block plus as promised an outdoor privy—again raised.

As I dragged my pack out of the Land Rover and jumped down the mute driver finally said, "my instructions are only to let you out here, I can't help with your pack or in any way help you with a fire, there is no lock on the door to the cabin as it's not deemed necessary. Inside you'll find cooking equipment, plus other essentials like oil, condiments, dried spices, dried herbs, chillies etc. It seems they wanted to at least give you a chance of making your foraged shit taste of something."

With his prepared speech given, he gave me an almost toothless grin and childlike laugh. Fuck me, where did they dig this hillbilly up from, the set of *Southern Comfort*? It all seemed a little clichéd, but I reminded myself we were in deepest darkest Northumberland and not the Louisiana swamps. I turned to him with my most endearing smile and kindly asked him to fuck-off.

With another gummy grin he said, "get yourself comfortable and the truck will be back in an hour to ferry you to the shooting range." And with that he was off, spraying dirt and grass ten feet in the air as he went skidding and sliding back the way he'd came.

I lumped my pack to the cabin, up the three wooden steps and opened the door. I was almost expecting a horror film style creak as the door swung open but no it glided on freshly oiled hinges without a sound. Bundling myself in I took note of the interior, not bad at all I thought, maybe twelve feet square and the bed was raised as promised.

The stove and fireplace were stocked with wood ready to be lit with a large chimney leading out through the roof and a guard for the fire which wouldn't hinder the heating of the room. There was also a metal sink and tap with running water, although I knew it would be best to boil the water first to purify before use. There was also to my surprise actually quite a decent larder of dried produce, such as rice, pasta, dried beans, dried lemons, sugar, rock salt, onion and garlic powders.

(I'd also noticed outside the cabin north facing near the door there was a large, sealed box attached to the wall, raised from the ground and lined with stainless steel, it was an ideal receptacle to use in winter as a cool box.) It would be enough food to keep me for a few weeks if I rationed it properly and trapped some rabbits and caught fish to give me some additional protein. I unpacked my bag onto the one shelf next to the bed, mostly changes of clothes, socks and winter wear.

I laid out my *Redline* sleeping bag which was capable of enduring minus forty-five-degree winters and set my hunting knife and sharpening stone just below the bed but in easy reach if needed. I didn't think I'd need the knife for our shooting practice this afternoon but from then on it wouldn't leave my person. My fishing gear I placed near the door along with the boxes of flies I'd brought, the candles and matches I placed on a small table near the stove along with the other provisions I'd brought along.

I opened up the map again and examined in more detail, where I thought my position was. Whilst they'd been careful to leave out any actual place names, I knew we were all situated within a few mile of each other between Otterburn and Wooler and spaced out along the River Coquet, so I thought I was most probably Barrowburn way. Still in the middle of a very large inhospitable area and especially tough on foot if I wanted to make a little sojourn to one of the other cabins.

Taking the lighter I set to work getting a fire going and succeeded on the first attempt. The gathering of wood and *dry* wood at that would be the immediate task at hand as a fire would need to be kept going at all times. The one glazed window in the cabin was adorned with shutters on the inside and out, which would help to keep the place at a reasonable temperature for the cold nights ahead. As well as the bed and table, there was a small uncomfortable looking chair which I placed in front of the fire, if nothing else it would be good for drying clothes.

Heading back outside I guessed I was only twenty to thirty feet from the riverside. After all the rain that had fallen recently the river had quite clearly encroached up the narrow riverbank and was proceeding towards the cabin. The only problem I could foresee if the rains kept up their deluge was that the grill would be rendered useless, fortunately the log store was raised to the height of the cabin also. The hammock was already full of rainwater and utterly useless, I thought to myself that they'd probably intended the competition to originally be a summer affair.

I wandered down to the swollen riverside taking in the surrounding area as the rain kept up its relentless downpour. It was such a beautiful untouched landscape and was an absolute pleasure to be here I thought. As I looked over to the other side of the river through the blurred sheet of rain, I could see what was now becoming an all too familiar scene.

The horrific face had loomed up out of the reeds and seemed to be in a worse state each time he appeared to me, with his horribly discoloured skin flaking from his scalp and one eye missing with black humour oozing from it. He made no attempt to cross the river, but I knew now that he was with me wherever I went and his vigil would remain.

I truly was haunted and alone with no one to confer with and I fully understood it was my own responsibility and burden to carry. Just then I heard the truck approaching and turned in the direction of the engine over revving and squirreling through the trees, when I turned back to the river my ghostly compatriot had gone.

***

The same driver who dropped me off slid the land rover to a halt in front of me spraying shit up my legs and grinning at me like the madman he was. I'd had enough of this prick and wrenched his door open.

I reached inside and dragged him out of his seat by his collar shouting, "Now, listen to me you cunt, it's your job to drive us to and fro, that's it. Any more shit like that and I'll take you over to the river and fucking drown you. Do you understand me?"

All his previous bravado had evaporated in a heartbeat, he spluttered, "Sorry mate, sorry, I'm only having a laugh."

"Yeah, well, not at my expense, you twat!" I replied and with that I punched him in the face and let him fall into the muddy puddles spitting and coughing the last of his teeth out through split lips.

With that I climbed into the back of the truck and waited for him to pull himself back up out of the dirt and into the driving seat. He caught his breath and remonstrated to me about how I was out of line and that when we got to the range, he'd be reporting me for misconduct and he'd get me disqualified.

I grabbed him again around his neck, choking him through the headrest and said, "listen to me you fucking inbred, you say one word when we get there and I'll snap your neck like a twig, you got that?"

"Yeah yeah," he managed to whisper as I increased the pressure around his throat.

"Not you nor anyone else will get in my way of this competition, not even that fucker who's trying his best to haunt me, are we clear?" I asked a little distracted as I realised what I'd said.

"What the fuck are you on about, you nutcase?" he asked but obviously didn't want the answer to, as he glared at me in pure horror through the interior mirror.

"Yeah, well, just remember our chat. Now, get me to the fucking range," I said while I released him and sank back into the seat.

Must be careful what I'm saying, they all think I'm mad to start with never mind coming out with shit like that. He gathered himself together and put the car in gear. With a last questioning look at me through the rear-view mirror he accelerated away from the cabin covering the grill and veranda in grime and wound his way up into the trees.

When we got to the range Alex was standing talking to the *Survival Man* and the gamekeeper; Subi and Orry were also there conversing together a little behind them. The driver jumped from the car as he brought it to a sliding halt and without so much as casting a glance at the others ran into a small Bothy they were using as a shelter and gun store.

As I emerged from the vehicle *Survival Man* approached me, "what's up with him?"

"Not a clue mate, maybe he's got the shits," I replied and sauntered off to the others standing in a huddle, desperately trying to shield themselves from the rain blowing in their faces.

I heard him say to himself, "*well, if he has got the shits he's fucked as there's no toilet in there.*" And with that he hurried into the store to check out the driver, who would hopefully keep his now denture free mouth tightly closed if he had any sense left.

We were to have a couple of hours practice this afternoon and the same four of us would be heading out first thing tomorrow on a hopefully successful hunt. While we were to be in a group of four tomorrow, as soon as any of us bagged a deer, a *gator* would arrive and transport us back to our respective cabins and then that was it, no more direct human contact until the judging commenced four weeks later.

The weather continued to deteriorate, the wind was getting stronger and the rain was incessant. We were completely soaked through, so no one spoke much and got on with the job in hand, my shooting was still impressive and I was confident that I'd be able to procure a decent sized Roe tomorrow. I repeatedly scored on all the targets I aimed for, when my practice had finished I watched the others feeble attempts.

Subi looked to be struggling to even pick the gun up, while Alex was clearly out of her comfort zone. Only Orry it seemed had ever fired a gun before and even then he was average at best. It would be an almighty struggle for any of the others to hit a barn door, never mind anything that moved.

I could only imagine how bad the likes of Pritchard and Cohen would be. Cohen would have to wedge the butt of the gun into one of his several substantial chins before he could comfortably take a shot. I wasn't sure whether Celestine would actually be sober enough to hit the middle deer of three, which no doubt that's what he'd be seeing for every single deer that was actually there.

Once our allotted time was up and all of us were soaked to the skin and thoroughly fed up with *Survival Man's* patter, we were bundled back into the Land Rovers and whisked back to the cabins. My inbred driver had obviously declined driving me back, so *Survival Man* drove me this time and repeatedly eyeballed me through the mirror, "so, what happened between you and that idiot of a driver?"

"Like I said nothing at all, is there a problem?" I asked.

"I've just never seen him this reserved; he was also sporting a split lip and I seem to remember he had at least two teeth left in his bottom jaw," he said this last with a half smirk on his face, but I wasn't giving anything away.

"At the risk of repeating myself I have no idea about him, maybe he hit his face on the steering wheel while bouncing off a tree after more of his shit driving. Anyway, the guy is a liability, what the hell are you employing a cunt like that for?" I asked.

"Up here there's not a great deal of workforce to choose from, he's a local lad with a couple of underlying issues, who actually does a reasonable job. Idiot he may be but he's my idiot, so not so much of the cunt, OK?" *Survival Man* replied.

I'd heard all I wanted to hear from this prick, so remained silent for the rest of the journey, smiling at him whenever I caught him looking at me. As we approached the cabin he said, "we'll pick you up at 6 *a.m.* sharp. It'll still be dark but we should be able to get a good head start up into the hills, so be ready."

Of course, I'll be ready you fucking muppet, I thought, what the hell else have I got to do tonight. With that I climbed out of the Land Rover and trudged off to the cabin without a response as I didn't feel it warranted one, I heard him spin away but I never turned to watch him leave.

I reached the cabin and searched around through the gloom and the rain for any unwanted visitors. But thankfully none were to be seen, maybe my unwelcome dead friend had made his point and was now gone for good, maybe.

7. First Night and Next Day

Entering the cabin was some respite from the cold and rain, the fire was still alight and the room was comfortably warm. I lit several candles and placed them evenly around the room to offer the most illumination possible. Outside was gloomy but not full dark, so for a few moments I contemplated collecting more wood but thought better of it and stripped out of my wet gear.

The chair was covered in no time with my steaming wet clothes and boots. I stood naked in front of the fire to thoroughly dry out and warm through, before I put a change of thermal underwear on, hiking socks and snood. Once dressed, I took down one of the large cooking pots from the shelf above the stove and cooked a little pasta, seasoned it, added a dash of olive oil I'd brought with me and settled down to my first meal in what would be my new home for the next month.

A welcome peace and contentment washed over me as I relaxed on the floor in front of the fire. I took the journal from my pack and made notes from the day I'd had, who I thought were the strongest characters down to the weakest. Alex and Orry were top, Bos had slipped dramatically as I felt my initial fears were misplaced.

Pritchard and that fat fucker Cohen were insignificant and would probably be their own downfall, as for Subi who knows but I couldn't see him being a threat. Celestine was a threat if he could sober up, then maybe he could muster up some kind of competition for me but the dreadful state we found him in today, he just didn't look strong enough to see out the first week.

So, my main rivals were Alex and Orry for the actual competition, except for their shooting. They'd be lucky to have pheasant or partridge, couldn't see them nailing a deer. But when it came to some fun and games, I had no interest in these two or Subi for that matter.

Subi looked like he had his own demons to deal with, he was weak and regardless of his cooking abilities, I couldn't see him surviving the month.

Pritchard and fat boy Cohen were who I really wanted to do some harm to, physically and psychologically. Bos also had it coming, even if he ran squealing to the officials, I'd still have my day with that bastard.

I placed more wood onto the fire and secured the fire guard in place. My clothes were almost dry by the time I decided to get a little sleep, so I pulled the chair further from the heat allowing more warmth into the room. Blowing out most of the candles but leaving the one lit closest to the bed left shadows in the furthest corner of the room, which left me slightly ill at ease.

I decided to crack open one of the several bottles of quality single malt Macallan I'd brought for this exact reason. Pouring myself two fingers I crawled into my sleeping bag and sat looking into the darkness with a creeping sensation that I could make out shapes moving in the half-light.

I must have fallen asleep as I woke a few hours later feeling rested but a little woolly headed. Looking down I was pleasantly surprised that I'd finished my scotch and placed the cup down by the bed without spilling a drop, although I had no recollection of doing so. Checking my watch, I'd been asleep four hours as it was approaching 5 a.m.; perfect, I thought, as I wriggled out of the sleeping bag and headed to the fire.

The room was still surprisingly warm considering it was only about six degrees outside. Using the old cast iron poker located at the side of the fire— along with a toasting fork and small shovel—I prodded and stabbed at the embers left in the fire. I added a couple of smaller logs and then placed a larger one once they started to take hold. Replacing the guard I stepped outside. Shit, it was cold after the warmth of the cabin but thankfully, it had finally stopped raining, how long for I didn't know but it was at least some respite.

Sunrise was still a couple of hours off, but I cautiously edged my way down to the river in just my cargo pants and boots using the limited moonlight to guide my way. Without thinking too much about it I plunged my head into a small pool just off the main river. The shock was immediate and the desired effect instant.

Any trace there may have been from the whisky was gone—that had been my first drink in months and surprisingly, the effects had been immediate—and I ran my fingers through my hair in a poor imitation for a comb. I stood breathing heavily from the shock of the water and stared into the dark, listening to the nocturnal creatures' scurry around me as I contemplated my day ahead. I yelled out incoherently at the top of my lungs into the early morning darkness, it felt wonderful to be alone.

Making my way back to the cabin I had a half hour before I was to be picked up, I quickly dressed in fresh warm under clothing and had a small bar of chocolate for my breakfast. Not something I'd do often but it was quick and easy with a little pick me up to kickstart the day.

I took my knife from under the bed and slipped it into my belt. Next I put my heavy-duty jacket on, gloves, snood and thick woollen hat, gators went on top of my boots and gloves last. I added more logs to the fire and replaced those inside the cabin with more from the outside store. I'd be lucky if the fire lasted until I returned but hopefully, I could shoot well and be back before it died completely.

Just as I finished replacing the logs, I heard the Land Rover approaching, I wondered who'd be driving this morning but as it came to a steady halt, I was surprised to see someone unknown to me, I closed the cabin door and a made for the truck.

A small stocky man of about forty with a ridiculous moustache—must be tough or very stupid to sport one of those—appraised me as I entered the truck and then gave me a warm smile.

"Morning, did you sleep well?"

"Good, thanks," I replied but was reluctant to offer more.

"Think the rain's going to keep off until mid-day, but it's going to be cold. It'll be pissing down by 2 p.m. and the temperature will drop to about two degrees overnight," he said then looked expectedly at me for some conversation.

"That's nice," I grunted and made it quite clear there was nothing more forthcoming from me.

Undeterred by my complete lack of interest he continued, smiling all the while, "my fellow driver phoned in sick today, would that have anything to do with you?"

"No," was all I replied.

"It's just that he was full of beans until he had to drive you here, not like him at all. And someone also said he looked like he'd been in a bit of a scuffle."

"Look mate," I barked. "I couldn't give two shits about your pal or even you for that matter. I'm here to do a job and I don't intend making friends along the way. Can you lot not get this into your thick heads?"

"No problem for me, just making conversation on this fine late autumn morning," he said through gritted teeth and an obligatory smile, whilst he fumbled about turning the radio on.

The radio programme was a retrospective look at results from yesterday's football. Being from Northumberland everyone fully expected you to be a Newcastle United fan, but I'd always followed the mighty Sunderland (for good or bad, mostly bad), along with my father and brother from an early age. Sunderland had nicked a win, while Newcastle and the supposed other north east club Middlesbrough had lost. The driver was grumbling to himself at this—obviously a Newcastle fan—but it was a pleasant start to the day for me.

It was a quiet journey into the hills from then on in. The sun was fiercely trying to break through the cloud cover but unfortunately, it just couldn't muster enough strength and we were to be in what felt like a perpetual darkness. We were to meet up with the guys from yesterday's practice by seven bells. As well as myself, Alex, Subi and Orry would be there, along with *Survival Man* and the gamekeeper who would supervise the shoot.

At least I wouldn't have to put up with the antics of the other reprobates. I might have ended up shooting one of them instead which didn't actually sound like a bad thing at all. Possibly considered by some as a kindness. We pulled up alongside two other vehicles and the other guys jumped out, they all seemed reasonably sprightly and I wondered how much of this was for effect.

Thank goodness they were all appropriately dressed for the occasion. Even Subi, who I'd had little hope for, had all the right kit on and even sported a large hunting knife at his side, which seemed to reach down to his knee.

Alex and Orry bid me good morning and I returned their pleasantries but that was all which was needed. Subi, feeling emboldened also said hello but then made no further attempt at conversation. We went to the back of the lead vehicle and four rifles were produced in their cases. All of them were the same single shot Winchester .243 calibre with one handed out to the each of us, while the gamekeeper and *Survival Man* each had a shotgun broken over their arms.

A packet of twenty seventy-gram soft nose bullets were handed out to each of us, although I secretly felt perhaps two or three would be enough, maybe even one if I were on parr.

"Remember guys," said the gamekeeper. "Head or heart shots only, heart will be straight through the chest, head is even more preferable. The cleaner and more efficient the kill, the more humane but also the better the meat you'll be working with as there will be less trauma. I've had the unfortunate privilege of working with muppets in the past who wait in tree 'hides' all day long then shoot straight through the back of the animal which completely destroys the saddle beneath."

At this he smiled sadly and shook his head in some grim recollection and then continued.

"Between us two"—here he pointed at our favourite *Survival Man*—"we'll be able to get you into position and within distance, I would imagine you'll need to be within two hundred metres. These rifles are good for three hundred metres, but the conditions are far from perfect and you're not all seasoned shooters."

He glanced my way at this and nodded ever so slightly, which I took to mean he believed I'd be able to bag a deer from further away than two hundred metres. A nice vote of confidence, I hoped not to disappoint.

"Remember safety is paramount, do not put yourselves or any of the team in jeopardy, for today only you are a team, remember that. Let's get started, we need to hike a couple of miles north and then we should come upon some suitably sized deer, possibly even a small herd. Right, if you'd all follow us; we'll be up there in no time."

The hike was over rough uneven terrain and within twenty minutes we'd all worked up quite a sweat; fortunately, the rain had kept away but we were expecting it at any time. Conversation was stilted at best and I personally offered nothing to the conversation. I didn't see the point as after this I'd not be in touch during or after the competition.

Survival Man tried to engage with me, but I only answered in one-word sentences, so eventually he gave up trying and concentrated on the trek ahead. *Such a wanker, I thought.* Approaching the next ridge, we were encouraged to remain silent with hand signals and get down onto our bellies and crawl arm over arm until we reached the top.

As we peered over the edge, a group of three roe deer came into view, grazing quite happily on the shrubs and grasses.

The gamekeeper motioned to me to crawl over to him and said, "two hundred-ish metres away, decent age and ready for you, are you ready?"

With a look, I hoped expressed utter contempt for him, I reached behind me, took the rifle from the case, loaded a bullet from my pocket and raised the rifle to my shoulder. Slowly cocking the trigger, I took careful aim, concentrating on my breathing I exhaled slowly and squeezed. The bullet was true and caught the oblivious animal directly below the jaw and exited through the back of its head, it was instant, painless and efficient.

I turned to the gamekeeper and said, "yeah, I think I'm ready."

The other deer had scattered and it would be a while before the others covered the distance to get another chance. Getting to my feet I reached down and picked up the bullet casing then I glanced at Subi; holy shit, this guy had gone green, no way was he shooting anything today. Alex and Orry looked suitably impressed as I re-slung my rifle and headed down to the kill site, I needed to get it bled and dressed before the *Gator* came to pick me and my spoils up.

Descending the hill to the animal I reached under my jacket and took out the *Bowie* knife. *Survival Man* was by my side offering advice, but I paid very little heed to him. The animal was most definitely dead, no need to check, although I knew you had to be careful as a wounded beast could be extremely dangerous.

Having dressed all kinds of birds and animals from pheasants, partridges, the odd stinking grouse then on to rabbits and then the larger deer. These needed to be quickly gutted to aid the hanging process, therefore protecting the meat. I flipped the animal onto it's back and sliced up from its anus to sternum. I then removed and reserved the heart, liver and kidneys as I needed these, then pulled out the remainder of the intestines and stomach and discarded these for any other wildlife in the area.

A surreptitious glance at *Survival Man* confirmed his approval as I turned the beast back over ensuring it was spread eagled to help it bleed out and then left it in this prone position for a little while. I then packed up the offal I needed into small freezer bags and went to clean my hands off on the grass.

When I returned, I picked up the rifle and handed it to *Survival Man*; "Thanks, Cecil," I said and turned away laughing.

I didn't see his face, but I could imagine it was a picture of shock that I actually knew his name and anger at how I could possibly have found out.

"The *Gator* won't take long, these guys may take a little more time than you. Are you OK to wait here while we carry on the hunt?" asked the gamekeeper.

I gave my consent with a slight nod of the head and sat down in the heather.

"Good shooting by the way," he said, "I'm impressed."

Alex smiled at me and raised her hand as she wandered off with the rest of them and a furious Cecil and headed down the hill in search of their quarry. When everyone was out of sight, I put my head in my hands. Just because I was a good shot didn't mean I enjoyed the killing of an animal, the complete hypocrisy of being a chef, I thought.

In the kitchen I could butcher any animal, but out here I didn't necessarily relish the act of the kill, I've always thought I could empathise more with animals than with people. It always left me feeling slightly hollow and a little sick if I'm honest but as long as it was to be eaten, as my father had taught me, then it wasn't just killed for sport and discarded.

Anyway, what was done was done. I could hear the roar of the *Gator* manoeuvring between the hills heading my way using the GPS tracker that we all had just for the day. I stood up, so he could more clearly see me, dragged my hands down my face a few times and pulled myself together before he arrived. God forbid I let anyone witness any weakness.

***

The guy driving the *Gator* was the same fuckwit with the tash who'd picked me up that morning, he was smiling that same inane grin as he was earlier. *Please no more conversation, I thought* and thankfully, none came. He helped me drag the carcass onto the back of the *Gator* and strap it down, then he jumped into the front looking my way and waiting for me to get in alongside him.

With a sigh I climbed in next to him and took hold of the side bar as I thought this is going to be a bumpy ride back to the cabin. With the now mandatory earth being churned up as we wheel span away, I wondered to myself how these idiots are supposed to be conservationists and yet they destroy the hills every time they got into a vehicle.

A pheasant exploded out of the heather as we descended towards something resembling a track. It very nearly collided with the driver and made him duck rather dramatically, which made me chuckle and receive a murderous glare from him as he fought to keep control of the *Gator*. Once we were on the track, we made good ground and arrived back at my cabin just as the rain started, lightly at first but intensifying with every minute.

Jumping from the *Gator* I took the offal I'd reserved and handed it to the driver.

"For the freezer," I said.

He looked at me with complete antipathy and snatched the bags from me.

"Are you for fuckin real?" he asked waving the bags in front of me.

"What the fuck do you want me to do? I need them freezing for two to three weeks and then bringing back to me, they'll be completely fucked if I store them here," I said.

"This isn't in my remit, it's bad enough I've got to drive you bunch of jumped-up cooks, never mind do your job," he barked at me.

"Look, just take them, label them and give them to someone at Kielder to freeze. We were assured at the beginning of the competition that this would be possible. Even if I preserve them somehow, they'll not last a month, will they?" I asked.

"Bah!" he said and placed the bags on the passenger seat. "Absolute bollocks this."

"Give me a hand with this carcass, I need to hang it out the back of the cabin, there's a hook already there," I said and he begrudgingly climbed out and grabbed the back legs, with me taking the front and we made our way around to the back of the cabin. Just as we approached the hook, he dropped the deer and turned back towards the *Gator*.

"That's as far as I go, hang the fucking thing yourself, you miserable cunt!" he said.

And with that he ran to his vehicle, jumped in and flipping me the finger sped off once again in the now expected manner throwing dirt into the air and covering the cabin door with all manner of weeds and shit, leaving me still holding the hind legs of my kill.

At this I looked down and started to laugh.

"Touché mate," I shouted and dragged the carcass the remaining distance, panting heavily I managed to heave it up and onto the hook.

I cleaned and dried the inside of the carcass with a rag then took out some polythene sheeting and draped it around and tied it securely. The rope and polythene had been stashed under the cabin in the hope we would find it for this exact purpose, at least that's what I presumed. I'd check on the carcass from time to time, but I wouldn't skin and butcher it for three weeks as the skin would protect the meat, giving it plenty of time to mature and tenderise.

With this done I went into the cabin and poured two fingers of whisky; job well done, I thought. I'd have this one drink then collect wood for the fire and build up the store while I still had the light, it was just past 1 p.m., so I only had a few hours of daylight left. The daylight went quicker from mid-November.

***

Entering the wood to the north of the cabin it became dense within what felt like only a few metres. Fortunately, the canopy of evergreen trees and thick bushes created a natural shelter and offered some protection from the rain and the wind. It was much gloomier inside the forest and once the sun went down, I believed the darkness would be complete. I gathered as much wood as I could carry, which was remarkably dry considering the rain that had fallen in the last few days and made my way back to the cabin.

On the way I caught movement in my periphery and as I turned the now familiar face appeared once again from behind a tree, "what the fuck do you want?" I hollered.

The fear was subsiding every time he appeared and as I looked at him, his dishevelled appearance, his worsening features I felt what I could only describe as a mixture of anger and pity. I fiercely shook my head to clear away any unwanted thoughts and dropped the pile of wood picking up a single log and screaming, I hurled it at him with all the strength I could muster.

The log bounced next to him and then hit him full in the chest. At least it appeared to hit him although he didn't seem to move a muscle and the log came to rest at his feet. He just stood and peered at me. He didn't come any closer, he didn't make any noise, just stared with his one good eye and his broken face as if willing me to come to him.

I took a couple of steps closer and then hesitated—*what the hell am I doing? I thought.* With this I bent down and picked up my collected wood, when I looked his way again, he'd gone.

"This is insane, I'm not crazy, you fucker. I know you're not real. How can you be? You're dead, I left you back in Jersey!" I screamed into the darkening gloom.

I turned and started back to the cabin, gently reassuring myself as I went. This isn't happening, impossible but then again how many times was I going to tell myself this. Maybe after this competition I could seek out some help but then again what would I say.

"Excuse me doctor, but there's this dead guy haunting my waking thoughts, he's someone I beat to death a while back!"

Yeah, that would go down well, it would be a one-way ticket to the loony bin. *Did people still call them that, I wondered?* My thoughts seemed to be coming more and more erratic.

The light was quickly disappearing as I hurried back to the cabin, I filled the outside wood store, hurried up the steps and slammed the door behind me. Once inside I felt a little more relaxed, though I still found myself checking the window and pondering what to do next.

Again, I asked myself was he intending me harm, could he physically *do* any harm? He had not tried to speak to me, he just seemed to be lurking when I least expected him. I wasn't even sure he wanted to cause any mischief or torment towards me. Maybe eventually he would have something to say? I thought I'd try conversing with him the next time he appeared as I was quite sure he would and as crazy as this sounded, he didn't seem to be leaving anytime soon, whether he was in my head or not.

Checking my watch, it was already 5 p.m., the day had gone by in a glance. Putting more wood on the fire and lighting several candles, I then dragged myself out of my wet clothes and poured myself a small whisky. I set my clothes around the chair to dry again, this was obviously going to be a daily chore as the rain did not seem likely to abate.

I realised I hadn't eaten anything since the chocolate first thing, so I rustled up some rice and beans with chilli and dried herbs and settled down in front of the fire, which was now happily blazing away. I noticed a wooden box beside the stove which I hadn't seen earlier, on opening it revealed wire snares for rabbits and hare, these were still legal in the UK, although quite barbaric. Not something I'd normally condone and didn't enjoy doing but needs must.

Protein would be needed for myself as well as the competition dishes, so I would set these in place tomorrow morning and hopefully, they'd be successful in their savage task.

The cabin also had a small, sheltered veranda at the top of the steps which led to the door, where the hammock was attached, but it was pinned at the very edge of the cabin's eave, therefore left out with no other purpose but to gather rain. I stood there under the cover of the overhanging roof looking out at the dark forest and river sheltering my whisky from the driving rain.

The weather was still grim, but the night was quiet, peaceful apart from the noise of the drumming rain and the odd animal cry or rustle in the undergrowth beneath the cabin. I found myself savouring the night, how serene it was and everything I'd hoped it would be.

I even found myself looking through the rain to see if my *"friend"* was out there waiting, biding his time before he revealed his real reason for being here.

8. Alone at Last

I woke early and felt this would be the norm for the rest of the competition. Even though it was unbelievably quiet outside with no traffic noise or late-night revellers to worry about, it was almost too quiet. It didn't feel natural not to have the normal small town nightly ruckuses to contend with.

No milkmen, no drunkards singing, no early morning papers delivered—not that I read newspapers, but the noisy bastards next door did. Jesus, I wouldn't even have the arsehole bin men and their over-the-top clatter to put up with.

I put logs on the fire and a pan of water on the stove to make a pot of tea, I had brought Lady Grey with me, one of homes small comforts (along with the whisky). It was a drink that could raise eyebrows when unexpectedly asked for by me in a busy production kitchen, when testosterone was the main dish on the menu on any given day.

I opened the door while waiting for the water to boil and peered out into the darkness, it was five-thirty and daylight was a couple of hours off yet. The rain was still persisting but nowhere near as heavy as it had been. I didn't expect this to last as it was forecast to piss down later. I wandered down to the little pool of ice-cold water as I had done the previous day and went through the same ritual of head dunk and then a scamper back to the cabin and the warmth in there.

I dressed, made tea and headed around the back of the cabin to check on the deer. The tea was delicious, that hint of orange was just enough but didn't overpower the tea itself. The polythene was keeping the worst of the rain from it and would help to stave off any frost. I figured that the weather whilst being very cold wasn't cold enough to freeze the beast as that would be an unwanted pain in the arse when I came to butcher it.

Not favouring breakfast today and as the day was just starting to lighten in the east, I headed out with the rabbit snares, with any luck I'd have a rabbit stew for tea. After setting the snares in places, where I'd found droppings and evidence of several burrows, I set off in search of mushrooms and any hardy herbs I might find.

Whilst being far too early to make anything for the final competition dishes, these initial stages were meant as a test of our survival first and foremost. I'd fish later but again for personal consumption only, maybe when we were into the penultimate week, I'd hopefully catch a salmon or a good-sized trout for gravadlax but for now, it was for my personal enjoyment.

Once the snares were set, I consulted the map. It must be getting lighter all the time although it could hardly penetrate the forest canopy and had little real intention of breaking through. I laid the map on the ground and turned my torch on to highlight the designated areas they had so kindly earmarked for us.

Using my compass, I headed in the general direction of the foraging area, thinking to myself that I could guarantee the likes of Pritchard and Cohen would be having all kinds of trouble with this. In all honesty, I couldn't see Fatty even being awake yet and it was now seven-thirty, the fat fucker would still be negotiating his way to the toilet at 9 a.m. Pritchard and that other cunt Bos wouldn't fare any better and poor old Subi looked like he'd be hoping to be back home by day three.

Obviously, I had no way of knowing if Subi, Orry and Alex had been successful on the shoot yesterday, I didn't hold out much hope for them. Pritchard, Cohen, Bos and the possibly sobered up Celestine would be going today and again, I feared they would fare no better. The gamekeepers and the *Survival Man—Cecil, ha, what a name that was*—had stated that they would not help with the shoot, only the tracking.

I wondered if they'd stuck to their guns or took pity on some of them and helped. I hoped to fuck they hadn't as this was a competition after all. With this thought of their impending disaster, I happily weaved my way through the forest to what I am told would be an abundance of mushrooms.

The forest was stunning, dense, dark evergreen foliage stretched out before me. It was so beautiful, all kinds of birds fluttered in the trees, animal shrieks of all description wound their way to me through the woods as I tramped my way in and around the natural serenity that surrounded me.

It was about an hour before I came across my first patches of mushrooms which were growing in a small clearing in the woods, within a slightly boggy area. I cannot imagine that these bad boys were what the organisers had had in mind for us to use. These were a small yellowy brown closed cap with long stalks, I had always been told to steer clear of these from my old man first and then from chefs I'd foraged with.

These were not to be cooked with, not unless you wanted a restaurant full of guests off their tits. Liberty Caps, hallucinogenic and if correctly used in the right hands, they make a great cuppa as we'd found out while experimenting a few times in my early cheffing days. Care must be taken when using Liberty Caps as the effects are similar to LSD and therefore, depending on the persons original demeanour, could increase an already paranoid person to dangerous levels. As well as this they would increase the heart rate and deepen any anxiety, especially with prolonged usage.

I entered the clearing and really noticed for the first time in a while how heavy the rain was without the protection of the forest canopy and picked every Liberty Cap I could find and it turned out to be quite a haul. I'd dry these out just for my own personal use, of course. Can't imagine the judges would be too happy if they were having some sort of flashback while trying to critique our dishes.

Nearby I also found some large clusters of Hen of The Woods, which would go very well with my eagerly anticipated trapped rabbits when I hopefully got back to the full snares.

All in all, I had a better than expected find, my pack was full to brimming with mushrooms and a short walk from these I found thyme and rosemary growing in abundance. With these collected I decided to roam further into the woods, I had marked exactly where this find was on my map and left a small marker of rocks to help me.

I was only an hour from the cabin and it was only mid-morning, so with plenty of time on my hands I decided to explore deeper. After a while of tramping through thick yellow gorse in a large clearing I got back out of the rain under the shelter of the woods. I took a seat on an ancient enormous fallen oak, which had crashed through dozens of other trees and created a natural avenue.

It felt warmer the deeper into the forest I got; apart from the constant patter of the rain, it was incredibly peaceful. I took a long draught of water from my canteen, rested my head back into the nook of a branch and dozed for a while, utter contentment washed over me as I drifted off. And time simply slipped away.

I awoke with a start as I had the feeling that something was snuffling about at my feet. Fearing it might be my KP companion I started to gather myself up but when the haze of sleep fell away from my eyes, I realised that there was a deer and it was only a metre or so from me. I remained where I was feeling exhilarated and desperately tried not to move a muscle. After what seemed an age but must have only been a minute, the deer looked up at me without any fear and simply ambled away with not so much as a glance back in my direction.

If only I had been allowed a camera or even my phone, it would have been an image to keep. Glancing at my watch I realised with utter astonishment that I had been asleep for over an hour, Jesus that never happened to me, I could not remember when I had last nodded off in the middle of the day. Gathering myself up and with a contented smile, I set off back the way I had come feeling the happiest I had been in years. Unfortunately, this blessed harmony and peace of mind was not too last.

Reminiscence: The Fence

As I got older and into my early teens, I found that I didn't need a great deal of friends. I not only grew to do without but also felt that it just wasn't my thing now. From time to time I took my younger brother Ben—two years my junior and nicknamed Chirpy for some long-forgotten reason—on what we always thought of as a grand adventure. But most of the time I was on my own and other kids my age steered well clear of me.

Mam and dad worried about me, but I was fine with it, I think that was why I started taking my brother along dripping after me just to appease the folks. Sometimes I'd take him on the three-mile hike to the old barns, which incidentally belonged to the same farmer who'd found Billy unconscious a few years back.

We would then happily throw rocks through what remained of the upper windows. God knows what the barns had been originally used for—maybe at one time they'd had dairy cattle on the farm?—but what remained was a particularly sorry sight.

It was an early morning in the middle of the October half term week (Blackberry picking week as we called it then), when I told my brother today we would go on one of these so-called adventures. He was buzzing, got his wellies on and was at the door hopping about like he needed the loo before I had even finished my breakfast.

Ten minutes later we were headed for the old barns, toast in hand for a little bit of window smashing; although truth be told, there wasn't a great deal of glass left in them to smash. As usual, it was raining and mam had made us wrap up as the temperature had taken a cold turn the last week. So, dressed in what would have survived an inordinately bleak Russian winter, we marched through the small, wooded area to the back of the house and on toward the farm.

When it was gloomy like this the "forest"—as I liked to call it in a complete exaggeration—always took on this ominous almost brooding look and we were always relieved to be out the other side. Thankfully, it was only about three or four hundred yards deep and maybe a mile long. Once through and with our backs to it we'd always forget about its menace until it was time to scramble back through on our return journey.

Once the spooky woods were safely navigated and not a soul from this world or the next had been seen, we'd run through a large field of scrub and then keep really quiet as we just about tip toed passed the farmhouse. It wasn't exactly private land here as a seldom used public footpath ran around the length of the farm, but it soon would be once we'd negotiated The Fence.

This wasn't just any old wooden rickety fence this was six-feet tall with inch thick spikes which adorned the top. There were small gaps between the spikes to help us over but if you slipped then you were in a world of pain. Many a story was passed around at school about boys who had been impaled on this fence and had to wait hours for the emergency services to arrive to free them, which in turn only made the adventure all the more daring if a successful window raid was complete.

With trouser pants tucked safely into our socks and wellies, as the last thing you wanted was to get hooked when about to leap from the top. Chirpy went first over the fence with me cradling his arse to help him over and then once safely down the other side, I leapt up and hoisted myself over, using the gaps to stand in and then jump down into the field.

The farm we were in was huge and scattered over several acres, so once we were safely at the derelict end the farmer couldn't hear much if anything drifting down towards his house. Which was just as well for us as he had two savage but strangely beautiful and almost regal looking German Shepherds, which patrolled the place but seldom came down this far.

Once there we made full use of the rocks and half bricks scattered around and hurled them at the now sparse windows. Few hit their target, but a muted cheer would go up when we finally hit one of the remaining glass panes. We'd normally continue this for thirty to forty minutes and then explore the empty barns and neglected broken farming machinery to see what treasures could be found.

Usually, not a great deal, as we'd scoured these barns for years now. On this occasion we headed for the old combine harvester, which was ancient and dilapidated. It had rats scuttling about in it, birds nesting in it and small trees growing out of it. It was a complete wreck, but it was like an adventure playground as you could squirm your way through into the bowels of the machine and then pray you wouldn't get stuck down there.

As we were both rummaging around in the middle of this prehistoric behemoth, we suddenly stopped and looked at one another at the same time—voices were coming our way. We slowly and quietly headed for the top of the harvester as that was the only way in or out and I cautiously peered over the top.

It was the miserable bastard of a farmer with another official looking fella with plastic bags tied over his expensive looking shoes. Shit, I thought, but then concluded that they are not going to be looking at this piece of old detritus surely. As I watched closer with Chirpy hanging onto my coat visibly shaking but more with excitement than fear.

The two men stopped next to another old tractor, which had always been covered in some old tarpaulin and something that we'd never really paid much attention too. Unbeknownst to us this must have been worth a few quid as they were haggling over the price at which to sell it. I motioned for my little brother to keep quiet and told him to make his way to the other side, which would obscure us from them.

Many times, I have replayed this scene in my head and wished I'd have just stayed put for a while longer as they can't have stayed out there all day and we could have just slipped away when they had gone back to the farmhouse. Anyway, as we slowly and silently climbed down the other side and started to make our escape, Chirpy tripped on some old wire hidden among the discarded junk and stumbled into a large empty oil drum. The noise was not exactly deafening but it was loud enough for the farmer and his cohort to come running.

We made a break for it, took to our heels and legged it! At thirteen and eleven respectively, we were pretty sprightly and I felt confident that these two 'oldies' had no chance of catching us, although they did set off after us at quite a lick and the chase was on.

We ran through the farm, passed his dogs which were thankfully tied up in chains, going absolutely nuts trying to break free and headed for the fence. Jesus, the fence, I'd never had to climb it in a mad hurry before and thought to myself there's no way Chirpy can get over quick enough without me.

Slowing down ever so slightly so Chirpy came up alongside me I yelled at him that he was going to have to leap as soon as we were there, grab the top and I'd push him as hard as I could to help him upwards and over. He grinned at me in the same excited way that he had when we first saw the farmer and I could almost see the adrenalin pumping through him.

As we neared the fence I yelled to get ready and as he leapt for the fence, he grabbed the top and I pushed with all I had.

I don't know how or what happened next but Chirpy screamed like no eleven-year-old should ever have to scream and then he just seemed to dangle on the other side of the spikes thrashing about. I leapt up and scrambled over then turned and looked up at him.

He was still dangling two feet from the floor but then I realised that he wasn't actually holding onto the fence, but the spike was thrust through the centre of his palm. It was clean through and sticking out the other side coated in gore. Then the blood started to flow, which was when Chirpy started to scream again.

I didn't stop to think what to do next just grabbed his hand and pushed, I thought it would come from the spike easy but no it was almost stuck and the blood running down my arms was making it difficult to get a decent hold. I also looked up to see the farmer baring down on us with a look of angry recognition on his face, "you again you little bastard!"

I pushed again as Chirpy screamed, God those screams were horrendous but what else could I do. Heaving with everything I could muster I managed to get his hand off the spike and we were away scurrying down to the woods with Chirpy cradling his bloodied hand.

With the farmer left behind shouting curses at us and exclaiming that he knew who I was and that my parents would hear of this. I thought in a moment of clarity, no shit Sherlock my brother has a hole the size of a ten pence piece in his palm, I don't think I can get away with this one.

In the woods I stopped for a minute to rest and took my welly off, then my sock which I wrapped tightly around my brothers' hand, amid his protests. He was desperately trying to crawl away from me with a look of abject fear etched on his face, but I knew I had to try to stop some of the bleeding. We made it home in record time and thank the Lord dad was still at work, mam quickly bundled us into the car and took us off to the hospital, driving like some wild banshee.

Chirpy had to have twelve stitches in his palm, while mam roared at me and he would also have to have a skin graft at a different time in the future. Mam was *furious and I could only imagine what was to come when dad got home. When we arrived back at the house the farmer was there waiting for us. As we got out of the car, before he even spoke a word, mam was on him in a flash, giving him the worst rollicking he'd ever had about leaving enticing old farmyard equipment out for boys to go rummaging through.*

He tried to protest and explain what had happened, but he never got a word in and mam hustled us through the door and into the house. I looked out at his utterly crestfallen face as he pulled himself into the car with a look of complete disbelief on his face. I stood at the window, smiled at him and gave him a little wave, then turned away before he could react.

Next day, I checked up on my little brother to see how he was feeling and to ask after his war wound. When I entered his bedroom, he was buried beneath the covers and was quite clearly pretending to be asleep.

"You OK?" I asked to no response, "Come on, Chirpy, what's up?"

"Nothing Jack," he mumbled.

"Hey, what is this, I thought you'd want to talk about our adventure yesterday?" I urged.

"Nah, I'm OK, I just want to sleep," he answered.

Felling quite put out by this as after all I did rescue him from the dreaded fence, I persevered albeit with a firmer tone.

"Come on, what's going on?"

And with this Chirpy almost burst from the bed clothes pushing his hand up into my face and shouted, "why the hell were you laughing at me when you were dragging my hand further down onto the spike?"

"What the hell are you talking about?" I yelled utterly bewildered.

"You pulled me back down onto it and kept it there you nutcase and it was the farmer who helped to pull my hand up and off the spike!"

He snivelled through the tears and snot now streaming down his face.

At this I simply looked at him dumbfounded, I didn't understand, it was me that had saved him, wasn't it? I was sure of it. I can remember being at the woods and wrapping his hand in my sock but when I really thought about it I couldn't actually remember freeing his hand from the spike. I honestly thought I had been the one to heave him over and become a hero in his eyes. I left his bedroom in a state of complete confusion and despair, if all that were true and I could do that unawares to my own brother then—

Thinking back, it was no wonder the farmer had been waiting for us at the house. He obviously wanted to try and explain what he had seen and then looking completely perplexed when mam had bawled at him and wouldn't listen to a word he had to say.

9. First Week

After my unexpected sleep in the woods, I headed back through the rain and wind to check the snares and was pleasantly surprised to find two decent sized rabbits caught, one of them still struggling. I quickly snapped their necks with the same feeling of guilt I always had. I then took out my knife and skinned, gutted and cleaned them then tied them together and carried them across my shoulder back to the cabin.

As expected, all was as I'd left it and as it should be and there was no sign of anyone having been anywhere near. Just then I heard a low buzzing from above and looked up out of instinct, forgetting we were supposed to act like they weren't there but it was incredibly hard to ignore a drone completely.

It lingered for a while and skirted the outside of the cabin; it would have made for good TV to see me with rabbits draped across my back and knife in hand. Also, with a pack full of mushrooms and herbs, which I duly obliged by conveniently opening it up and revealing the contents.

It would have also taken in the deer professionally dressed and hanging at the back. I wondered what cheesy commentary Schroder would be adding to these pictures and so dearly wanted to flick the drone the finger but managed to restrain myself.

Thankfully, within a few minutes it took off, looking for some other competitor—*good luck with their catch of the day I thought*—so, I quickly jointed the rabbits and took them inside to make myself something to eat. Rabbit stew with thyme and foraged wild mushrooms was a decent effort for being stuck in the middle of nowhere, all washed down with a couple of cheeky snifters.

The next few days went this way. Some days I'd forage, some I'd set snares and some I'd simply sit at the riverbank amongst the reeds and the mud, usually in the rain and fish in a state of blissful contentment. I had caught several good-sized trout which made for some simple but tasty meals, along with the larder that had been provided it could make for quite a feast.

When the rain had actually let up one day, I cleaned the grime from the grill and using some of the firewood I grilled the trout alfresco. It was deliciously smoky with a lemon dressing I'd made from the olive oil I'd brought and the dried lemons, which I'd rehydrated.

My KP *"friend"* visited with me most nights now, he sat hunched in the corner of my cabin amongst the deep shadows and watched my every move. His appearance was most definitely deteriorating and in all honesty, he was quite unrecognisable now. I conversed with him most of the time, I mean why the hell not?

He never took my offer of food or a whisky or even my *special mushroom tea*—which I brewed most nights as a substitute for the booze—he was a cheap house guest but if it were an apology he was after, he could well and truly get fucked! I felt no guilt at what I'd done and if he wanted to spend his eternity sitting with me then good luck to him.

He obviously wasn't there to harm me, at least not physically, so he'd have to try harder if he wanted me to lose my mind as he wasn't exactly good crack. Maybe I was crazy? *A loony*? *Gone fishing*? If that was the case then fuck it, it felt OK with me.

I knew I had slipped back into the bad habits of the demon booze and my newfound love of the hallucinogenic mushroom tea, but I had none of the everyday work stresses and as long as I remained fed and watered then what was the harm. Even with the copious amounts of tea I was now ingesting on a regular basis, I didn't feel any more anxious or paranoid than I usually did.

Now, that we were finally here in the middle of nowhere, the end of the competition seemed such a long way off. I also had a fair idea of what I'd be cooking for those final dishes to be judged by Clements and Co, so I felt no immediate pressure to do anything more than simply relax and enjoy myself.

Keeping track of the time was useless and not particularly necessary, so I seemed to favour just going by the light of the day instead of wearing my watch as I didn't exactly have deadlines to meet. I kept religiously on top of my daily chores. Washing my clothes in the river, cleaning and drying the inside of the deer, collecting firewood, as I went through copious amounts to keep the fire going all day and night.

Rabbits and fish were in abundance, so I felt I had no worries on that score. I would also take several more trips to the mushroom fields—which appeared to stretch forever—to gather just enough for a few day period.

The weather—if one was worried about it—was grim every day, mostly raining with some blustery winds and becoming very cold, it must have been somewhere between three and four degrees. It was approaching the end of the first week when feeling particularly bored and a little melancholic I decided to go further afield and explore south west.

I knew that some of the other cabins were this way and wondered if Fatty Cohen had given up the ghost yet. I thought I would creep down to his place and have a looksee if I manged to get close enough, but I felt he would probably be long gone by now.

Packing my map and compass I set off early before first light and worked my way through the trees with the aid of my torch for the first couple of hours. As always of late it was raining hard, the ground was a bog and it was tough going, the forest was unyielding almost as if it were refusing to allow me to traverse this way.

As the weak sun desperately tried to break through the rain clouds and then penetrate the forest roof and after fighting for a good half an hour with a particularly dense—and suspiciously man-made part of the forest—I forced my way out into a small clearing. The sweat rolled down my back, so I sat down on a rotting tree stump for a two-minute breather.

I took a drink of water and looked at my surroundings, glancing down I noticed footprints in the mud leading away to the other side of the clearing and quickly got to my feet. With my heart racing I stashed my canteen in my pack and raced across the open ground and into the safety of the trees. Once under the cover of the natural forest canopy I stopped, calmed my breathing and listened closely.

***

At first very little could be heard over my own heartbeat pounding in my ears, but as I gradually became attuned with the natural sounds of the forest, I could just make out intermittent voices somewhere off in the distance. As I moved towards the voices to make out a little more, it now appeared to be only one voice having a heated conversation with itself.

I crept ever closer trying not to make a sound, but I need not have worried as it was a manic full-blown argument. Amazingly, it was Cohen quite clearly alone and arguing with himself outside his cabin. He was pacing up and down the veranda, sometimes dropping down into the mud, wandering around there for a while and then back up onto the veranda again to keep up his ridiculous monologue.

"Why the fuck did I let myself get into this? You are a fucking idiot, Cohen, do you realise that? What on earth were you thinking about?"

I could only sit and stifle my laughter, I knew he wouldn't be coping but this was ridiculous, why hadn't he just got in touch with the organisers and been picked up? What a ridiculous specimen he was, he was dirty, inappropriately dressed for such a cold day in cargo shorts and t-shirt and he still had on those ridiculous flip-flops.

He had no logs in his outside store and there was no smoke coming from the cabin's chimney. I surreptitiously skirted the outside of his cabin, keeping within the cover of the treeline. At the back it was not a surprise to see there was no deer hanging. This useless bastard was unravelling after just one week, surely the drones must have seen this. Then again I suppose we had been told implicitly that it was up to us to pull the plug if that's what we wanted.

On everyone's map there was, along with the best foraging spots, a large red cross highlighted, which was where the emergency phone could be reached. It was easy enough to get too and would take each competitor a mere thirty to forty minutes from their respective cabins.

I looked even closer at Cohen; he wasn't just dirty but filthy. He looked like he hadn't washed all week, his feet and legs were covered in cuts and abrasions as if he'd been out in the woods in his shorts and idiotic footwear. What a useless wanker was all I could think, absolutely pathetic.

The cabin was surrounded in chocolate wrappers and coke cans. He must have brought a huge stash of these to be his basic home comforts but had obviously been living on these things alone as the lazy bastard will not have been able to cook if he couldn't even get a fire going. By now, it must have been heading towards midday or possibly even later, so I decided to head back to my place.

I would have some food, freshen up with a change of clothes and then I'd come back out here to see if I could put the shits up him during the cover of darkness. It was about time I had some fun with this blimp, such a dislikeable man that I think everyone would approve of me making his Northumberland stay as uncomfortable as possible. He always liked playing the big man when he had his bosom buddy Pritchard with him, so let's see how big he was when on his lonesome.

I felt confident I could tip this excuse of a man over the edge and he'd soon be running scared and asking to be taken home to his equally fat mummy and that would also mean one less in the competition to worry about.

Heading back was easier as I had a little bit of a skip in my step with the thought of tormenting Cohen. I must try to avoid the drones while I'm this far south of my cabin as I didn't want anyone putting two and two together and realising what I had in mind.

The organisers obviously knew that there was bad blood between myself and some (well most actually) of the other competitors, so I would imagine they were trying to keep a close eye on us. Arriving back at the cabin I estimated it was about a two-to-two-and-a-half-hour hike to Cohen's place, I would set off back there at around 10 p.m. to arrive just in time for the 'witching hour'.

This made me laugh out loud to myself, when you are as afraid as Cohen quite clearly was then arriving as I planned at around midnight would without doubt add to his abject terror.

I had collected as much dry wood from inside the forest on my return journey from Cohen's cabin and stacked it just inside the door as my wood store was full outside. The fire was getting low, practically embers, so I added freshly chopped sticks—which I'd left indoors to dry out—and then once they took hold added larger logs. I then prepared a meal of braised rabbit thighs, with some rice and herbs. The legs would take a little while to cook as they were best cooked slowly.

Stripping out of my wet clothes I headed out into the cold late afternoon, strode down to the river in just my underwear, stripped out of these then without any hesitation plunged full length into one of the pools, which had recently formed since the river had burst its banks. The water was freezing cold and the rush was instant, my whole body seemed to respond to the intrusion and I, at once, felt completely invigorated and cleansed.

Climbing from the water after enduring as much as I could bare, the shock of the wind hitting me was like a double whammy, but I found it was equally thrilling. Then looking to the sky and inwardly sighing I heard the now familiar low buzz of the drone to spoil the moment. I ignored it as I had been requested to do so and headed back to my cabin butt naked, if they wanted a show then they could have it.

Quite frankly, I was past caring what they thought of me and slowly climbed the wooden treads to the cabin and stepped inside, with the door closed to the elements and the fire now blazing, the room was gratifyingly warm and felt almost sensorial against my chilled body.

***

I sat there in front of the fire until completely dry then dressed in fresh clothes, took out my journal and made some notes on my progress and Cohen's subsequent disassembling. I was increasingly curious to know if everyone was still competing and whether we had had any early dropouts yet.

Subi and Celestine I had backed to be gone first but you just never know. Maybe Subi had found his balls and Celestine had sobered up and sorted himself out—maybe pigs might fly—or maybe one of them had the same idea as me about sabotage. It was tough not knowing if the others had settled into it with the same ease in which I had.

I made more notes on where Cohen was and what state of mind I thought he was in; Pritchard would be my next port of call but as he was further afield I'd need provisions and would have to be prepared to be out most of the night.

Celestine was north of me along with Alex and Subi; Orry and Bos were possibly further north still. At least, I thought they were, but I had only briefly seen the map and couldn't exactly recall—helped somewhat by the mushrooms and whisky I felt—so Orry and Bos could be anywhere. These would have to wait for now as Cohen was first on the list.

After the rabbit legs had been slowly braising for about an hour, I added the rice and let that cook out, thirty minutes later I was enjoying a meal that gave me the sustenance for a long night ahead and a meal that Cohen could only dream of. He must be freezing cold, deflated and feeling utterly wretched and his body would be hungry and screaming out for any kind of nourishment.

I could not believe he'd taken on this challenge without any kind of proper research into what we were expected to live like. It crossed my mind then and I wondered if the silly twat had had the forethought to have brought candles? He probably thought he had full electricity, Sky Q and a widescreen TV. I could just imagine him sitting there shivering in the dark with no food except a chocolate bar and some coke, he couldn't even make a pot of tea if he were too lazy to gather wood to build a fire.

I gathered together a few essentials for tonight, I had my watch on with knife strapped to my belt, map, torch and a couple of chocolate bars I stashed in my pack along with my canteen for the journey ahead. I waited patiently until ten, downed a quick whisky, felt and savoured the burn in my throat and set off for Cohen's place. I was in no mad dash as I had plenty of time to get there, he wasn't going to be going anywhere.

Eventually I came to the thicket, which seemed even tougher to negotiate at night. I managed to force my way through and for a moment wondered if the organisers had built this up for this exact reason, as some deterrent for the likes of me but then I dismissed the thought out of mind. I crossed the clearing and came to the treeline above Cohen's cabin.

As expected, it was in complete darkness with the shutters spread wide open—I was right about the candles—but again I could hear a voice, it was soft and feminine like and strangely not at all unpleasant.

I soon realised that this time the crazy fucker was singing too himself, if I wasn't mistaken it was a Neil Young ditty, "*I'm gonna give you till the morning comes, till the morning comes.*" He just kept repeating this same line over and over; Jesus, this guy really had lost it. Maybe he felt this was his last night and he'd get out tomorrow?

It put my own sanity into some sort of perspective, not mentioning any dead kitchen porters that is. I checked my watch to find it was a little after 12:30, happy with this I began to creep down to his cabin desperately avoiding the potentially clamorous coke cans and other detritus he had left lying around like a booby trap (albeit an unintentional one).

The rain—it was always raining these days—helped to conceal my arrival as I climbed up the steps to his door. It drummed against the roof of the cabin and I proceeded to slowly crawl along his small porch to the single window, avoiding the hammock which was strewn across but still tied by one end to the roof.

The fat bastard must have tried to relax into it and it couldn't hold his sheer bulk and subsequently snapped–*how I wish I had been here to see that I thought* with a barely stifled giggle. The cabin was exactly the same purpose-built structure as my own and as I neared the window and was about to raise myself up to peer in when the floorboards creaked.

"Who's out there?" shouted Cohen from inside, his voice quivering as he said it. "Come on, I can hear you, who the fuck is it?" he whimpered.

I remained silent desperately trying not to laugh when I heard him say to himself, "Jesus, William, come on get a grip lad!".

William? *Ha,* I didn't think anybody called him that never mind himself. Now, it really was taking all my strength to stifle the laugh waiting to explode from me. I gathered myself up firstly onto my haunches and then into a full standing position and sneaked a look in through the window. I could just make him out in the little moonlight available, he was crouched in the corner with a tatty blanket wrapped around him and what looked like a saucepan in his hand raised in front of him like a weapon.

That was it, I couldn't contain myself any longer and burst into laughter and almost fell from the porch into the mud and shit left by fatty himself. It was then I heard a guttural roar from inside and Cohen came bursting through the door with a crash, pan raised high, blanket falling from his shoulders and revealing an enormous sagging belly.

"*Cunt-ingham,* you really are an utter cunt!" he screamed and ran straight at me.

I sidestepped off the veranda and dropped into a rather dramatic roll into the disused coke cans, wrappers and dirt. As it turned out, this little manoeuvre was completely unnecessary as Cohen in his rage tripped on his semi discarded blanket and rolled down the three steps, dislodging one, cracking another in half and only halting his furious descent when his head hit the outdoor grill with a sickening crunch.

After a minute or two I managed to get my laughing under some kind of control and steadied my voice.

"Cohen?" I shouted, "Cohen? Come on stop fucking about and get up, you useless sack of shit!".

But he didn't move, not at all. Gingerly creeping towards him I shone my torch in his face, "Oh shit!" I muttered.

This guy was quite clearly dead, no if's or but's about it, there was no need to take a pulse or try CPR, he was undoubtedly dead. His head probably caused by the sheer weight of the fat bastard had split like a melon. There was blood everywhere and grey matter was seeping down his face and onto his comfort blanket. That gave me the giggles all over again as all I could think of was Charlie Brown's mate Linus sucking his thumb and clinging tightly to his security blanket.

The rain was still sheeting down washing the blood from Cohen's face as quickly as it oozed from the crack in his head and the wind was picking up desperately, trying to whip his blanket away from being entangled in his feet and out into the forest. I had to think for a minute, there was no fear of drones as I'd only seen and heard them during the day, plus the weather was atrocious and it would have been impossible to navigate one in this.

I knew I should simply work my way to the emergency phone point and call for help but everyone involved knew of the animosity between us and I would surely be blamed in some way. More importantly, if he were to be discovered, the competition would be over. I could not let this happen, I had to win, the competition had to be finished, no matter the cost.

And let's be honest, was anyone going to miss this fat useless slob of a man, I doubt it. Possibly his bosom buddy Pritchard but I'd take care of that cunt anyway. I realised that my only answer was that I would have to put Cohen in the river, dispose of his wreck of a body, it was that simple.

***

As I turned to look for helpful materials, a lone figure lurched out of the dark and dragged itself towards the prone figure of Cohen now lying in a pool of blood and filth. It casually sat down and appraised the situation staring between the body and me.

"Look, if you've nothing constructive to say and are not here to help then fuck off for a while, yeah? You're not going to sit there and judge me, it wasn't my fault anyway, he fell and hit his head, so just let me crack on and resolve this situation will you?"

I shouted at the KP through the wind and rain. Not that he gave much acknowledgement of my outburst, he just sat there staring and with a slight shake of his head, which could have been disapproval or possibly just some kind of dead man's palsy.

Using the light of my torch I searched for anything of use and found the polythene sheet tucked under the cabin, which should have been used to cover his non-existent deer. Laying this at his feet as best as I could and holding the corners down with rocks, I slowly heaved his body onto it.

Wow, this guy was heavy, it took everything I had just to roll him over. There was also rope beneath the cabin, again probably the identical one I had used to secure the deer in place and I wrapped this around him in stages securing the polythene to Cohen's body. As I got to the head my fingers sank into the head wound and brain matter squeezed between my fingers making me wretch.

"Bah, even in death you dirty bastard you make me want to puke!" I hollered into his sagging face just as a large fart escaped him. "Jesus, is there no end to your repulsive habits!"

The smell then hit me and that was it, I ran slipping and sliding over to the river and puked, not so much from the fingers that had slid into the gaping head wound but just the odour emanating from this repulsive body. I'm positive my KP companion would have been laughing at me if he'd had any semblance of a mouth remaining to laugh with.

Wiping my face and cleaning my hands of gore in the icy cold water of the river as it furiously raged by, I gathered myself together and got back to the task at hand. Gathering heavy rocks from the outskirts of the forest, I then placed them inside Cohen's parcelled body and resecured the ropes to the corpse.

I was still worried that he'd float back to the surface even with the weight of the rocks and so, I sat there for a few moments to think what else would be best to do. Would puncturing the body help? Surely it would fill with water and aid the sinking process, otherwise the eventual build-up of gasses would bring him back to the surface and it would be game over. I was reasonably confident my DNA would be all over this fucker and there was no way out here to even attempt to get rid of it.

"Bollocks," I mumbled to myself surreptitiously glancing at the KP who was still keeping his *single* watchful eye over me. Then making a decision and quickly disregarding his look of disapproval, I knew this was something I would have to do and drew my knife from my belt.

***

Plunging my knife into his belly was not as gross as I had expected, it just felt like I was boning out a shoulder of pork, it actually slipped into him easier although the smell was a hell of a lot worse. After several puncture wounds and another trip to the river to expel the last of my previous meal of rabbit, I sat back on the broken steps of his cabin.

I considered what I'd done and knew that if—*when*—he was found I'd be definitely screwed. I rested for a minute or two nibbling on one of my chocolate bars to try and replace what I'd thrown up then returned my cleaned knife to my belt. The KP remained looking on but offered up no useful advice or help, just sat there with what I imagined a contemptuous look.

After I felt somewhat restored, I began the wretched job of hauling Cohen's body with the addition of heavy rocks towards the river. I couldn't imagine he'd float downstream too far even though the river was raging as this guy weighed a tonne, as long as he was submerged and stayed that way, I didn't care.

It took me what seemed like an eternity to get him there but thankfully as we neared the riverbank, or at least what remained of the riverbank, the mud and water aided me and I was able to drag and slide him into the river. He sank immediately beneath the dark waters but then instantly resurfaced bobbing towards the centre of the river. As I started to feel the first semblance of panic and feared I'd have to try and retrieve the body somehow, he again slowly slipped beneath the surface and mercifully and with a massive sigh of relief didn't re-emerge.

Trudging back to the cabin I needed to try and cover any third-party involvement, just in case they actually did notice the big fucker was missing. Checking my watch, I was startled to see it was 3:30 in the morning, I needed to get a spurt on. Running into the woods I snapped a large leafy branch and brought it back to the channel that had been almost gouged into the mud, where I'd dragged him to the river.

Furiously slashing it backwards and forwards I tried to disguise it as best I could along with any boot prints I could find. I threw his discarded cans and wrappers about to also better hide the tracks and scattered sodden fallen leaves as haphazardly as I could.

Under the ever-watchful eye of my up to now useless KP companion, I ventured into Cohen's cabin. As I expected, it was a complete and utter shithole, his supplied larder was barely touched, he hadn't even bothered to try and re-light the fire once the initial cache of firewood had been used.

His limited wardrobe was strewn everywhere and all of it seemed to have been soiled in some way shape or form. How can anyone live like this? Looking through his allowed quota of personal belongings, there was nothing of any use and knowing time was of the essence, I quickly left the chaos of Cohen's cabin.

The blood that had come from his head wound was seeping into the mud under the incessant rainfall, by morning I couldn't imagine there'd be much obvious trace especially from the aspect of a drone. Closing the door behind me I left the cabin pretty much as I had found it, minus the fat man, of course.

I searched the area around the cabin one last time from the veranda and finding things to be as they were supposed to, I climbed down and around onto what was almost a duckboard at the base of the cabin and dropped down into the reeds near the riverbank. I then made my way within the rushes and shrubs until I could get to the treeline, therefore leaving no more unnecessary boot prints.

I had one last look back at his place from the woods and satisfied that all seemed well—as well as could be expected—I took off back to my own place double-time. I made good progress through the forest and even the thick dense bushes, what I feared to be a man-made barrier seemed less of an obstacle and I was back at my cabin by six. The KP was sitting waiting for me in his usual corner of the cabin amongst the shadows and I could not help but think, how the dead travel fast.

First thing I did was add some wood to the fire, then put a pan of water on for some special tea; while this was brewing, I downed a large well-earned whisky or two. I felt exhilarated, the adrenalin was still pumping and I stripped out of my clothes ignoring the KP and sat naked in front of the fire. The heat prickled my skin, but it felt good, I felt truly alive.

I stayed there with the blaze of the fire almost too much too bare, drinking my tea and alternating it with quality single malt until the first signs of light crept through my window and until I was well and truly off my tits.

10. The Cohen Aftermath

I awoke late to what felt like birds ceaselessly twittering inside my head. The noise was unbearable as I got to my feet, staggered bare arsed to the door, ripped it open and screamed at them to fuck off. They scattered into the sky and headed for the security of the forest, soon to return and continue their chattering.

My brain was on fire and felt like it was trying to burst from the top of my skull. I decided I must ease off on the tea at least for a day or two to recover my senses somewhat; wow, that shit was strong, coupled with the whisky it was a highly potent concoction. I stood at the door for a few minutes and tried to orientate myself with the circumstances of last night and the realisation that it wasn't any kind of dream and that Cohen was most definitely dead.

It wasn't my fault, I was convinced of that; he should have been better prepared then he might not have been so spooked when I arrived at his door.

Remembering him sitting there with his saucepan for protection caused another laugh to suddenly burst from me, what a muppet that boy was. I wondered how long it would take the organisers to realise he wasn't there? He'll have been almost a recluse this first week, so they probably wouldn't think much of not seeing him around the cabin and as long as I hadn't been seen then nothing could be proven.

Bad blood between us or not, they would have to be able to prove I had actually been in that area and without his body then hopefully we'd get to the end of the competition before they got wind of what happened. Right now, that's all I was bothered about, nothing much else concerned me except the competition and getting to the end of it triumphant.

I decided to take a plunge and freshen up in what I now thought of as my very own ice bath near the river. The rain had briefly stopped again but the sky was dark and the black ominous clouds remained. I couldn't see the weather improving a great deal as the competition wore on if anything it would probably worsen.

Weaving my way down to the pool feeling still drunk and a little high, I stood at the edge and braced myself for the freezing waters. I'd taken to not even bothering with clothes—not even the obligatory underwear—for the few yards to my early morning dip. It wasn't like there were any crowds to offend and it would be up to the producers discretion to relay whatever the drones picked up if one happened to pass by.

Again, the replenishing powers of the pool ripped through my body and the insufferable hangover and the recovery was instantaneous. I stayed submerged within the pool as long as I could stand it until the cold and the fear of passing out was overwhelming, then crashed through the surface and slowly pulled myself up and out into the wintery midday gloom.

I looked down at myself and while I had taken every precaution in looking after myself, I noticed I'd still lost several pounds this first week. Ribs that were not normally apparent were quite visible and while this in itself wasn't too much to worry about, I couldn't let it worsen.

I must make sure I eat more, the pasta and rice were provided for this exact reason and I have to make use of them. It's imperative that I keep a certain level of fitness what with my nightly exertions using up a lot of my bodies stored fuel, replenishment was the key.

Back inside the cabin I dressed in warm gear for the day, re-stocked the fire and taking heed of what I'd just discussed with myself, started a lunch of trout, rice and beans. I looked at the whisky and whilst sorely tempted I decided against it and brewed some tea, not the hallucinogenic kind.

After I had eaten a hearty lunch and cleaned up after myself—could never live in a shithole, unlike some dead fat people I could mention—I sat down and planned the day ahead. More firewood as usual was needed—another thing that Cohen had neglected, it was vital to keep a fire going—I would also re-set the snares for a couple of rabbits as my stocks, I kept in the outside cool box, were all but diminished.

I might also fish later but I intended heading back to Cohen's place first as I wanted to see from the safety of the trees what the area around the cabin looked like in the broad light of day. Under the cover of darkness it might have looked OK, only to find I had left some glaring mistake for the drones to capture. I would have to move quickly as the days were getting shorter.

Once the wood was safely stored away and the snares were set, I packed lightly and headed off at a good pace to Cohen's cabin. The forest was as serene as ever, the floor was soft and silent under foot caused partly by a blanket of dead leaves and moss. The wind had dropped and the rain had not resumed as yet, but I was sure it was just a matter of time.

Two hours later—an excellent effort I mused—I was at the edge of the treeline scanning the area for anything I may have missed. The rain had worked its cleansing magic and there was barely a trace of the track left by dragging fatty's humongous corpse and I could not see any sign of boot prints whatsoever. So far so good.

I next looked along the water's edge where Cohen had been consumed by the river, nothing remained of him. I had had a terrible nagging feeling while working my way over here that he was going to be floating with his arse sticking up out of the reeds or his bloated face poking through the polythene set in a rictus grin. Thankfully, nothing of the sort appeared and I breathed a sigh of relief.

The river was still swollen and flowing fast but didn't seem as fierce or relentless as it had been—but if the rains persisted as expected, this river could and would be deadly—and I wondered how far Cohen had been dragged along the riverbed. Probably not that far as he would be hopefully stuck in the silt at the bottom because of the sheer size of him.

Just then I heard the low buzzing and looked up to see a drone heading towards Cohen's cabin doing the rounds for the day. I quickly buried myself in the undergrowth as best I could and with the shelter of the trees, I knew I would be impossible to see. It headed towards the cabin, circled around it and then paused, it looked to be trying to see inside the small window. Shit, I should have draped a sheet up at the window or at least closed the shutters, but it was too late now.

The drone hovered for a while, obviously trying to get a better look inside, but it would be very difficult to see anything through the gloom along with Cohen's detritus spread everywhere. After what seemed an age, it moved slowly away and circled the cabin again, trying to see if there were any signs of Cohen apart from his discarded coke cans and confectionary wrappers.

They must have been used to Cohen's inactivity and boring no-show by now as after a few agonising minutes for me when I thought the game would be up, it took off at speed and headed for the top of the treeline. Luckily, it wasn't anywhere near my secreted position and I heard it quickly retreat back to wherever they were stationed.

Well, for now it seemed my little secret was safe, at least for the time being, so a little hesitantly I crawled from my hidey-hole and headed back into the forest. It was slower going on my return journey as the rain recommenced its deluge, the crack of thunder overhead shattered any peace the forest had given me and I worried as to how bad this storm was going to be.

I could not imagine Schroder venturing out in weather like this to do his reports, he would probably be pissed up in his elegant trailer. They—the producers—would probably set up a fake scene, whereby Schroder would be a stone's throw from his trailer but offer the appearance of being stranded in the deep forest like some Grim fucking fairy-tale. He would do his carefully prepared lines and then he would dash back under the cover of his palatial surrounding's.

I bet he so wished he hadn't delayed proceedings with his imagined injury, complete piss head that man.

While negotiating my way back, I wondered how my fellow competitors were getting along. I imagined Alex would be adapting fine, Subi I have no doubt would be home by now. I was not sure of it but had the feeling that Orry may be OK, still I was not a hundred percent on that one. I could guarantee Bos would be bullshitting some farmer somewhere and trying to get eggs and supplies from them with his considerable charms. Pritchard would be contemplating making the journey to his pal Cohen—well, good luck with that one.

Celestine though, now that was a puzzler, would he or more to the point could he have sobered up? If so, he undoubtedly could be a formidable opponent, but I simply could not see it, I was curious as to whether he even wanted to sober up. It was probably some cry for help coming here, but I fear he would find very little sympathy after the torment he had caused to the profession. He was probably already dead in his cabin, having choked on his own vomit in a drunken stupor.

***

Nearing my cabin, I headed towards my rabbit snares and to my delight— and then subsequent feeling of guilt—I had two good size adults, although they were half mad with fear and one had almost pulled the lower part of its leg off trying to scramble free. I snapped their necks and skinned and gutted them a hundred yards from their burrows. Tying their legs together I slung them across my shoulder and continued on home.

The light of the day was all but gone and as I was nearing my adopted home but still within the safety of the trees, I heard voices and could see torch light flickering in the direction of my cabin. Dropping to the ground and taking my knife from my belt I cautiously approached the edge of the forest and peered through the downpour at the scene before me.

It was Cecil the *Survival Man* and one of his flunkies, the smug dude with the ridiculous tash. I noticed in their *Gator* there were two shotguns almost set out as a display, so they could be seen by anyone in a show of assumed power and they were braying on my door and shouting my name. They had obviously had a recce of the surrounding area as I could make out fresh boot prints all around the cabin and I was infuriated to see that they had also trailed mud right up to my door.

Emerging from the forest and slowly making my way towards them— making sure they could see me wiping my rabbit bloodied knife on the grass—I made a show of replacing my knife in my belt as they watched me approach. The *Tash* made an involuntary motion towards the shotguns and Cecil gently placed his hand on his arm to arrest his movement.

I shouted a greeting as I got ever nearer, "good evening, Cecil," with a beaming grin across my face that never quite reached my eyes.

"Evening, Jack," he replied through gritted teeth and as I looked at his companion, I could see the hint of a smile on *Tash's* face at me using the big bad *Survival Man's* real name again.

"What can I do for you gentlemen on this fine late autumnal evening?" I asked sarcastically as the rain suddenly increased its ferocity beating down on us and another crack of thunder rumbled up above.

I did not invite them into my cabin to get out of the atrocious weather, I stood looking at them unable to hold the grin any longer as it was replaced with a look of utter contempt.

"I thought there was to be no contact between us and the outside world? This is what we were told, did you two not understand?" I enquired.

"We're just doing a bit of a search for one of the competitors who hasn't been seen about for a few days," the flunky explained with a look from Cecil as if to say, shut the fuck up, this is my show.

"Oh really, that's interesting, can I per chance ask who?"

Unbeknownst to these two morons my heart was beating furiously, the noise in my ears said clearly they must be able to hear it, but they just looked at me through the rain inquisitively. It had only been a day since Cohen had been consigned to his watery grave, it surely could not be him, could it?

"Celestine is missing, he hasn't been seen since Thursday, that was the last we saw of him before the weather closed in and we had to pick and choose when to send out the drones. He was heading into the woods this way, but we know that means nothing as he could have gone anywhere," Cecil replied.

Relieved, but hopefully not visibly I continued towards them and slung my rabbits into the outside cool box.

"Well, I haven't seen anyone and that's just as it should be. Wait a minute, should I be worried that he was heading this way? Is that why you're here, are you warning me in case he tries anything funny? What if he sneaks into my cabin tonight, ties me up and buggers me?" I asked sarcastically holding my hand in front of my mouth in mock surprise.

"That's not why we're here, I'm sure you can look after yourself," Cecil says while taking in the cabin and surrounding area and the fact that I was quite clearly thriving. "No, we just wanted to make sure you were OK and that you'd not come across him in the forest somewhere, possibly in trouble?"

"Look, Cecil, I know what I am and I know I can be a cunt but come on, if the guy was in trouble regardless of him being utterly incompetent, drunk and pathetic, do you honestly think I'd leave him lying in the forest to die if I came across him?" I answered with the most sincere look on my face that I could possibly conjure without breaking down and laughing.

"Fair enough, Jack, we're going around all the competitors asking if they've seen him as the drones haven't been out since earlier today as they are pretty much useless in this storm," Cecil replied.

"If he happens across this way, I'll be sure to tell him to get in touch. By the way seeing how we're all getting on so well, can I ask if everyone is still in the competition, has anyone scarpered yet?" I asked trying to disguise my little jibe.

"Sorry but unfortunately, I'm not allowed to relay that information, Jack; everything must remain confidential regarding the other competitors," he smugly explained taking far too much pleasure in doing so.

"For fuck's sake, *Cecil,* are you for real you jumped up errand boy? This isn't exactly army manoeuvres, it's not like it's going to make any difference, now, is it?"

But he was ignoring me and walking away head down against the storm back to his *Gator*. What an absolute dick that man was, the name most definitely suited him.

As his flunky ran passed me hurrying to catch up, he turned towards me and through the rain mouthed, "Subi," then made a throat cutting action with his finger. And with a sinister smile as if he had actually *cut* Subi's throat, he was climbing into the vehicle alongside miserable Cecil.

So, Subi as predicted had gone, no real surprises there as the kid looked in a perpetual state of fear. With Subi gone and Cohen indisposed somewhat and with Celestine missing in action that just left the five of us. Celestine had lasted four days, Cohen albeit with a little help from me had lasted a week and Subi even less than that. I would take a close look at Pritchard and then hopefully get to Bos, the other two I had no desire to get at and therefore, would leave them to their own devices and allow them to compete.

That night after those two muppets had left, I went inside, lit candles, added fuel to the fire and changed into some dry clothes. It had become one of the most laborious parts of the competition, trying to keep clothes dry and ready for the following day.

I prepared dinner, which was pasta with seared rabbit loins, *Hen of the Woods* mushrooms, olive oil and tarragon. It was delightful and washed down with a small whisky. I brewed tea—Lady Grey—and sat in front of the log fire surrounded by the smell of damp clothes and the almost painful but gratifying heat prickling the skin of my face, contemplating the events of the last two days.

Things had escalated quickly out of control at Cohen's and while I accepted some responsibility—notably provoking him—I still figured he should have been better prepared. Actually, he should not have been allowed entry into the competition in the first place, considering his total lack of preparation and fitness, which amounted to a misplaced arrogance.

Putting these thoughts aside and finishing my Scotch, I wriggled into my sleeping bag and settled in for the night. The KP—who was now becoming the one constant in my life—was there keeping his usual vigil in the corner as I blew out the candles but by now, I no longer cared or even thought of him as a threat. His actual purpose I knew not, so therefore until things changed significantly with him, I would not worry myself about his presence.

As unhinged as this may sound, being in close proximity to a corpse—at least my mind was telling me that he was a corpse—I was actually beginning to enjoy the company as I had always been such a solitary person. With the obvious exception of his repulsive appearance of course.

***

Next morning, I woke early and felt completely refreshed. I could still hear the rain beating hard against the wooden roof of the cabin, but it was now almost soothing in its ferocity. The storm had raged all night, thunder rumbled and lightening flashed at times illuminating the KP slouched in the corner but again, he didn't cause me any fear. He almost felt like my own assigned security detail sitting there as watchful as ever, although still an incredibly poor conversationalist.

The storm was still going albeit just the rain and wind, but it felt like the roof was going to detach itself from the walls at one point. In fairness, the cabins had been very well constructed and stood up to the task at hand. Regardless of the weather I clambered from my sleeping bag and poked some life into the fire, then I decided I would take part in my what had now become early morning ritual of the plunge pool.

It was still dark as I emerged from the cabin into the freezing temperatures and I immediately observed a pair of glistening red eyes staring directly at me through the rain and inky sky only a few feet away. Aiming my torch and finding on closer inspection—and some relief—they revealed themselves to belong to a large badger. There were two actually as the other was close by, trying to keep out of sight but keeping a wary eye on me also.

I'm not stupid enough to approach or agitate one of these beasts as they could be such a formidable foe, so I waited atop my steps until they'd seen enough, got bored and headed back into the forest. I then resumed my stroll down for my early morning dip, I was deep in the heart of Northumberland and its wild beauty was truly astonishing.

I made a breakfast of seared trout simply with a little olive oil and using the dried lemons—which I'd soaked previously—added these for a little vitamin C. I brewed tea and took it outside onto the sheltered veranda and with a blanket clutched across my shoulders watched the barely visible sun rise above the forest through the pouring rain.

I kept a watchful eye on the ever-expanding river as it crept closer to the cabin and fortunately for me, this morning the wind was blowing from a northerly direction and was, therefore, battering the back of my south facing hut keeping a modicum of shelter for me under the roofs awning while I contentedly sipped my tea.

Today, I'd set out North and see what lay past the mushroom fields and beyond. I'd imagine I would run into a farm or two at some point and while strictly forbidden, I may try and beg—or steal—a couple of eggs from a farmer, just to alleviate the boredom of rabbit and trout. With the storm persisting it seemed prudent to stay within the canopy of the forest rather than any open ground as these massive old trees would offer at least some protection from the elements.

I'd think of how to torment Pritchard and hopefully Bos while I'm walking, as it'll take me some time to breach the forest and navigate past more cabins, wasn't sure who's I'd come across first but with Subi gone, that just left Alex and Orry north of me, again I wasn't sure about Bos. Maybe he would also be north, but I couldn't remember the original map, obviously our personal maps only had places of relevance for each competitor, such as the emergency phones and best foraging spots.

Wrapped up in my warmest clothes for the day ahead and refilling my rucksack with water canteen, dry socks and chocolate, I set off after having first checked my maturing deer. Thankfully, it seemed OK considering the atrocious weather we were having and luckily, it hadn't been cold enough to freeze as that would be a major pain in the arse when I came to butcher it.

Once in the forest beneath the trees the rain could hardly manage to penetrate through the canopy and it felt warmer the further in I ventured. I could hear the wind howling far above but I felt safe and secure in this magnificent woodland refuge.

After maybe two hours of hiking and negotiating over and through a rough terrain of felled trees, rocks, marshland and streams and with the sweat rolling down my back, I could feel the woods begin to thin out. Then within minutes I was beyond the protection of the forest and was hit with the full force of the storm.

The freezing cold wind and rain lashed my face with renewed ferocity and for the briefest of moments I considered turning back and dashing into the protection of the forest. Just then I noticed through the downpour one of the cabins perched as mine was dangerously close to the river and my inquisitiveness as to whose it was got the better of me.

So, I slowly made my way towards it. There was a deer at the back of the cabin and as with mine, it had been professionally prepped, cleaned and hung. They'd also used the same sheet and rope in which to cover it with and it looked in good order, albeit a little smaller than mine.

I crept closer but wanted to remain unseen, the billowing rain and generally gloomy morning did offer some protection, but I wanted to see who's cabin it belonged to then get back on with my days sortie. As I neared the door it was wrenched open and Alex stood there, brandishing her knife, wearing only the skimpiest of inappropriate underwear, woolly hat and her hiking boots. It was a rather peculiar and yet strangely alluring attire and I flung my hands into the air in mock surrender.

"Whoa, whoa there tiger, it's only your friendly neighbour and fellow competitor Jack." I shouted through the ever-increasing storm. "Jesus, who were you expecting!" With an almost imperceptible sigh Alex lowered the knife and indicated with it to come inside.

"Come inside, Jack, for fuck's sake; it's freezing out here," Alex said.

I noticed she made no attempt to cover herself up and I thought yep that's what living out here does for you. Even though it had been just over a week since coming out here all of your normal inhibitions (not that I thought she had many anyway) seemed to erode away. Once inside and out of the storm, I took off my hat and gloves and stood in front of a good to see blazing fire with lots of wood stashed inside the doorway.

I asked Alex, "what's with the warm welcome?"

"Some cunt has been trying to wind me up, lurking around here during the last couple of nights; at first I thought it was you, don't ask me why please, but turns out it's that inbred local driver. The one who's teeth you quite happily knocked out," she said without any sign that she had been frightened by this turn of events.

"You're shitting me?" I asked. "That useless little fucker, I warned him a week ago not to mess me about, I thought he would have taken that to mean all of us. Hang on a minute, why the hell did you think it was me hanging around?"

She ignored this question and continued. "He can't seem to get it through his rock of a skull that firstly, I'm married and secondly, it's to a fucking girl," she said as she sat on her bed and started talking.

"Two nights ago, I could hear something scuffling about outside and when I got to the door thinking it was an animal of some sorts, I saw someone scuttling off into the woods. So, last night I set up camp just on the edge of the treeline and waited. He came from the south and passed right by me, that's when I realised who it was. Even with his hood pulled up I'd recognise that shambling gait anywhere."

She took a sip of her drink—not offering me one, so I knew I wasn't going to be here long—I assumed it was tea and then she resumed her story.

"I watched him creep down to my cabin then up onto the porch and peer in through the window. I'd left a couple of candles on and the silly fucker kept looking, even though he could see quite clearly I wasn't there."

Another sip of tea and I also realised I'd never heard her talk so much.

"As he was gaping through the window, I carefully snuck up behind him, grabbed him by his hood and dragged him off the porch and into the mud. He nearly shat himself as he spluttered an apology, his intentions were honourable, he said. Absolute shite, he was obviously hoping to catch me naked, the fuckin pervert; he was holding onto his dick the whole time he was pleading with me."

Here, I had to agree with the inbred that that would be a pleasing sight and worth taking a chance of getting a beating but remained quiet and let her continue. She still hadn't made any attempt to cover up and sat open legged with her elbows resting on her knees and mug in hand.

"Once I had calmed down, I told him I'd be using the emergency phone and calling to explain what had happened and that he was to be dismissed immediately. But ten minutes of him begging with me, I let him off with a cuff round the head and with a warning never to come back or I would castrate the bastard.

No grovelling would help him then and with that I let him go with a kick up the arse and he scarpered into the woods. That's why I came at you like I did, I thought he was back when I saw someone come out through the woods."

"Well, as you can see," I gestured to myself, "I'm not him and I doubt he'll be back after the warning you gave him," I said.

"So, what are you doing this far North?" she asked suspiciously.

"Just having a hike up this way, I wanted to see what's what and who's where, you know," I replied innocently.

"In this?" And with that she pointed outside at the weather.

I shrugged my shoulders nonchalantly and asked, "you see anyone else up this way?"

"No contestants, only that survival wanker and one of his arsehole staff. Apparently, Celestine has gone missing and they were out searching for him."

He's not the only one missing I thought and said, "yeah, they came to see me also, I can't say I'm surprised as the guy was a liability from the start. The organisers will be shitting themselves if anything's happened to him. They'll be worried about a lawsuit coming their way, even though we signed all kinds of waivers."

"Yeah, we signed insurance waivers, but they must have realised that he shouldn't have been allowed out on his own, the guy was smashed on opening day. Do you know if everyone is still in?" she asked.

"It's not from the most reliable source but I think Subi has gone, didn't last the week, that came from Cecil's sidekick, the one with the tash. I haven't heard about anyone else," I lied.

"He was another one far too removed from his comfort zone, he nearly put a bullet through the survival guy after we left you with your kill. He was a nervous wreck with a gun in his hand, although seeing the fear in that dickheads face when the bullet whizzed by his nose was priceless," she laughed.

"He went totally nuts with Subi, literally leapt on top of him and then ripped the gun from his grip and threw it into the gorse bushes, Orry and me had to physically restrain him to calm him down. I think, that'll have definitely helped Subi make his mind up to leave. It was still quite funny, all the same. So, how far north are you going to be heading?"

Glancing at my watch and seeing it was pushing mid-day I said, "shouldn't be much further, have you seen any farms or any signs of life around here? There's nothing indicated on any of the maps they supplied us but there must be some close by."

"I've seen one small farm about an hour's tough trek north along the river, but it didn't look up to much, no animals around and the actual farmhouse looked in desperate need of repair. Have you eaten anything decent? I've just been living on rabbits and mushrooms. I'm not much of a one for fishing, so haven't even attempted any.

I never could be arsed with the waiting game and all the different flies etc you need for different fish. I did happen upon some intriguing mushrooms though if you catch my meaning," and with this she gave me a conspiratorial wink.

"I've been living on the same as well as some fish, plenty trout in the river, I also stumbled across those bad boy mushrooms, can't imagine the organisers intended us to find anything on that score. I bet that useless cunt Schroder would love to get his greasy paws on them though," I said sniggering to myself.

Alex agreed with an uneasy nod, but I began to realise that maybe I was overstaying my welcome, so I quickly said, "well, I'm off then, cheers for the chat and best of luck to you for the rest of the competition."

She raised a curious eyebrow to my niceties—as I'd offered nothing at all back at the beginning of the competition—and then offered her hand in response which I shook warmly.

"Yeah, good luck to you too," she almost stammered.

Heading back out the door and into the constant rain and with the sun desperately seeking a way through the clouds, I felt a sense of relief as I had never been the greatest at small talk and have always felt slightly uncomfortable in those situations. As I marched towards the trees, I glanced back to see Alex standing on her porch, still in a state of undress watching me go and when she saw me turn, she raised her hand in farewell. I returned the gesture and disappeared into the trees.

She was a strange cookie that one, I for the first time inexplicably began to think that maybe winning wasn't everything and that I possibly could be beaten by someone like Alex. The thought of not winning didn't seem to offend or upset me anymore as it once would have and with that mulling around inside my head, I continued on through the forest feeling rather enlightened.

Although I might not go much further considering Alex had said there wasn't much to be found heading north. Orry was out there somewhere but I actually didn't mind the kid and felt he'd do just fine, he didn't need me adding to his worries. I considered that maybe I was softening after all these years then suddenly remembered what I'd been capable of with Cohen just hours previously. No, I was still the same old me and one civil conversation with someone, I felt vaguely attracted to, hadn't turned me saintly.

11. The Body in the Woods

I worked my way back through the forest after I had headed north a while to find just as Alex had said, very little. I decided to take a different route and headed a little further east once I'd past the mushroom fields and stocked up on Liberty Caps and Hen of the Woods. The woodland was just as deep and still provided plenty of shelter from the elements, although from time to time a large clearing would emerge as if out of nowhere with no explanation as to why and the full force of the storm would resume its relentless battering of me.

Rabbits, foxes and deer were in abundance here in this undisturbed—and untouched by human hands—sanctuary and barely glanced my way as I passed, seemingly more interested in keeping out of the escalating storm. From time to time a crow would heed a warning to me with its harsh cry then take to the air in an almost mocking cackle.

After a while of heading east I turned back south west in the general direction of my cabin, nothing more was to be discovered this way and the afternoon was rapidly diminishing. It would be dark by the time I got back but by now, I was used to traversing the area at night and equipped with my torch and compass, I'd reach the cabin safely.

Up ahead in the deepening gloom I could just make out something of a brighter colour lying prostrate that didn't quite seem to fit with the rest of the forest surroundings. Approaching with caution, I gradually came closer, only to find it was someone slumped against a felled tree. On reaching the now what could only be described as a body as there was no life left in this husk, I realised as I turned it to face me that it was what remained of the missing Celestine.

By the look of him he had been here a while, his almost blue bloated face was set in a look of utter bewilderment as if even at the end he had had no idea of what was happening to him. His nose and ears had become a mealtime for some of the forest inhabitants as they had been chewed off along with his ungloved fingers.

Lying next to his butchered hands was a large empty bottle of Scotch, a cheap one at that. One eye had been plucked out, most probably by the birds and the vitreous humour along with the grime of days unwashed, had left a black stain running down his cheek. Even his boots had been ripped apart to get at his feet which looked like they'd been squeezed through a mangler.

He'd obviously ventured out whilst completely intoxicated as he wasn't even wearing a jacket, just a flimsy jumper and a grubby pair of jeans. There was no evidence of a hat, backpack or even a pair of gloves.

Having clearly lost his bearings without any hope of rescue, he'd wandered aimlessly into the forest unawares he was getting himself deeper and deeper into trouble. Hopefully for Celestine, he'd have been in such a drunken stupor that he wouldn't have perceived the danger he was in until it was too late, that's if he had realised at all.

Hyperthermia was most probably the cause, but it could quite easily have been a heart attack judging by the sheer disregard he'd held his own body in. He was mostly just skin and bone and on lifting his clothing I found bruising up and down his arms and legs, which could have been needle marks, along with old scarring down his wrist, which could have been an earlier attempt at suicide. His life was clearly over long before he set off into these woods.

I could not and would not feel sorry for him as he was a terrible person and he had most definitely reaped what he had sowed. But I did wonder how someone who had been as successful as he had could end up like this, we all loved a drink but, Christ, you had to be stronger and draw the line at some point. There would be very few people if any to mourn this guy.

He'd been in his time one of the most feared and reviled chefs in the country. Granted he had mentored and created some of the best chefs in his regimental style of kitchen, who would go on to national renown but at the same time, just as many young lads—and lasses—had been crushed and driven into the ground by his ruthless and execrable qualities. In his early days, he had made me look like Mother Theresa.

I sat next to him and considered what to do with his corpse. Again as with Cohen, if I reported the body then the competition would come to an untimely conclusion, which I would regret as I desperately wanted to get to Pritchard and Bos before that happened. So, the question was, should I bury him?

The ground was soft enough with all the rain that had fallen that a shallow grave would be easy enough to dig, therefore not out of the question. Would he give a fuck what I did, I very much doubted that? He must have known the damage he was doing to himself and what condition he was going to end up in. Yet again, I felt the organisers were without doubt to blame, they should have for several reasons not let him enter this competition, a man in such obvious state of dissembling was always going to be a problem.

Regardless of how bad the weather had become—as this would surely be blamed for Celestines demise and not the producer's incompetence—the powers that be had fucked up as this should have been a summer event. Northumberland in late autumn was not to be taken for granted, not that it mattered to me; of course, I was in my element.

After some deliberation I decided to leave him exactly where I had found him. If *Survival Man* or one of his ridiculous cronies stumbled across him then that would be it, but I doubted he'd be discovered for a long while yet. No one would be coming out this way soon or this deep into the forest, there was just no need or reason to venture this far out.

I made a mark on my map as to where I thought we were. At least in the same vicinity and once all this was over, I'd inform someone where he was; well, at least, maybe, I would. Stealing a last look his way and leaving him to the bidding of the forest creatures I set off once again for the refuge of my cabin, what after ten days I began to think of as home.

I made good time on my return journey. Up above I could still hear the storm raging and when finally breaking through the last of the trees towards my cabin, I staggered back as it hit me with its full force. Leaning forward almost horizontally into the storm I pushed my way towards my haven and slammed into the door and on opening it I knew the fire had gone out.

There was a residual heat, but nothing compared to the warmth and comfort I'd had of late. I made this the opportunity to clean the old cinders from the fire and rebuild a new one. I was freezing cold and soaked through, so it was a laborious job but once I had the fire built and then lit, it soon started to give me the warmth I craved.

Once I had the familiar and heartening roar of the fire in front of me, I stripped out of my wet clothes—again—and huddled in front of it. It didn't take long to warm my chilled and aching bones and I soon felt rejuvenated enough to get dressed, set out my latest instalment of sodden clothes around the fire to dry and start to prepare some food.

It would be a simple affair of pasta and olive oil, lots of it as I intended paying a visit to Pritchard within the next day or two, so I needed to stock up on fuel. I also brewed some tea with my new batch of Liberty caps and greedily drank this down.

I must have fallen asleep because when I roused myself it was bang in the middle of the night and I felt increasingly anxious at having slept so long, obviously fuelled by the mushrooms and the several whiskies I had sunk. Sweating profusely and feeling more drunk and erratic than I'd felt in a long time, I began pacing the small cabin in what I can only describe as complete paranoia.

The KP was in attendance in the corner reclining in his usual indifferent manner and offered me no comfort whatsoever.

Anger surged through me and I screamed at him, "fuck off and leave me be, have you not seen enough yet, what do you actually want from me?"

Unperturbed he just sat there and what I can only assume glared at me. His unsightly visage was still deteriorating and his body seemed to be giving up the ghost. I lunged at him and took a couple of wild swings at his putrid head but obviously, I didn't connect with anything and my last punch hit the cabin wall beyond him drawing back bloody knuckles.

I screamed out in shock more than pain and dropped to the floor. Blubbering to myself in some noncoherent garbage, I looked up at him cradling my bloodied hand in an almost beseeching pose. I then apologised to him, almost begging forgiveness for my outburst then fell face down onto the wooden floorboards and proceeded to pass out.

***

When I next woke it was daylight and I'd slept the rest of the night, the fire was low but retrievable and sadly, there was no sign of my only friend. I had somehow managed to wriggle out of my clothes during the night and lay naked on the floor with just a blanket over me. I painstakingly got to my feet, leaving the blanket on the floor and threw some logs on the fire, disregarding the sparks that were sent flying out of the grate and onto my legs and floor.

In the somewhat dishevelled state I found myself in, I at that moment didn't give a shit what happened to the cabin. Luckily, none landed on anything that would readily ignite and I figured—and hoped—the fire would be blazing in no time. I didn't feel like eating, couldn't face my usual offering of rabbit, so I brewed some tea, Lady Grey that is and sipped this as I staggered to the door still naked to peer out.

The storm had abated somewhat and the rain had actually eased for the first time in days. It would be a thankful rest bite as the river was massively swollen and all the while creeping closer to the cabin. I reached back inside the door, pulled the blanket from the floor, wrapped it around my shoulders and sat on the veranda, it was freezing cold, but I needed this to clear my foggy head.

Overhead a drone was buzzing, ignoring it completely I sipped my tea and thought about the day ahead I was planning. I would hang around here today with no excessive exercise or unnecessary stimulants, revive myself fully and then check out Pritchard's cabin tonight. It'd be at least a four-hour trek, so I'd have to prepare better.

I was hoping to find him in much the same state as I'd found fatty but for all I knew, he may have adapted a little better. Annoyingly the drone seemed to be hovering a lot longer than usual, maybe I looked like shit, therefore making for better TV. I stood up, dropped the towel exposing myself fully and raised my cup in mock salute. The drone spun around and took off up and over the trees in seconds, maybe I wasn't much to look at after all.

It probably wasn't the wisest decision but, in my journal, as well as notes on my competitor's abilities I kept an account of what happened to Cohen that night as some kind of justification and also how I had found Celestine's body in the woods. Whilst I was fully aware that Cohen shouldn't have been dumped unceremoniously in the lake, I wanted it on record that I hadn't killed him, at least not directly.

And Celestine's demise had absolutely nothing to do with me whatsoever. That responsibility lay at someone else's door, his own, as the drunken bum had brought it all on himself. OK maybe I should have tried to inform someone but again, what would have been the point? The guy was dead and nothing could change that. Well, at least that's how I saw things and that was all that mattered.

While I was writing up my notes, I heard a vehicle approaching through the trees. Considering there was supposed to be no contact with us, this was happening far too often for my liking. I hid the diary beneath my bed and quickly threw some clothes on along with my boots and hat.

I slid the knife into my belt and opened the door to greet my visitors just as they skidded to a halt outside my door. Cecil—*super hard Survival Man*—and to my complete surprise Schroder climbed from the Range Rover, obviously as Schroder wouldn't slum it in a *Gator* and cautiously made their way to the door.

"Jack, how the devil are you?" asked Schroder jovially while proffering his hand out to shake. I made a show of scratching my balls then took his clammy limp dicked hand with a sly smile and enjoyed immensely Schroder's look of utter abhorrence.

"Gentlemen, how are we?" I responded while watching Schroder surreptitiously wipe his hand on his trousers.

"Celestine is still missing," *Survival Man* pressed on without the niceties of Schroder and then added, "Cohen is also missing. It's been a couple of days since we last picked him up with the drone. You see anyone about? From what we can gather you're the most well-travelled out of all the competitors," he knowingly insinuated.

So, they knew I was covering some miles but obviously didn't know exactly how far I'd gone or what I'd got up to, I'd have to be careful of this wanker.

"I thought the whole point of this little excursion into the wilds was to be isolated and therefore, see how we cope under the stress? Is this not the case?" I asked pleasantly and then pressed on not so nicely. "If so, then why are you here again for starters and also why the fuck would I know or even want to know where any cunt else is?"

"You seemed pretty interested the last time we spoke how the others were getting along, we just wondered if any of them had been hassling you or hanging around? We know there's bad blood between some of you," *Survival Man* asked.

Very slippery, I thought, Cecil, turning it around so it looked like you were worried for my safety. "I asked last time about the others as it was the obvious thing to do, we are after all in a competition, are we not chaps? And no, no one has been hassling me but thanks for your completely sincere concern, Cecil."

"Yes, yes," Schroder interjected, "You are of course right, Jack, that would be the prudent thing to do, asking after the other contestants, we're all just a little worried for their safekeeping as I am sure you can appreciate."

"I can indeed, Phillip, I just feel like things are being directed my way by certain parties," here I glanced at Cecil. "And I'm not particularly fond of the insinuations as I'm sure *you* can appreciate."

"Look, Jack, let's cut the bullshit," Cecil barked, "there's two men out there who could be in danger, we just want to know they're all right and move on with the show. I'm sure even *you* can appreciate that."

"Yes, why don't we cut the bullshit and while you're at it why don't you two get back in your nice little motor and fuck off back to civilisation and your plush trailers!" I yelled, "how does that sound for appreciation of the situation?"

"Jack, we're very sorry to have disturbed you and we'll be leaving now, if you see either of them will you please get in touch using the emergency phone, I implore you. And good luck for the rest of the competition," Schroder grovelled as he laid a restraining arm across *Survival Man's* chest and backed away.

I could see Cecil was raging and desperate to be at me, but his better judgment overruled him. I don't think Schroder's feeble attempt to suppress him would have worked if he'd actually cut loose and attacked me. I can't imagine the show's producers would have been particularly happy with him, but if they only knew what I had done and had planned for Pritchard then they probably would have pinned a medal on him for his timely intervention. Hindsight is a wonderful thing.

"Not to worry, chaps, I'm sure Celestine is blind drunk in some shithole bar in Wooler, not quite knowing where the fuck he is. And Cohen is probably eating himself into a coma at some all-day buffet somewhere as we speak." And with a dainty little wave, which again nearly tipped Cecil into the abyss, I ambled back into the cabin and slammed the door.

Peering out of my window I could see them arguing as *Survival Man* Cecil obviously wasn't finished with me, but Schroder was pleading with him to get into the car. Cecil obviously wasn't convinced of my final assumption that the two missing parties had simply up and left.

I'd have to work quickly over the next few days to complete my sabotage of Pritchard and Bos, just in case old fatty's body decided to make some untimely reappearance. I also began to regret not burying or at least camouflaging Celestine's body because if they did decide to do a full search of the woods, he'd be found, eventually anyway and then that would be that.

12. The Hunt for Pritchard

I spent the rest of the day recovering from my previous night's exploits, the combination of whisky and shrooms were beginning to take a hold on me. As much as I knew they would be my eventual undoing, I was quite sure I wouldn't be giving them up anytime soon. What with my almost constant KP companion and the brutal but *accidental* death of Cohen, I felt the drink and drugs were helping me in keeping it together.

I managed to get a couple of hours of sitting at the riverside, supposedly fishing but for some reason the river wasn't yielding me with anything worth eating. After another hour I gave up on my fruitless mission and packed away my gear. Trudging the short journey back to the cabin and then running as the rain resumed its deluge, I happened to glance up towards the edge of the forest and noticed a sudden flash of movement.

It wasn't my KP friend as he was sat keeping vigil in his preferred daytime position on the veranda and rudely, I thought, not even looking my way for once.

I dropped my fishing gear, slipped in the mud, got my feet back under me, then took off towards the woods at pace. But as I reached just inside the treeline I tripped over some exposed roots and fell heavily headfirst down a slight embankment and came to rest in a bed of uncomfortable prickly gorse bushes. I did manage to see just before I fell a large lumbering shape disappear deep into the trees, a shape that could belong to no other than Pritchard.

It must have been him as no one else I'd come across was the sheer size of that bastard. I thought of heading out again after him but by the time I dragged myself from this gorse, he'd be well gone. I was amazed he'd come out this far, it was a good few hours if not four to his place, maybe he just wanted to talk? But then why did he run?

I very much doubted he was here to chat. His hatred for me equalled Bos' so he must have had some other ulterior motive as to why he would drag his big arse up here, it would be one which involved my discomfort and downfall, I had no doubt.

Spurred on by this peculiar turn of events, I felt happy and justified in my original idea of sabotaging the bastard's chances. I returned to my cabin, picking my fishing gear up along the way and deposited myself inside to wait for the night. I would eat again, replenish my energy and then set off. As well as a giddy excitement I was now also angry that someone like that prick could try and get to me. The sheer audacity to think he could come out this far and try to catch me unawares.

One positive thing to come out of this was now he would be exhausted by the time he got back to his place. Big unfit fucker like him, I'd likely have the benefit of surprise as he will undoubtedly be collapsed snoring like a baby when I arrive. I brewed tea and waited on the porch alongside my dead compatriot, both keeping a vigilant eye on the trees; as always, we had a one-sided conversation. This time it was about Pritchard and his chances of survival; unfortunately, my friend offered no opinion either way.

Nothing stirred in the woods before me, the coward would not have had the heart or the balls to travel by night. That's why the fool had attempted to ambush me during the day, therefore making it easy for me to see his approach from the woods.

When it turned seven and feeling back to my old self, I grabbed my map, compass, torch and backpack with chocolate and my water canteen inside. I also had a change of socks, trousers and a blanket, in case I got caught out and needed to rest in the forest. I put on my hat, heavy jacket and gloves and fastened my knife to my belt. The temperature was still dropping and it was now very cold, but thankfully the rain had stopped.

The clouds had lessened and a half moon could be seen providing a little natural light. It would be a tough hike through the forest as the ground was now similar to a quagmire in parts and the streams through the forest had widened making it even more difficult to navigate to Pritchard's cabin.

I would have to take it steady as I wanted to reach there without being overly exhausted. I'd also have to skirt around Cohen's place as I didn't want to leave any of my boot prints or run into anyone in case they'd set up a welcoming party for his return. I would not be checking up on his body and hoped that the river had kept its secrets and managed to keep him submerged in its murky waters.

It was still a gruelling journey, even though I had been cautious and not pushed too hard but at almost midnight, I noticed the trees starting to thin out slightly. Encouraged I turned off my torch and ploughed on. Crawling to the edge of the trees and taking in the scene—ever thankful for the meagre moonlight—I noticed Pritchard's cabin had fared a little better than Cohen's.

I could see a funnel of wispy smoke drifting into the partially clouded night sky. Well, at least he had managed to keep a fire going. I could also see faint candlelight coming from the solitary window, amazed he had actually remembered some, but I was confident he would be asleep. I skirted around the cabin as silently as possible and noticed that to my utter amazement he had managed to bag a deer.

As surprised as I was by this turn of events, normal service was then clearly resumed as he hadn't wrapped it for protection from the atrocious weather we had had. The idiot hadn't even bothered to hang it or even gut it, the wretched thing was just lying half submerged in the mud at the back of the cabin and some of the forest's wildlife had been happily nibbling on it.

The beast was ruined, it wouldn't even be good enough for dog food. The intended wrapping for the deer was scattered along with the rope amongst the bushes behind his cabin, he obviously hadn't had a clue as to its use. His grill hadn't been used, but in all fairness, there hadn't been a great deal of weather for it. The outside wood store was also empty and then creeping up to and inspecting his cool box I found that also bare, with no trace of anything ever being in it.

Keeping my eyes and ears open for any sight or sound, I crept up onto the veranda and carefully edged my way along to the window to peer in. As expected, Pritchard was flat out on his bunk, snoring gently. His feet were comically dangling over the edge as the bed wasn't long enough for him, the candle was dangerously close to his head and the fire was nothing more than embers and wouldn't last the night.

His larder from what I could see was almost completely used up and like Cohen, the place looked in utter disarray. There were clothes scattered everywhere and the floor was littered with used tins—which he must have brought with him as his allowed quota of home comforts—and mud and general detritus from the meals he'd actually bothered to prepare. Disgusting to think, along with Cohen, these two supposed chefs ran kitchens and preached to young commis chefs about hygiene and the importance of it.

I tiptoed back along the veranda, down the steps and headed up into the trees to rest a little. Here, keeping a watchful eye on the cabin, I took out my water canteen and sated my thirst, then replacing it in my pack I stowed my gear—camouflaged as it was—amongst the trees but left it within easy reach if I had to bolt. I then headed unhindered back down to Pritchard.

Again, I crept as slowly and quietly as I could to the window and surveyed the situation.

Pritchard was gone.

Panic and adrenalin coursed through me as I realised this useless oaf had somehow outwitted me, how had he emerged unseen from the cabin? All I could think was I must have taken my eye from the door as I stashed my backpack amongst the trees.

Suddenly sensing someone's presence behind me, I turned to see Pritchard standing at the bottom of the steps smiling malevolently up at me. In his hands he held a large wooden club, which he had fashioned from a branch and with his eyes never leaving mine he was passing it menacingly between his hands as if testing its weight. In the torchlight I took note for the first time of his deep-set eyes, high forehead and bulbous nose, he really was an ugly fucker.

"You were at my place today, I caught a glimpse of you just as I tripped but it was most definitely you, Pritchard," I stated. "Your big ugly fuckin mug is difficult to miss, even in the middle of a darkening forest."

"Yeah, that was me, I was out searching for Cohen and I wanted to ask you a few questions about him," he asked.

"So, why didn't you stop and ask me earlier about Cohen? What's the useless shite done now?" I replied.

"Like what have you done with him, you fucking psycho? He hasn't been seen for days by any of the drones or by us searching in the forest. And the officials have said his family haven't seen him either. It must be you, no one else would give a shit but you, you always take it too far. You hate Cohen and me, you always have," he said.

"You sound like a petulant child who's lost his big fat teddy," I taunted him further. "Have you lost your teddy?" I said, sticking my bottom lip out and mimicking a child.

"You know what, *Cunt-ingham*? Enough of this shit, I'm just going to beat it out of you."

And with that he lunged at me brandishing his club high in the air. As he came at me wielding his club like some neanderthal, it crashed into the low hanging roof above my head. And thankfully—with splinters of wood and guttering raining down on me—it gave me ample time to kick him with as much ferocity as I could muster into his substantial gut. With a loud 'oomph' he staggered back and almost toppled over.

One hand was cradling his stomach and the other clenching his homemade club planted in the ground like a walking stick. Furiously exhaling, he managed to right himself and with a desperate groan, which then quickly turned to rage, he raised his weapon again and barrelled towards me.

While Pritchard was blowing out of his arse and readying himself for another attack, I leapt from the veranda and planting my feet in front of his lumbering body, rained blow after vicious blow at his monstrous head and shoulders.

As big as Pritchard was, he wasn't fit and he quickly started to weaken under my barrage of well-placed punches as I kept up my relentless onslaught. He finally let go of the club, which was now dangling limply down his back and with his last strength and my overconfidence, he defended a couple of blows and grabbed me by the throat.

Surprisingly, all of the fight hadn't left him as I'd hoped. And even as I proceeded to pound his midriff his fierce grip tightened around my windpipe gradually cutting off my air. I could feel myself weakening and with my last strength ebbing away and black spots creeping into my vision, I dug deep into my reserves and somehow brought my knee up flush into his groin.

The pressure on my throat lessened for just enough time for me to get my hands into his grip and take hold of his fingers. I yanked down as hard as I could and the welcome sound of his fore and middle finger breaking, followed by his scream in pain was like blessed music to me. The constriction around my throat was released and gasping I took in great lungful of air and desperately tried to get some oxygen back to my brain.

Whimpering like the child he was, Pritchard fell to his knees holding his misshapen hand in the crook of his elbow. Taking this opportunity I kicked him as hard as I could, connecting flush with his chin, he spun around and with a thud fell face down in the dirt.

Judging by his splayed legs and arms and the fact that he wasn't making any effort to get his face out of the mud, I guessed he was unconscious. Bending down on closer inspection while still fervently keeping my guard, the steady breathing and blowing of dirt and foetid breath in my face seconded that.

Reminiscence: The Intervention

After the incident with the fence and if what had unfolded was true, my brother understandably wanted very little to do with me. Even being in the same school he wouldn't seek out my help if he were in trouble. He preferred to sort it himself, although he didn't get a lot of hassle coming his way because of the threat I could have posed.

Oh well, I thought if nothing else it had taught him to stand up for himself. Deep down I was upset by what had happened as after all he was my little brother, but at least he hadn't told our parents about the incident, although mam obviously knew there was something not right between us.

I'd been barred from ever going near the farm again and mam had blatantly refused to speak to the farmer on a couple of more occasions when he had tried to engage with her and explain what he had seen. Until finally exasperated, he had given up. Dad had been apoplectic with the whole accident but had eventually put it down to boyhood jinx and we all, except my little brother of course, tried to move on from it.

A year or so later with me not having any mates or even a kid brother to hang out with, I began feeling increasingly angry and demonstrating more and more anger issues. On a regular basis I would be dragged to the headmaster's office at school for fighting or disrupting a class. My schoolwork suffered and my parents became all the more worried.

Finally, dad had had enough and dragged me down to the local boxing club, somewhere I would normally have avoided like the plague as this was quite simply not the place to be seen. Surely, dad didn't want me in here I thought as I looked around at kids from all kinds of backgrounds—and many different schools, mine included—but mainly dog poor.

Granted we weren't rich in any sense of the word, but I knew we were better off than most in here. Dad seemed on good terms with the owner/coach and before I could protest, I was quickly fitted with a dirty spit slicked mouthguard and a pair of ragged old gloves that smelled of ancient sweat and something quite metallic, which when I think back now must have been old blood.

"Just have a go, son," dad said, "let's see if you enjoy it."

This seemed completely insane, what on earth would I enjoy about hitting someone and being hit back for sport? Fighting at school was different, it was illicit, here it was simply entertainment. And more to the point who had taken my dad away and substituted him with this other fella? As far as I was aware dad was always against all kinds of violence; yes, he watched the fighting on TV and he was a big man, but it never crossed my mind that he had ever boxed or could possibly enjoy this.

"Now, jump up in the ring lad and let's see what you're made of," said the coach.

Jesus, I thought these fuckers are serious; for a while I just thought they were trying to scare me, but they mean to go through with it. Oh shit, I thought! Well there was nothing for it, I couldn't let dad down, so I climbed awkwardly through the ropes with too big gloves, slightly shaking knees and up into the ring.

The lad standing opposite me looked a lot meaner than me and a lot bigger to boot and as other lads stopped their training, wrapped towels around their sweat soaked necks and gathered at the edge of the ring; I thought, right ya bastard, I'll have a go.

Dad had stood back, the coach approached and said to me, "now, son, just take it easy, you've seen a boxing match before I take it?"

At this I nodded after dad and me had spent many a Saturday night watching Fight Night, never thinking I would end up in one.

"Keep your hands up and defend yourself at all times that's the most important thing. Then if you think you can hit him, have a go at it. Nobody is judging you on this alone and your old man is just over there, see?" I could see dad watching from behind a few of the smaller fighters, "and he won't let anything bad happen to you, now will he?"

"OK," I said and felt a steely determination to not let dad down and hopefully not embarrass myself in the process.

Suddenly coach shouted, "box" and we both advanced to the middle of the ring and for the first few seconds we circled each other like wolves around their quarry. Being this close I realised that this lad was even bigger than I had first thought and he was all muscle, what had I got myself into?

The first blow I didn't even see but Christ, I felt it; he caught me just above the temple and for a split second I thought I was going down to the canvas. Then quickly pulling myself together, shaking my head and breathing hard I swung a *wild hook, probably with an open-faced glove and only narrowly missed. But in the process I left myself open to take the next blow.*

This time I saw it coming, albeit I couldn't do much about it, but I did brace myself for it. He caught me in the ribs and even fully prepared for it I blew out my mouthguard, shit that hurt. But even before the coach could shout break, I'd quickly bent down and stuffed the guard back in.

More determined than ever and noticing the other lad grinning at me like I was finished, I advanced towards him. My blood was up now and I started throwing punches—to a couple of encouraging hoots from the other boxers— and yes, they were wild but in my defence, they were consistently wild and systematically brutal. At least for a fourteen going on fifteen-year-old anyway, until finally one landed square on his jaw, wham!

The lad staggered and went to one knee, yes I thought, I've got the bastard! Next thing I knew he was back on his feet, antagonistic smile gone and coming towards me with a look of absolute rage on his face. For the next few minutes, I must confess I took a bit of a beating. But I never hit the canvas once and then finally the coach called time and I got to sit on the edge of the ring leaning back on the ropes, nursing a split lip, rapidly swelling eye and bruised ribs.

Dad came over with a beaming smile as I looked up and apologised, "sorry, dad, thought I would have done better."

"You thought what?" he said, almost laughing now, "Better? That lad there is the over fifteen junior champion for Northumberland, he's a hell of a fighter and that was the first time you've ever been in a ring. You put him on his knees at one point. He was just going to show you the ropes for a while until you clocked him, then it got a bit more serious."

I looked at dad a little bewildered, not just for the fact that he was pleased with my performance but that he'd actually put me in with someone as accomplished as this guy. Shit, I could have been pummelled.

"Oh right," was all I could say through my bleeding lip. "I've got a funny feeling, mam won't be particularly happy."

"You let me worry about mam, Jack, she'll understand. Now, do you think you'd like to come back to the club next week?" Dad said. "I've had a word with Mickey"—that was the coaches name—"and he is keen to take you on, I'll get you some gloves and a gum shield of your own though, eh? What do you think?"

"Yeah, I'd love to, dad, as long as you think I'll be good enough and you square it with mam?" I said.

Dad just ruffled my hair still beaming at me, just then the lad who I had fought with came over to us and removing his gloves shook my hand.

"Well done mate, good effort, welcome to the gym". And with that he was off to continue sparring with someone else.

Walking home with dad I have to say I had a feeling of utter euphoria. I'd had my first actual fight (a legitimate one anyway) and somehow dad was unbelievably pleased, this was absolute madness and would probably take a while for me to make any sense of.

Mam was waiting for us when we got back home and the shouting went on for most of the rest of the evening. That was once she'd given me the once over with plenty of tutting, rubbing and painful prodding, along with copious amounts of 'Witch Hazel'. While the shouting went on in the next room between mam and dad, I tried to speak to Chirpy to tell him where I had been and what had happened, but he just sat watching TV and ignored me. I persevered for a while but to no avail. Oh, well, I thought, I couldn't please them all.

***

I knelt there on my hands and knees in the cold mud for a moment breathing heavily and trying to regain some strength. Pritchard was out for the count blowing bubbles into some filthy puddle, but I didn't know how long for, so I had to think fast.

The rope that was meant for the tying of the deer I'd seen at the back of the cabin. So, getting gingerly to my feet I trudged through the mud and bushes to find it, hurried back to Pritchard and tied his hands as tightly as I could. As I was tying his feet, he started to stir and come round so doubling my efforts, even though I'd had to take my gloves off to tie him and my hands were freezing cold in no time, I managed to get his feet also bound.

It was comical watching him regain consciousness, the confusion etched on his face as he urged himself out of his enforced nap. I sat and waited for him to come fully back to the land of the living and caught the distinct whiff of urine and realised he had pissed himself. God, what was it with these two repulsive individuals, first the stench from Cohen's arse and now this animal.

As his head cleared and seeing me sitting there, gazing at him with the rope binding his hands and feet, he realised his predicament and genuine fear entered his eyes.

I gave a hearty laugh at his plight, "this is a fine situation we find ourselves in, Joe, is it not?" I asked using his Christian name.

I thought, well, if he is quite happily pissing himself in front of me then we must now be intimate friends, mustn't we?

"Go fuck yourself, Jack," he replied whilst struggling against his bonds and trying to raise himself out of the dirt.

OK so maybe not close friends I sniggered lost in my own thoughts. I then asked, "So, Pritchard, what are we going to do now then?" Reverting back to our more formal Sunday names. "It's a good few hours until sunrise," I looked at my watch, "six actually. No help coming for you, you useless sack of filth, I should just kill you and dump you in the river like I did with your tubby friend."

At this he looked up at me and started to cry. I didn't know if his tears were because he'd lost a supposed mate or because he had just realised that his situation was much more grave than he first feared. Through his childlike blubbering and with snot running down his face to mix in with the blood from the boot to the mouth, he began to plead for his life.

I sat there and listened with the broadest grin on my face. While I hadn't really had any intention of killing him earlier when I had set off on this little escapade—at least not consciously—I now thought why the fuck not. The winning of the competition was getting further and further from my thoughts and yet again, I found myself wondering if I had turned a corner and lost all interest in the prize.

"Come on, Jack, you know you don't need to do this mate," he gasped sucking in mud and grimy water as he spoke.

"Oh, mate now, is it? You can fuck right off with that one, you know I can't stand the very sight of you and I know the feeling is mutual so you can cut that shit out," I replied drawing my knife from my belt and resting it across my knees.

Seeing this his crying increased and he again started to struggle trying to raise himself off the dirt floor, if he'd been in better shape, he would have been able to do so. Just then a distant rumble of thunder interrupted Pritchard's sobbing in the clear night sky above us but looking to the east I could see no stars as there was heavy cloud cover and the imminent arrival of rain.

With one final effort and with a gasp and a pitiful groan he managed to raise himself into a sitting position just as the first raindrops started to fall. I quickly got to my feet and tucked myself beneath the sheltered canopy of the veranda and watched him squirm in the mud.

Looking to the heavens I said, "Okey dokey, Pritchard, I suppose we had better get on with this, eh? Can't hang around here all night just to get soaking wet, talking shit with the likes of you, now can I?"

Pritchard straightened himself as best he could and with his last remaining dignity yelled, "you know what, Jack, fuck you! You've always been a twat, so fucking get on with whatever it is you feel you have to do, I couldn't give two shits!"

"My oh my, we are in a bad fettle aren't we lad? And the language coming from you is quite atrocious, I'm in utter shock," I mocked.

And with that I got up off the veranda, casually walked down the steps twirling my knife, grabbed Pritchard roughly by the hair and slammed his face into the mud. I then lifted his bound feet up and pulling my blade across the back of his ankle sliced clean through his Achilles tendon.

"You see now, Joe, the benefit of wearing good quality hiking boots and not low-cut flimsy trainers?" I stated matter-of-factly releasing his legs and sidestepping to avoid the gore.

Pritchard howled and the blood spattered to the ground, lots of it. He wriggled around in the mud, his face contorted with agony and utterly filthy now and the lower part of his legs were covered in blood. He was shouting and swearing at me offering vague threats that he had no hope of fulfilling.

"You're a total spineless cunt, Jack, cut me loose, you bastard, why don't you fight me fairly like a man?"

"Fight fairly?" I said incredulously, "just like you were going to do when I turned up this evening?" I yelled at him, "with your homemade club raised like some caveman about to smash my brains in. I had no intention of this you fucking idiot," I gestured to the knife, "until you came at me with the sole intention of doing me in. I was just going to wind you up a bit, sabotage your deer, although to be honest you did that all by yourself you inept twat. You've ruined that beast all by yourself by not covering it, gutting it and hanging it you absolute muppet."

I went on, as Pritchard squirmed beneath my tirade not giving a care about the deer. "You need to learn, Pritchard, that I'm not some sap you can try and bully like that slob Cohen, did you honestly think you could better me? He (Cohen) liked to hang on your every word because he had no self-esteem, he was weak. Whereas me, well, I'm managing just fine on my own. I'm strong, I don't need anyone like your pathetic self to try and manipulate me to their will. Now then, enough of that. Shall we continue?"

Pritchard tried to wriggle away from me. Where to God only knows, as he couldn't exactly get far with a slashed Achilles and bound up as tightly as he was. I once again grabbed him by his hair and slammed his face into the dirt, again and again until his moaning and struggling stopped. Next, I took my knife and pressed it down into his mouth horizontally, sawing through his lips into his cheeks only stopping as the blade ground against his back teeth.

"I'll make that smile bigger, you ugly fucker," I shouted as I withdrew the knife.

He squealed then quickly realised that to scream only made it worse, so he desperately tried to stifle it as best he could by keeping his mouth closed. With the blood streaming down his face, hands and feet still bound tightly, I could see it in his eyes he was acutely aware that his plight was inevitable.

He made such a pitiful site, I actually thought about letting him go and hunting him down in the forest, just to prolong his agony—and my fun—and see how far he could possibly get. Or maybe I could just leave him for the animals and the same fate as Celestine. I must have drifted off in my own thoughts about what I was going to do with him and by not paying attention, when I did finally come out of my revery and look up, he had slithered almost to the river in the vain hope of escape.

The mud and water had made it a little easier for him to use his knees and elbows and slide himself along inch by inch and he had nearly made it. Nearly.

As the storm clouds gathered and the rain recommenced its deluge, I ran towards him slipping and sliding, then on reaching him I grabbed him by his leg ropes and plunged my knife through his right thigh. Forgetting the damage I'd caused to his mouth, he screamed again and then with a loud gasp and then a sigh, the fight simply left him.

He collapsed face first into the mud as comprehension finally dawned on him that his brief hope of escape was futile and the end was only a matter of time. Pulling the knife from his leg, I then heaved him over as I wanted my face to be the last one he ever saw. Exhausted but smiling triumphantly into his ruined face I propped myself up on top of him, placed my knife above his heart and pressed down with all I had.

The knife slowly sunk into his chest and through into the riverbank beneath him. Pritchard's expression was one of shock then blessed relief, as the life left his body and he sank further into the dirt.

I rolled off Pritchard's lifeless wreck of a body and lay there in the mud panting. The sweat ran down my face and my knife slipped from my grasp because of all the blood. With the rain pelting down and the occasional crash of thunder overhead, I slowly picked myself up and got to work disposing of Pritchard. I must stop killing people so large, I thought with a mirthless chuckle.

Once again, it was with an immense effort that I managed to untie him, get him into the polythene sheet—which I'd recovered from the bushes behind the cabin—then re-tie him in the polythene along with once again some heavy rocks. Thankfully, there were no disgusting smells like there were disposing of Cohen except for the distinct smell of piss that is, as I edged him the last couple of yards towards the water.

As I neared the now raging torrent of the river, my head down dragging this monstrous lump with me, I heard a twig snap directly in front of me and then a childlike manic giggle. And when I looked up through the rain, it was into the bloodshot eyes of Phillip Schroder.

Shit!

13. The Gradual Breakdown of Phillip Schroder

Unbeknownst to us as competitors and with us now camped in the middle of nowhere, Schroder had been putting a brave face on for the last few months. Once he knew he was going to have a shot at redemption and this new style of competition, he had made a conscious effort to get clean, as it wasn't just the drink that was fucking up his life.

Drugs, albeit recreational drugs. What this actually meant, he didn't know because to him they were all recreational, at least everything he had tried. He could in one night alone do coke, ecstasy and shrooms all washed down with a good quality Talisker. How he was still alive was beyond him. He'd even tried peyote (whatever the fuck that was) from some beautiful red head he'd been sleeping with, I mean peyote for God's sake.

He had found out later after an incredibly bad trip that it was a fucking cactus of all things! Trying to get clean was a struggle for Schroder, not just because of his health, but because he enjoyed it too much, I mean really enjoyed it. The temptation was always there, why go out for a drink or two when you could get fucked up, stay out most of the night and end up back at some chick's flat (his words).

Unbelievably, he had actually broken his ankle, which caused the postponement. And yes, I had still been right, he'd been off his tits on some pill that was apparently going to change his life, that's what he'd been told anyway. Well, it put his life on hold if nothing else. As he'd been dancing naked with the redhead on his balcony, he then attempted to leap from this into the pool below.

At a height of about twelve feet and having just had his pool cleaned, it hadn't been refilled yet, luckily for him he'd landed feet first and only broke his ankle and not his thick skull. Being so high, he'd hardly felt the snap and when the paramedics finally found him, he was trying to hobble, still naked except for a towel across his shoulders the four miles to the hospital. Thankfully, his rented house was reasonably remote, so not too many neighbours were exposed to his, by now shrivelled, genitals and lily-white arse parading down the lane.

Schroder's breakdown wasn't a recent thing, he'd gradually got worse since the court case, whereby with just the skin of his teeth he'd been acquitted. He had known she was underage. OK only by six months he said, but still she had been all over him and she was in a nightclub for fucks sake. I did point out that yes she may well have been in a nightclub, but the next two times you met up with her was in the cold light of day and one time she had been in her fucking school uniform. Point taken he'd conceded and then went on with his story.

After the court case no one—especially his so-called friends—wanted anything to do with him, his agents—and there were many of the blood sucking bastards (again his words)—all snubbed him and wouldn't return his emails and phone calls. They wouldn't even come to the door of the office when he had turned up one day, albeit a little dishevelled and the worse for wear.

That encounter had ended bad as whilst being ejected from the building he'd thrown up over the security guard and subsequently taken quite a beating. As he lay bleeding at the entrance to his once place of work, a stray dog had—favouring the heap of what it thought a discarded heap of clothes in the doorway—pissed on him and then slowly wandered off. He finally knew and understood what the bottom rung of the ladder looked like.

After months of almost begging for work, he finally gave in and simply lost himself in the drink and drugs, it was the easiest choice and the only thing left he could do. He was wealthy and it was always his favourite past time anyway, from there his life had spiralled out of control. He'd been photographed in a thousand compromised positions, falling in and out of taxis drunk and being ejected from parties to name but a few. He had once again become the talk of the papers and TV, but for all the wrong reasons.

When one day out of the blue, through a drunken and drug fuelled haze, a young pissant director had turned up at his door with a pitch for a new show, he'd leapt at the chance. Well, he'd actually staggered about a bit then fell over. This young director—he looked to be about eighteen, not sure if he had even started shaving yet and this must surely be his first real gig—had said Phillip had been the first choice on his list.

But deep down he knew even through his drunken stupor that all that amounted to was utter bullshit and he was most definitely this guy's last chance at getting this competition off the ground. Even with his reputation and career now in tatters, a sober, clean Phillip Schroder could easily deliver the goods and to be honest, he thought the scandal would probably add to the attraction. All he had to do was get sober—that would be easier said than done.

Getting himself sober had been tough, he had had to do it in stages. First, he'd binned off the hangers on, the flunky's who would say or do anything just to get a fix or a drink out of him. Next, he stripped the house of all his pills, coke and drink, even the 'secret' caches that were carefully concealed around the house. And finally, he hit the gym.

With the help of the muscle-bound Adonis who lived in the next house down and could probably have any woman in the land, just a pity then that he was a raging homosexual. He hit the weights, pool and anything else with a commitment he previously thought had left him. Anything which would help sort his desperately beaten-up body and mind, he even tried yoga and meditation.

All he had to do was stick it to the Adonis once in a while and look like he was enjoying it. Didn't matter to him, while strictly speaking he wasn't gay, it was no hardship and therefore, just another means to an end for him as there was nothing he wouldn't do to get another shot at the starlight.

He'd stayed clean for three whole months.

He'd been doing so well with his cold turkey and fitness regime until the redhead turned up. Fuck me, this girl was like some kind of devil and he couldn't, no matter how hard he tried, resist her charms. She arrived one evening at his front door, armed with a bag of coke, poppers and some exceedingly good single malt.

She had many other things in her bag of tricks that you would normally have to pay a lot of money for and things that would make a decent fellow blush. She promptly threw out his remonstrating young Adonis back to his own place and as quickly as that he had succumbed to her will. Three days of utter debauchery had followed until the night when the balcony incident had taken place.

After the so called 'accident' and the ankle break and the subsequent umpteen apologies to the director, producers and anyone else who'd listen. He then explained how well he had been doing to get back on the wagon and that it had only been a blip on his road to sobriety, it would never happen again. But alas no, it wasn't to last.

Once his ankle was on the road to recovery, he hadn't gone back to the gym or the meditation—or the neighbourhood Adonis—he'd started drinking and within no time at all he was almost back where he started, albeit a little more functioning. Then disguising his habit as well as he could he'd finally met all of us, the competitors, it had tipped him further into the abyss. An absolute set of cunts he called us and I couldn't have agreed more.

He had realised that without his *little helpers* he was never going to cope with the day-to-day mundane work of trying to fill in the gaps of what was essentially an incredibly boring TV show for the viewers. He felt the producers had fucked up with firstly, the selection of chefs and secondly, the impact they thought it would have on the general public. After all, it was basically watching people fish and sleep. Quite perceptive for a man who was for the most part whacked off his tits.

He then told me that after he and Cecil had paid a visit to me last week, he'd come to blows with the *Survival Man* and that had been the last straw for him, he'd hit the bottle hard that night. He'd been astonished at the treatment I'd received from Cecil and challenged him about it.

Once they'd vacated the car back at his trailer Cecil had set about him and Schroder, emboldened by the booze had rightly retaliated. The director had had to intervene and Schroder had been suspended from the project. They would get someone else to do the voice over parts and they had a stand in for the "action" shots and said that he was now just too big a risk for the project.

Disgusted by his treatment Schroder had taken off into the woods with a stolen *Gator,* having first stopped to fill it with supplies of smoked salmon, caviar and other fine delicacies from his personal catering team. Along with whisky and his hidden stash of coke and pills he had been living for the last couple of days in Subi's vacant cabin. He was sure they had no idea where he'd gone and hoped they thought he had departed Northumberland for good.

He had been enjoying his little sojourn in the forest when the idea occurred to him to pay me a visit to apologise for Cecil's "positively indecent" behaviour. He thought, he could find my cabin and when at first he'd lost control and ditched the *Gator* in a small ravine and thought, that's it, he'd fucked up, he then luckily happened upon Alex's cabin and knew he was heading the right way.

Alex had appeared at the door—always watchful after the stalking inbred— and asked if he was OK and if he needed any help. But he'd pleasantly declined and continued on his merry, if somewhat stoned way. This had been earlier today. When he'd neared my cabin, he'd seen me emerge and wondering what I was up to—and unbeknownst to me and a little slack on my part—he'd somehow followed me here unnoticed and unfortunately, seen and heard everything.

***

After listening to Schroder's story, I had to hand it to the fella, getting to my place and then following me here must have taken some doing. Looking at him you could see he was as high as a kite, I don't know what he was on but fuck me, it'd given him some balls. His wide bloodshot eyes stared excitedly down at me like an expectant child waiting for pudding.

Rather irritated with the whole situation I found myself in, I asked him, "so, what the fuck do you want with me? You may have noticed I'm in a bit of a tight spot here. I understand you've been through a *lot,* Phillip, but a little bit of help would be greatly appreciated."

"Yeah, yeah, no *problemo,* my friend," he said like an over eager to please kid. Not sure about the friend bit but I needed a hand as I was sweating like a pig. "I'd like to have seen you trying to dispose of Cohen on your own," he sniggered.

"Let's get the big fucker in the river and then we can have a clean-up round here and see if he has anything of use in the cabin," I ordered and Schroder was only too happy to oblige.

We dragged the body the last couple of paces and on the count of three hurled it as far as we could into the maelstrom of the river. Pritchard's body sank immediately and was gone from sight and just like that I'd now killed two people and caused the death of a third.

I knew I'd be caught soon, it's impossible to think I could bullshit my way out of this, no matter how crazy I'd found myself becoming. Schroder looked mighty pleased with himself and helped me to next disguise the boot prints and any sign of a scuffle as best we could. Then we both entered the cabin.

Sitting in the corner with a face that now looked like it was slipping from his skull beneath but somehow still managing to look smug was my friend and confidante the KP.

I said to him, "where the hell have you been? Could you not see that I needed a little help out there?"

Schroder on hearing this looked at me rather puzzled, "Who are you talking to, Jack? I'm over here and forgive me if I'm wrong but I'm pretty sure, I did help you out there."

I turned and looked at Schroder, "Er yeah, sorry about that, Phillip, I'm just talking to myself, feeling the strain a bit," I answered laughing nervously and looking to my dead friend.

Schroder looked unsure about this exchange between us for about a heartbeat then slapped me on the back, "don't worry, Jack, I'm here now!" He exclaimed like he was some *Marvel* superhero. I thought, yeah, well, that doesn't exactly reassure me, you mad fucking junky.

The cabin was as just as I'd noticed earlier, a mess. In fact, it was worse now I was actually on the inside. How on earth these people lived like this I would never fathom. A couple of logs remained at the side of the fire and I placed these on to it to keep the fire going as long as possible, therefore hopefully creating the illusion that the cabin was still inhabited.

Checking my watch and seeing it was pushing 3 o'clock, I realised that the time was getting away from us. One last glance around the cluttered cabin left me in no doubt that there was nothing of any value or use.

Turning to Schroder, my apparent new partner in crime I said, "We need to leave now, it's a good four hours to my cabin and if we hurry we'll get there before sunrise as long as you don't hold me back."

Schroder looked happy to be involved and that he had thankfully been invited. I had to stop a minute and think how fucked up the last few days had been, this latest turn of events with Schroder had obviously reshaped my life going forward, on this I had no doubts. There was also the small matter of the recent murder to consider.

All I could think about now was finishing what I had started, granted things had dramatically changed from what I had first wanted to achieve from this competition but there was no going back on that now. Bos was where my attention turned to now, I wanted that bastard and Schroder—if for once he could keep his shit together—could help me procure him.

Schroder was an absolute ball breaker on the way back to the cabin, I'd have to make sure he kept up his recent daily intake of hard drugs if I wanted him to be of any use. I had to constantly shout at him to stop pissing and moaning and seriously considered a knife to his throat at one point.

Finally and with lots of cajoling and fierce encouragement and the odd threat of quick and brutal retribution and with the sun desperately trying to break through from the night and rise towards a new day—looking like another wet one—we were at last approaching my cabin. I felt like some kind of vampire along with his *familiar* desperately trying to get back before the sun turned me to dust.

Breaking through from the treeline and heading for the cabin I instantly felt that something was most definitely wrong, something was amiss. At first, I couldn't put my finger on it and then suddenly it hit me, my deer had disappeared.

"What the fuck? My bastard deer!" I shouted at Schroder grabbing him by his jacket and screaming in his face as he was the only one here looking—as was usual lately—particularly vacant and totally uninterested in my plight.

"It's nothing to do with me, I haven't touched your precious deer," Schroder finally said snapping out of his wool-gathering state and remonstrating his innocence.

"Where the fuck is my deer? How can my deer have gone? It's not like there's a bear in the woods that could lift it off the hook and carry it away now, is there," I shouted at Schroder again and then suddenly it dawned on me—Bos! It had to be that cunt.

He is the only bastard that pathetic and sly to not have the balls to take me on face to face and wait until I wasn't here. And then of all things stealing my fuckin deer; my deer, for Christ's sake! Was this what he had been planning all along? It's a bit pathetic if I were honest. Here's me turned into, by my own admission a brutal psychopath and the best Bos could manage was looting a dead deer. I suddenly had a terrible thought and raced to my cabin, barged through the door and took in the scene.

***

Nothing, he had done absolutely nothing! What a pitiful spineless individual he really was. I think, at that moment, I hated him even more for not trashing my place. Why hadn't he at least smashed up my supplies and pissed on my bed, I know I would have if the roles had been reversed. Following me through the door Schroder looked somewhat confused at my anger but relieved he had somewhere he could get warm, take some pills and then at last get his head down for a while.

He liked to remind me—as he had done several times on our trip back here—how exhausting it had been defending me against Cecil. How difficult his struggle had been through the miles of forest on his own to catch up to me and that a little appreciation would be nice.

I always answered him with the same, "shut the fuck up, Phillip! Just give it a rest, for fucks sake."

I left him to it and inwardly seething wandered down to the river pool that was currently being pelted with rain, stripped off my soiled clothes and plunged myself below its now distinctly murky depths. It wasn't the cleanest of ice baths—ice was starting to form around the edge now and the days were most definitely getting colder—I'd ever had as the water was now full of the river embankment's dirt, but I desperately needed to clear my head. When I'd stayed in the freezing pool as long as I could bear, I climbed out into the freezing morning, gathered my strewn clothes and headed back inside.

Schroder was flat out on my bed snoring peacefully, what a strange predicament I found myself in. Who would have thought I'd be sharing a cabin with this worthless sack of shit. I suppose he had tried to defend me against Cecil, so maybe I owed him one. One though and that would be it.

I got to work reviving the almost dead fire and within minutes it was already producing some heat. The cabin was cold but not as bad as I'd imagined it would be. I filled a pan of water and set it on the stove for tea. It'd take a while, but I felt I needed a cup of strong tea to help me think on how to approach Bos.

If he were in this area then he obviously wasn't as far away as I'd first imagined him to be. I knew what kind of a person he was and therefore, knew the lazy bastard would never have trekked too far to reach me. This was good fortune as time was not on our side. Once Schroder was rested and we'd had some much-needed sustenance, we'd set out and find him.

I didn't know how long we would have until they found my gruesome river gifts and called a halt to proceedings, so I had to work fast. For all I knew with the river full to bursting, Cohen's arse was at this precise moment as I sat here contemplating, floating into someone's back yard. I was also regularly losing track of the days, had we even been here two weeks yet?

All the long nights were blurring into one, I was feeling more and more paranoid, more anxious and angrier by the minute. And while I should have been having an invigorating cup of Lady Grey, I placed a healthy portion of liberty caps into the pan and left them to brew.

Instinctively smelling this through his slumber—how he managed this I will never know—Schroder woke up looking a lot more refreshed than I felt. And together, even though we were both very well aware that this was not the right thing to do under the circumstances—we cracked a new bottle of single malt and alternatively drank this along with the magic tea.

Before long we were both merrily battered and regaling the previous night's events with a lot more hilarity and gusto than there should have been. At the end of the day a man—albeit a worthless sack of shit of a man—had lost his life. While Schroder and I were completely smashed, I attempted to introduce him to my KP friend, who as always was keeping his watchful eye over me in the corner of the room. But at this seemingly polite introduction Schroder burst into a laughing fit and called me crazier than him. Yep, I thought, I do believe I am.

14. Time Is Running Out

I woke to an incessant banging on the door and someone hollering my name, "Come on, Jack, open the fuck up!"

Fucking Cecil again!! What the hell did he want now? My head felt like someone was trying to break out of it as I sat up. The banging persisted—this cunt was relentless—and eventually, I acquiesced and shouted, "Alright, Cecil, keep your fucking hair on!"

Checking my watch, it was midday and then glancing to the floor I was surprised to see Phillip Schroder sprawled in the corner with his head almost in the KP's lap. For a moment I had no idea how he'd got here and felt completely at a loss and then bang! It all came flooding back, God I hoped he would actually be of some use later.

I staggered semi naked to the door and looking down I was thankful I'd managed to at least put some underwear on at some point after my dip, but with the fire just mere embers I gathered a blanket around my shoulders and opened the door.

Cecil and two of his inept cronies stood on the veranda desperately trying to look menacing while keeping out of the rain, again it was pissing down.

"Now then, chaps, you three been up all night sniffing each other's crotches?" I asked matter-of-factly.

At this one of the lads, the inbred I'd pounded the first day and sporting a dazzling set of what looked like borrowed false teeth as they didn't fit his mouth whatsoever, lurched towards me shouting, "I'm gonna fucking have you ya prick."

And in the exact same instant Cecil—while I also didn't and probably couldn't move a muscle – grabbed him roughly by the neck and through him off the veranda. He fell down into the rain and the mud and as he hit the ground with an oomph, his nice new teeth flew out and landed in the dirt.

"Just calm down, boy, for fuck's sake!" Cecil said to him and the lad at least had the decency to look shame faced, while urgently trying to ram his soiled dentures back in place.

"Jack, we need to talk, we're missing Cohen, Celestine and now Schroder. The latter took off in our Gator, raided his trailer of food and booze and then disappeared. We're also not a hundred percent on Pritchard."

"And this has what to do with me exactly?" I asked suddenly alive to the situation but feigning exhaustion and gently closing the door behind me, so they couldn't see Schroder's prone figure.

"I've been here getting wasted all night from pure boredom because of this incredibly poor and disorganised competition as I'm sure you can tell just by looking at me, here I pointed to my face. I cannot and in all honestly do not want to help you with those missing nitwits gentlemen and to be honest, I couldn't give a shit. So, why don't you and your two little pant sniffers just fuck off!"

Cecil was raging and grabbed hold of me by the blanket and thrusting his face into mine—and suffering the morning breath of the drunk and wasted—he growled, "This is your last chance to help us, Jack, you utter cunt, the police are being called and search parties are being organised. If you have had anything to do with this, I'll make sure I'm the one to personally bring you in."

"Alright *Columbo*, you do what you think you have to but for the time being get the fuck off my porch."

I broke his grip on me and pushed him off and away.

"You also might want to ask that little turd rolling around in the mud about how he was trying to cop a look through Alex's window and wouldn't take no for an answer. And while you're at it ask him where he got his new teeth, *Horse and fucking Hound*?"

Cecil's sidekicks looked confused as to what to do. Especially horse teeth down in the mud and probably well aware he was going to get another bollocking for stalking Alex. But with a nod from Cecil they retreated (Cecil grabbing the retard by the scruff of the neck and dragging him up and away) to their Land Rover, parked precariously close to the riverbank.

With the now predictable wheelspin and cascade of dirt they disappeared down the track and were gone. As I was just about to turn, Schroder appeared at my shoulder. He looked decidedly more sober than I felt and asked, "what the fuck are you standing with the door open for? It's as cold as some Baltic state out there."

Completely oblivious as to the recent altercation.

**

"Listen, Phillip, I've got some things I need to get done and they start tonight. It isn't going to be pleasant, so if you think you saw enough last night and want nothing more to do with what's coming then you need to get dressed and leave now," I said to Schroder, as for some unknown reason I felt a newfound sense of responsibility for his welfare.

"Is that the way you're going to treat your new partner?" asked Schroder, it seemed he had taken my little speech as a personal affront.

"I know what went down last night and I'm quite happy to dish out the same treatment to that other unspeakable cunt Bos. He constantly took me apart with his self-professed silver tongue when I found myself alone with him, the bastard was incessant with his personal jibes and all-round defamation of my character. I promise you, Jack, he was a major factor in me not retaining my sobriety."

"OK, Phillip, OK," I said placatingly. "You know I had to ask the question, so don't go getting squeamish if things turn very dark very rapidly yes?" I said to him but wasn't quite convinced that Bos had had anything to do with his alcoholism, he was long gone by the time Bos had turned up.

"We need to cover the ground fast to his cabin, it can't be as far as what Pritchard's was, so we'll leave later tonight; if he's there, great but I have a funny feeling he'll have sort better suited accommodation elsewhere."

"What the hell do you mean, Jack?" Schroder asked.

"I know him, Phillip, he's a real lazy bastard and tries to manipulate other people in doing as much for him as they can. We'll head past Alex's cabin and then on to Subi's, pick up a couple of well-earned supplies from your stash if you catch my drift," here I winked at him. "And then head off in search for Bos."

Schroder looked excited and smug with himself when I mentioned using his ill-gotten gains and then turned to me, "I'll get the tea on, nothing can be achieved without a mind replenishing brew first."

I agreed and decided to prepare us some lunch with the last of the rabbit legs along with some rice. The last thing I felt like doing was eating but we needed fuel to see us through the day and night ahead, within a few hours we'd set off north again. I'd retrace my route past Alex's and then on to Subi's place. Orry was also out that way but I wasn't sure how far north and I had no intention of paying him a visit anyway.

We could rest a little at Subi's, refuel and then push on. I hoped to be at Bos's place at the very latest by the early hours of the morning and from there we'd find out where the flash fucker was. I was more and more confident that the little prick had stolen my deer but not for his own use.

God forbid he would have to prepare his own food, he'll have dumped it as soon as he couldn't carry it anymore, just to wind me up even further. I was also struck again that winning the competition had taken a back seat and it was all over for me. All those months of preparation and planning gone and I had been fully committed to victory but now, I had another objective.

Furthermore, I had somehow unintentionally picked up a passenger in the shape of Phillip Schroder and even more unbelievingly made him an accomplice, albeit a very willing accomplice.

After eating we sat back and relaxed awhile. Schroder as if by magic and with a dramatic flourish produced a finely rolled toothpick of a joint and—this being the strongest thing we would partake in today—we smoked that chatting about what lay ahead. I regaled my triumphant story of flattening Bos outside a pub when we worked together previously in Kendal and that we'd met only on another couple of occasions. But still the hatred for the man remained and that if I'd come this far with Pritchard and Cohen, then I may as well go all the way and indulge in the destruction of Bos.

I had no doubt it was clear I would be caught and locked up after achieving this, so I'd better make the best of things while it lasted. I wanted more than ever to wipe the smile from Bos's smug face and fully intended on doing just that.

Time pressed on, getting ready we dressed in several layers of clothing, which would be needed for this little expedition to keep us safe from the elements. And with my knife fastened to my belt and backpack full of essentials, change of clothes, torch, map and the ever-present chocolate, we left the cabin. Schroder had no pack with him, but he assured me he was ready and up to the task.

I glanced back at the cabin as I entered the woods and felt a slight pang of sadness at my departure. I had enjoyed my time here but knew it was coming to a conclusion and this would probably be the last time I set foot in there. Hard to believe this had all unravelled in only two weeks.

As I looked at a fiercely determined Schroder, I had the distinct feeling that he knew his brief tenure of being in the spotlight was well and truly over for him. And the realisation that things on his return had not quite gone according to plan if he'd even had one in the first place.

***

We had set off just as the last of the light was fading, although it did seem lately what with the atrocious weather it never really got light, we seemed to be stuck in a perpetual dusk. Schroder was quiet but seemed unwavering in his task and didn't complain. Even when he lost his boot to a bog and it took the both of us to extract it, the look of disgust as he squeezed his foot back into it was almost comical.

His usual jovial self-had gone, no doubt caused by the lack of amphetamines in his blood. The forest felt more resilient than on previous visits, denser and foreboding, malevolent almost. As if it knew what we were planning and was determined to try and prevent us from seeing our journey through.

Every bush seemed courser, every stream wider, every bog deeper, it was an incredibly harsh environment I knew but whereas on previous visits it had been an enjoyable task, now it just felt like cumbersome obstacles had been placed in the way to distract us from our final goal.

As we were nearing Alex's cabin, a low rumble of an engine could be heard up ahead and light could be seen through the thinning trees, so I immediately brought our progress to a halt. Telling Schroder to wait and stay hidden in the forest, I took off my backpack and leaving it with him, edged quietly to the treeline to try and make out what the noise and light source was.

Crawling on my belly slowly and silently through the wet forest floor then carefully looking through the thinning leaves but keeping as low as possible I could see two vehicles outside Alex's cabin. Both had their engines running and lights ablaze. Keeping out of sight I slid from the trees and staying within the long grass dragged myself toward the back of Alex's place. Then I slowly edged myself underneath the cabin and then the veranda just enough, so I was as close as possible to hear what was being said.

The freezing cold mud was thickest here and I could feel myself sinking down into it a couple of inches at a time. Cecil and the gamekeeper, who I hadn't seen since the day of the shoot, along with three other men (the Tash and the kid with his new dentures were both there) were talking to Alex.

She had wisely remained inside and had the door open just enough to engage with, what I can only describe as a hunting party. It was hard to hear what with the driving rain and the sound of the motors, but it sounded like Celestine had been found and that the competition would be abruptly coming to an end.

Alex seemed nonplussed about Celestine and felt the competition should be able to proceed. She rightly said, it had been expected we would lose people along the way, granted they would have left under their own steam and not actually upped and died. I almost burst out laughing at this but quickly got myself under control.

"For God's sake, Alex, losing people to disqualification or retirement from the competition is one thing but someone dying, albeit by their own ineptitude is something altogether different," the gamekeeper said. "We can't honestly continue, what with Celestine dead and two others missing."

"Two others missing. And who might that be, that cunt Cohen isn't missing, is he?" Alex asked.

"As a matter of fact he is, you wouldn't happen to know anything about that now, would you?" asked Cecil. I hadn't thought it'd be long before he intervened, he liked the sound of his own voice, that cunt did.

"No, not a thing, but it doesn't take a genius to work out he wasn't exactly up for this. He's probably hiding in a hotel until the month is up, so he can boast to his family and friends that he stayed the course. Who else is missing?" Alex asked.

"We think Pritchard," said the gamekeeper. "He's only been missing a day or two, the problem we have had is it's been hard to get the drones out in this weather, plus those two are not the most outgoing or active of contestants, so they did pretty much fuck all to start with."

"Well, I've not seen either, Schroder went dashing by a couple of days earlier, but he had very little to say and I've not seen him since, nor the other two at all," Alex said. "And in all honesty, I don't want to see any of them."

"Schroder you say, that's interesting, we thought he would be long gone," said Cecil. "While I'm here I also want to apologise for this little prick," he said gesturing to the retard boy with the fine set of new gnashers. "He admitted to me that he'd pestered you for a couple of nights, he was told under no circumstances to approach anyone, so all I can do is apologise."

"As long as I don't see him again," Alex said a little exasperated, "I'm not bothered and please think again about the competition, some of us have invested a lot of personal time and expense to take part in this. If a couple of arseholes—and both close friends at that—have decided to cut and run, then the rest of us can't be held responsible. Yes, I know Celestine is dead and I will even pretend to be sad if you would prefer, but that fucker was on borrowed time anyway by the look of it. So, why not let's try and get through the next two weeks without further incident and then fuck off home, yeah?"

I don't think Alex had ever spoken so much in her life and hiding there underneath the cabin trying to stifle a giggle was becoming increasingly difficult. Cecil and his party looked in complete disarray as to how to progress and at the end of the day, it wasn't their decision to call a halt to proceedings. That would be up to the producers and if they thought they were going to lose money—more money after having wasted plenty on Schroder—they wouldn't be the happiest of bunnies.

"Look, all we can do at the moment is keep searching for them. Celestine's body has been taken away but there doesn't seem to be anything suspicious about it, looks like he wandered off into the forest drunk, got lost and unfortunately died of exposure," the gamekeeper said.

"After this whole debacle it'll be up to the bosses what happens from here on in, so you'll just have to hope that they want to or are even allowed to continue. If by some chance you see any of the missing parties, including Schroder or even if you see Orry around, would you kindly explain to them what's going on please."

"Schroder will likely turn up when he runs out of booze and pills. I've no doubt on that score," said Alex. "Again why the *'Competition of the Year'* well *supposedly* that is," here she waggled her fingers in the air like imaginary exclamation marks, "would want to engage the services of these deadbeats is beyond me." And with that she turned and slammed the door in their faces.

I backed out from under the cabin and then crawled further off into the reeds near the river and squatted down keeping out of sight. Just then *The Tash* came ambling around the back of the cabin heading my way and looked to be staring straight at me. How on earth could he see me as it was pitch black now, my heart skipped a beat and the adrenalin began to course through me. I wasn't going to be caught now, after I'd come so far.

I reached down for my knife, slowly withdrew it and held it ready as he got ever closer. Just as I was readying myself to launch out of the reeds thinking my cover had been breached, he unbuckled his pants, took out his dick and unleashed a furious jet of urine the likes I'd never thought possible. Jesus, I thought, relaxing slightly and letting out my breath slowly. You oblivious fool, you have no idea how close you just came to getting your throat cut.

"Come on, get a shimmy on for fucks sake!" I heard Cecil calling in my direction as *The Tash's* seemingly unstoppable flow finally began to subside. And with a last couple of dribbles and shakes and a grumble of discontent about how he never gets time even for a piss, he was tucking himself away and retreating through the reeds towards the trucks.

I heard the trucks engines screaming away from Alex's cabin and then gradually fade into the night. With an audible sigh and then puff of the cheeks as I knew how close my discovery had been, I stepped out from the reeds and headed back towards Schroder, who by now would most likely be beside himself with fear.

Reminiscence: The Fight

I had been boxing two years, mainly as a way of controlling my anger and secondly as a hobby and way of keeping fit. Mam wouldn't come and watch and I couldn't really blame her, seeing her just turned seventeen-year-old son fighting wouldn't have been a pleasant experience for her.

Chirpy wouldn't come either as by now we weren't even brothers anymore, just two boys who shared a room, nothing else. He had his own friends and from the snippets of conversation I'd had with him, I was known by his friends as a psycho and was to be left alone, under no circumstances was I to be engaged with. Seemed a bit harsh but I didn't let it bother me too much.

The boxing had been good for me, I'd had a reasonable amount of success within the club, but I had no allusions or expectations that I'd be able to go further than the local club at any point in the near future. At school, I had produced the qualifications that I'd required to get into college and I'd be attending a two-year full time catering course starting in the upcoming September. I'd always enjoyed the idea of cooking and it seemed like the right thing to do.

I had also for some reason toyed with the idea of joining the police for a while and during a careers evening at my school a police officer was present handing out flyers and engaging with some of the students who might fancy a career in the emergency services. On seeing an opportunity to speak to the officer I took my chance and asked him several questions about pay, working conditions and all the usual topics.

On seeing my genuine interest the officer posed a question to me, he said, "So, you have been given a report of a woman in danger at a local housing estate and you are to proceed to the property immediately. On arriving at the said house a woman answers the door and is in obvious distress and looks to be trying to shield her face from view as she has clearly been a victim of domestic abuse."

I listened intently as the officer continued with his scenario. "Asking the woman if she is in danger, she hesitates and then apologises for causing a fuss and all the while she is looking over her shoulder at someone close behind her. At the same time, a man can be heard telling the woman what to say.

When you ask if you can come in for a chat just to ensure that there is no danger, the woman is wrenched away from the door and a big man takes her place shouting abuse at you and telling you in no uncertain terms to leave and that the woman asked for it."

The police officer then asks me, "are you still following me OK?"

"Absolutely," I say.

The police officer then said, "So, my question to you young man is with the woman obviously in distress and the man in question has quite clearly been beating her, therefore the woman is still in immediate danger, what is your next move going to be?"

Without any hesitation I answered. "Drag the bastard out the door and kick the shit out of him!" Knowing in my heart and without any doubt that this was exactly the right thing to do.

The officer looked down at me and said with an almost fatherly smile, "and that's why you have no future in the police force, son." And then he simply turned away and engaged with another student leaving me standing there completely bewildered at what I had said wrong.

Around this time I had also been seeing a girl from my school, Bernie, who would also be going to the same college. While I wouldn't exactly say it was true love, we were close and I'd become very protective of her, maybe a little too much at times.

We'd normally try to procure some cider and head to the local park to get particularly pissed and then partake in uncoordinated sticky fumbling's that I can imagine weren't exactly fun for either of us. Heading back from one such shindig on a late summer evening, we encountered three guys of roughly the same age as us. I had a vague recollection of one of them but couldn't remember exactly where from.

I attempted to walk by them, but they spread themselves across the narrow path and laughing amongst themselves, decided to try and block our retreat from the park. I also noticed that apart from the fact all three of them were bigger than me, they were also in a worse state of inebriation than us, they'd obviously been drinking a lot longer and deeper than we had.

As my senses started to clear with the introduction of a little adrenalin, I endeavoured to push through them keeping my Bernie in tight behind me. Obviously, they were having none of this and pushed back, all the time looking lasciviously at Bernie.

"What's the hurry, mate?" A particularly ugly pock faced lad with unfeasibly long arms in proportion to his body said, "where are you two love birds off too?"

The whole scenario of a young couple being set upon is so clichéd to think now, but this sort of thing happened a lot back then. Nowhere was particularly safe and we should have known better than to venture into the park after dark. Too late.

"Come on, lads, I don't want any bother, we'll just keep going and get home, yeah?" I said but to no avail as the first punch landed at the back of my head and that was it, they set upon me with some stinging blows and kicks to the head and body. The bastards even slapped Bernie to the ground and one of them was on her, tearing her blouse and trying to get her trousers down, while Bernie hung on desperately, screaming for all she was worth.

I managed to get to my feet and swung with a few wild blows but not really connecting. One guy was trying to get hold of my arms and I managed to fling my head back and it connected with his nose. With a scream he let go his feeble attempt at pinning my arms and as the ugly bastard with the ape like arms threw wild punches towards my head, I dodged past them and placed a boot into the face of Bernie's attacker. He fell with a heavy thud and Bernie was at him with her fingernails in his face causing all kinds of damage.

Just then, whilst sparring with the ugly bastard and realising that he had fought before and had me on reach with those ridiculous Mr Tickle *arms, I heard shouting and saw two blokes heading towards us. With this the three possible would-be rapists all scarpered, the last to get away was Bernie's attacker as she wasn't finished yet and raked her nails down his face one last time screaming at him.*

The two blokes chased them off and helped Bernie to her feet, "you alright, flower?" one asked and Bernie tried her best to compose herself and smile, but the tears were coming now.

She understood she had been so close to being raped and the realisation of this was hitting her hard. I thanked the fellas for their help and we left the park together, me cradling Bernie while trying to staunch the blood from my nose. I explained that the police would have to be informed but she wanted none of that.

Bernie and I didn't last long after the incident, while she didn't exactly blame me, she didn't feel safe anymore and wouldn't leave the house, her parents eventually wouldn't let me into the house or anywhere near her as if it were all my doing.

After this I put every waking moment into the boxing, anyone the coach could throw at me I'd happily take on regardless of size, shape or ability. I wasn't interested in friends at the club, just opponents. Two months after this and while preparing for college we had an inter-club boxing competition between my club and another in the next town that produced equally good fighters.

It would be fought under real conditions, all the usual precautions would be taken, head guards etc would have to be worn. I was first to put my name down, I normally fought at featherweight, but I was quite happy to go up a weight or two, I was nine stone dead when the competition day arrived.

On the day of the competition dad was really keen to come but I asked him not to, not because of a fear of being beaten but because since the incident in the park my whole persona had changed, worsened in fact. Boxing had previously brought some kind of solace to me but now, I feared I was right back where I started and I didn't want dad to see it.

He agreed not to come but was unhappy, which hadn't been my intention whatsoever. All the fighters at the club were in attendance and were up for it, bragging rights between any club is always important. For me, I knew this was my last day at the club regardless of what happened, I'd had enough, not of the fighting but of the restrictions and restraints within the fighting community. I'd be starting college soon, so I'd endeavour to put all my energies into that.

I got ready, boots on, headguard in hand and my hands taped up and then wandered out of the changing rooms and into the gym proper. Most of the other club had turned up by now and the coaches were exchanging pleasantries, obviously well known to each other. I looked over the visiting club members and instant recognition dawned on my face as I stared into the eyes of one of my park assailants.

A face like that I should have known he'd be a fighter. I'd thought at the time that he had some experience, but now here in front of me, no amount of experience would help him. I stared at him with complete hatred. Fury raged in me, not just because of the park attack but he was also to blame for Bernie and me not being together anymore and just as the coach was approaching, the bastard smiled at me. He knew exactly who I was and quite clearly, felt no remorse.

"Coach," I called. "That big ugly bastard with the ape arms, I want that to be my first fight, I know it wasn't my allotted bout, but can you sort it?" My eyes had never left his as the coach, somewhat confused wandered back over to the opposing trainer.

This wasn't protocol as fights had been arranged and bouts had been pencilled in, it was only supposed to be a friendly competition between two local clubs, so I hoped the coach could sort it. I saw their coach speak to ape boy and he nodded vigorously, right it was on.

Looking past ape boy, another familiar face stood there but obviously wasn't competing today as he was sporting some deep scarring to his cheek, nose and eye. Well done Bernie was all I could think, pity the bastard hadn't lost the eye. Staring at him he dropped his eyes to the floor, clearly not as confident without the booze and an audience.

Coach came back then and said, "Fight's on if you really want it, Jack but he's welterweight, you're giving away about a stone and a half, it's your shout kid."

"Yeah, that's fine coach, no problem, I need this fight."

"OK then it's yours, don't know what's going on but don't get carried away in there. Yes, he's an ugly bastard but he's a decent fighter," Coach said. "Their gaffer rates him highly."

"Just get me in the ring coach," I said.

146

What felt like no time at all I was through the ropes and in the ring, gum shield in, head guard on, gloves laced up and ready to go. I never took my eye off him, I felt a cool calm wash over me and looking at my opponent he didn't seem quite so big or confident when he was facing me. I might be giving up a lot of weight, but I knew my rage would see me through.

From the first bell I raced out and set about him in the middle of the ring with such an onslaught of vicious blows he never stood a chance. Every shot I'd been taught I rained down on him, uppercuts, hooks, hardly had to jab as my domination was so complete. I don't even remember taking a blow to the head or body. Towards the end of the first round, he stumbled and I caught him with a sweet right hook.

As he went down to the canvas, gum shield flying out, I followed him down and leapt on top of him and kept beating him. All style and grace left me as I continued to pound his face until both coaches had floundered into the ring and managed to pry me off him. I was screaming incoherently about being left alone to finish the job as coach manhandled me to my corner and held me there pressed against the ropes.

The kid was out cold. Bleeding from his mouth, eyes and nose and the opposite coach was trying to revive him with smelling salts, while simultaneously stemming the flow of blood from several deep facial cuts. He also kept looking at my coach and wondering what the hell just happened. I was kept pinned in the corner by coach until he could signal for one of the big heavyweight lads to get me out of the ring and into the changing rooms.

Coach was too stunned to say anything to me as I was dragged away, just kept looking at me in utter bewilderment. Everyone was amazed at what they'd just witnessed and looked at me with complete confusion, the competition was over and like I'd thought at the beginning of the day, my boxing was finished.

No one had ever known what had really happened in the park, but as I left the gym for the last time, I thought if nothing else I'd been able to hand out some sort of retribution and give my ever worrying mind a little reassurance.

***

Passing Alex's cabin, the door suddenly flung open and she stood there looking at me as I'd try to scurry past unnoticed.

"What the fuck have you been up to, Jack?" she shouted through the pounding rain.

"Things have gotten a little out of hand, Alex; in fact, I would actually say they're spiralling quite quickly out of control! We're just heading off to pay our friend Bos an overdue visit," I said.

"What do you mean, *we*?" she asked. And just then Schroder came bustling out of trees to join me.

"Jesus, Jack, I was beginning to worry," he said and then saw Alex and beamed at her. "Hi Alex, we're on an exciting adventure!"

At this, Alex looked at the pair of us in complete exasperation.

"What the actual Jesus fuck is going on? And you two together? Never saw that one coming."

I said, "I can't see the competition continuing, Alex, and for that I'm truly sorry but if it does and you can win then I'm pleased for you. I want nothing more to do with it, it's all yours."

Looking perplexed and somewhat scared Alex said. "You look after yourself, Jack, you too, Phillip, don't know what you've got yourselves caught up in but whatever you need to get done then do it quick. From what the gamekeeper and that other prick said, you haven't got long before the police arrive. Also, one more thing. That dickhead Bos isn't north of Subi's place, he's west still following the river."

And with that piece of advice and a last melancholic smile she closed the door and left us standing in the pissing rain.

15. Bos's Last Stand

I should have realised that Bos's cabin would be west, a slight misjudgement on my part but nevertheless, Schroder and I ploughed on. I felt more determined than ever and when we reached Subi's old place, it was a welcome rest bite from the cold and the rain. The wind had also picked up somewhat, but I considered this to be good news as it would help to conceal our arrival at Bos's place.

Schroder had stolen—albeit from his own personal trailer—some first-class single malt and once we had slaked our thirst with plenty of water, we threw back a couple of whiskies for the road, spooned great handfuls of Oscietra caviar into our mouths and finished off with the last of my chocolate.

I had not seen my original dead companion since the previous night's exploits but looking out into the storm, I noticed him standing in the rain. His countenance was by far the worst to date, he now only vaguely resembled the KP I'd killed all that time ago and I fear I would probably have trouble in picking him out of police line-up.

He cast a sorry figure standing there as the rain and wind pelted his head and body. Nevertheless, it didn't seem to cause him a great deal of concern or for that matter actually touch him, it just seemed to pass right through. And I think for the first time I realised what his purpose was, why he'd come back to what I thought was originally to torment me.

I fully believe now he was some prophet of impending doom, a kind of omen or Jonah as whenever he appeared bad things happened or at least were about to. Feeling a little uneasy and slightly nauseous from this latest revelation—and the unholy combination of whisky and caviar—I was never more hell bent on murder.

We got our things together and set off back into the night with the storm raging but a certain spring in our step as to what lay ahead. Schroder looked quite possibly as manic as I felt and I was certain that could only be a good thing, the fact that he'd popped a pill as we were leaving probably had something to do with it. We had exchanged very few words since this morning, but both of us remained in silent agreement that what we were doing was justified. At least, in my mind it was; fuck knows what was going on in Schroders addled brain.

Knowing we didn't have as far to go as first thought was also a great sense of relief as we battled our way through dense forest, gorse, bogs and streams. We passed very little wildlife as it all seemed to have buried itself away out of the atrocious weather, possibly hoping for better come the morning. Or maybe it too along with the forest knew what we were planning and decided to steer clear.

I'd lost all sense of time when we found some cover in a particularly sheltered part of the wood and sat down to rest. Looking at my watch it was pushing midnight but hearing the distinct roar of the river not too far away I knew at some point in the very near future we'd happen upon Bos's cabin, he couldn't be much further along.

I thought of Orry then, tucked away in his cabin oblivious as to what was happening as he was so far out of the way. Maybe for the best I thought, who knows given time he may give Alex a run for her money.

Sitting in this dry sheltered place with Schroder and feeling distinctly relaxed, I once again pondered what I'd done and what I was about to do. It wasn't that I felt a great deal of remorse or regret with it all, but I would when all this was over miss the flat and the job I'd grafted so long and hard for. I knew there was to be no going back now and glancing up even Schroder looked lost in thought.

"What are you thinking about, Phillip," I asked.

"Not much truth be told, Jack, I could not give two fucks about what we're about to do. I've already made my peace with it and that suits me fine. Did I ever tell you what that cunt Bos did to me?"

"No, you didn't and I didn't like to ask," I answered thinking, oh please no, I don't really *want* to know this, but that was it, he made himself comfortable and proceeded to tell his story.

***

"At the start of the competition some of us were holed up in a hotel just outside of Alnwick, waiting for everyone else to arrive. Myself, Bos, Pritchard and Cohen were there and we were having a drink in the bar after dinner. Yes, I know everyone thought I was supposed to be off the booze and I was to keep up the façade. But hey ho, that's just the way it is and like I said, meeting you lot was pushing me to my already precarious limits.

I was exhausted, having been through a lot of late and then what with the long journey north and so on. So, after quite a few cheeky sherbets I passed out right there in the bar, embarrassing to say the least."

He continued, "Anyway, when I finally came to and woke up, I for some reason couldn't move and found I'd been moved to Bos's room, stripped naked and they'd hog tied me with a table lamp cord.

They then took turns pissing on me while filming it with their phones. They just kept laughing at me, it was horrible, Jack. I desperately tried to obscure my face and wriggle free but having been tied so tight it was impossible. Clearly, this was just a big game to the likes of Pritchard and Cohen, nasty devilish cunts that they are. Sorry, *were.* Now, you can understand that when I saw what was happening with you and Pritchard, it was easy for me to be a willing collaborator, revenge is sweet my friend."

At this—and not wanting to hear anymore—I tried to interrupt but Schroder was in full swing now and telling me his tale, must have been purely cathartic for him. He went on.

"So, when eventually—and fuck me it took an eternity—their beer enhanced bladders had run out, they proceeded to manhandle me, to torment me further. A toe in the ribs or a well-placed heel in the bollocks, then one of them—that fat fucker Cohen I think it was—grabbed my recently healed ankle and twisted it violently.

At this I screamed the roof off, the pain was all consuming. I think because of my scream and obvious pain, it gave them such a shock and brought them back to their senses and thankfully that put paid to Pritchard and Cohen's involvement. I think they were visibly shocked at what they had been doing to me and backed off remonstrating with Bos that they were done.

It had all gone too far and they quickly headed for the door and were gone. That left me alone in the room with Bos and he had this look in his eyes as he just stood there staring down at me. I'll never forget it, he is pure evil, Jack; I'm telling you, there's something seriously wrong with that man.

I tried pleading with him to let me go but he just left me lying there while he went into the bathroom and came back with the biggest toilet brush I had ever seen."

My eyes widened at this and I had to stop myself from bursting out laughing while again attempting to get him to please stop his story, but Schroder ploughed on regardless.

"He took the brush and rammed the handle in my ass, Jack; right up to the hilt and the bastard didn't even lube me up first!"

That was it I burst out laughing and immediately begged Schroder's forgiveness, apologising as I held myself shaking uncharacteristically with sheer enjoyment.

"It wasn't fucking funny, Jack, the pain was excruciating and Bos just stood there laughing like a school child and taking pictures. Once again, he just stood there staring at me with that evil look of his and he was most definitely aroused by my predicament. I'm sure he had a hard on, Jack. He then simply turned around, left me bound like that and went out of the room for what felt like a lifetime.

When he finally came back, he sat down on the piss-soaked carpet next to me. He pulled the brush slowly—and purposely as it ripped me apart—from my arse and said he would cut me free but if I so much as tried anything or told anyone at all, he'd send the pictures he'd taken to every tabloid he could think of."

Visibly upset in the gloom of the forest, eyes brimming with tears and with just my torch acting as a spotlight on him like he was back on the stage, Schroder finished his story.

"So, when he finally cut my bonds and released me, I quite rightly went for him. I leapt to my feet—painfully aware that my arse was bleeding, the blood was running down my legs and my dick was lolling about—and wrestled him to the ground.

I wanted to kill him there and then but I knew I'd be fucked, not in the same way as the toilet brush had so recently managed, but it would be equally painful. He kept yelling at me that he'd release the pictures, so leaving him lying there, I tentatively got to my feet and stinking of piss and feeling complete humiliation, I grabbed my clothes, got dressed and left. What the hell else was there for me to do?

You will have noticed that when we were at Kielder two weeks ago, as well as the fact that my chance at sobriety was well and truly cancelled, I couldn't have been nicer to everyone. I was walking on eggshells and now, you know the reason why. I despised the evil cunt, but he had my bollocks in a vice. Every time I spoke up or laughed with someone, even when we had lunch, he was watching me with that same creepy stare and smiling at me. The bastard!"

I had been having trouble getting control of myself after the toilet brush story, as horrific as it was, it was still a damned funny one. Once I was sure I wasn't going to break down in tears again, I turned to Schroder and said "Well then, when we capture the rapist cunt, you can take your time with him, make him suffer in the same way he made you."

At this Schroder smiled. A genuine yes, I'm going to make him fucking suffer alright type of smile.

***

We picked ourselves up and continued on. Schroder kept popping pills, but I wanted to keep my head clear, this man somehow had the constitution of an ox, how he was still upright was beyond me. We fought our way through the forest until finally it started to thin out and become easier underfoot, the rain and the wind again hit us hard, but we kept our heads down and pushed into it.

Emerging from the woods, the river was right there in front of us and was now a furious raging torrent. As we hiked alongside the gradually shrinking riverbank, I was desperately hoping there'd be a way to get across as it would be impossible to swim. Fortunately, about a mile along, we came to a small, old but well-maintained bridge, it must have been here for the movement of sheep between fields as we weren't exactly on a public bridleway.

The water was actually starting to flow across the top of the wooden boards now that the river was so high and I pondered how long the bridge would stand. And whether if we actually managed to have a return journey it would still be here before it crashed downstream with all the other debris that looked to be destroying anything and everything in its path.

Once safely over the bridge and following parallel to the river we kept on heading west and within the hour the familiar sight of one of the competition cabins came into view. There was no smoke from the chimney or any light in the window, but I still commanded Schroder to wait behind a stone cairn set a little way back from the river. If there were cairns here, then worryingly the trail we were following may be used more frequently than I'd hoped.

Circling Bos's cabin and seeing with absolutely no surprise whatsoever that he didn't have a deer hanging, I silently crept up onto his veranda and peered in at the window. All the while consciously aware that Pritchard had caught me out doing this exact same thing.

It was pitch black inside and unless he was asleep tucked up in the far corner, which I sincerely doubted then the place was just as I had thought, deserted. Signalling to Schroder to join me and watching him scuttle along like some drugged-up commando, I carefully opened the door. Completely empty.

Shining my torch around the interior of his cabin it looked like no one had been here for a while, at least not for a prolonged stay of any kind. The larder had been systematically emptied of everything of any use and the fire had not been lit for a long time. So, where the hell was Bos? I knew that sneaky fucker hadn't been playing by the rules, I just knew it.

I turned to Schroder and said, "told you that fucker would be elsewhere, didn't I? We need to get out and find him, its nearly 2 a.m. already, I want the bastard tonight."

"So, where can he be, Jack? This is utter madness, do you think he's bottled it and done a runner?" he asked.

"Nah, that little prick will be holed up somewhere taking advantage of some lonely young farm wife and her wares. All while her husband is at some dickless show, drinking copious amounts of pissy ale and parading his prize fucking pig!"

I was angry even though I'd had the feeling for days that he was whooping it up somewhere, while we were all working hard to make the competition work.

"So, where to next?" Schroder asked while desperately trying to roll a spliff as we sat there contemplating.

"Let me think and if you have to smoke that then give me a quick tug on it, I need something to keep me calm," I said snatching the newly rolled spliff, lighting it and taking a long slow drag.

"We'll keep following the trail along the river." I mused, "we must come across something or somewhere at some point as that lazy cunt wouldn't have ventured too far. But just in case he does come back though." And saying this I took my dick out of my pants and pissed all over his bed and sleeping bag.

Schroder, giggling to himself and obviously having just topped up his drug intake, did the same. Then not completely satisfied he unzipped fully, loosened his belt, dropped his shorts and started taking a dump for good measure.

Heading out the door and looking back over my shoulder I said, "That's a little too much for me, Phillip. I'll wait outside for you to finish if it's all the same to you and I'm taking the spliff with me."

Back outside we set off along the trail and noticed that it quickly started heading in and away from the river. We seemed quite satisfied with our nightly pursuits and Schroder happy at his part in destroying Bos's cabin kept sniggering to himself. He was now only a shadow of the man that used to be one of *the* major hosts in British television, who could have thought that someone could drop so far after being at the top for so long.

Regardless of what I'd had to do to get by and get on, I still felt deep down that I had some semblance of dignity. But then, would I know if I had fallen too far, what if I was crazy? Would anyone see things my way? I doubted this very much, I'd have to face up to things, eventually when the proverbial *they* caught up with me.

I quickly disregarded these thoughts, what was done was done. Finally, being on some sort of trail and a more solid ground was easy going compared to the usual trek through the forest. Having sure footing and not the usual sludge that we'd got used to was a blessing and made for us making steady progress.

Old derelict farm buildings started to appear, some with caved in rooves, others with trees growing from previously used windows, few at first and then increasing in number and slightly better condition. At last, we had reached some kind of civilisation if still somewhat remote and I had the distinct feeling Bos wasn't faraway. If he could have wormed his way into the first farm he came across, then I knew he wouldn't have gone looking any further for any better.

The track then opened up and out onto a surface of loose chippings resembling the closest thing I had seen to a road for two weeks and up ahead there was a foreboding looking farmhouse. It was a little run down but not beyond repair and as expected it was in total darkness, after all it was nearly three in the morning.

Schroder started to speak but I hushed him and told him to crouch down near an old decrepit barn, while I waited patiently to see if the household truly was asleep. After maybe fifteen minutes of us anxiously waiting and Schroder fidgeting incessantly because of the speed he'd just rubbed round his gums, we slowly and silently approached the house.

Unusually for a farmhouse and especially one as remote as this, I couldn't see any signs of dogs, maybe they were kept at the back of the house and they had kennels there.

We carefully worked our way through the clearly disused farmyard towards a large side door and there, just as I thought they would be were Bos's brand-new boots. Still shiny with a few smatterings of dirt up the sides and sat on the doorstep alongside a much smaller set of older worn boots. That bastard had been ensconced here for quite a while it seemed and was obviously living it up in the lap of luxury. Well, at least the meagre luxury an almost derelict farm could offer in the middle of nowhere.

With my inhibitions now seriously reduced owing to certain recent events, I pushed down on the door handle, it was unlocked. *Yes,* I thought, at last a bit of good luck and proceeded to push the door slowly inwards. After what I had done of late, breaking into a farmhouse in the middle of the night held very little fear for me now, so with Schroder tagging along close behind me like an obedient puppy, we entered.

Just then an explosion of light hit us and all hell broke loose.

***

I was caught completely unawares by the light, it felt like a solar flare going off just behind my eyes. I stumbled and fell to my right just as a cacophony of noise exploded into being, followed by an angry triumphant bellow and then screaming. Falling heavily to the side and hitting my head – but thankfully not enough to cause too much damage – had been incredibly fortuitous for me but alas not so much for Schroder.

I looked back just in time to see him projected through the now wrecked open door from which we'd just entered in a cascade of blood, clothing and wooden splinters. Turning back from the door to face what was in front of me I almost burst out laughing. The smallest, frailest, oldest woman I had ever seen with the most determined look on her face was wielding a huge double-barrelled shotgun and desperately trying to reload the behemoth she held.

She'd let loose both barrels into Schroder's chest in a devastating blast and I thought it very unlikely he'd be alive out there.

Quickly scrambling to my feet, I launched myself at the old dear and subsequently flattened her with the gun wedged between us and a torch flying from her grip then into the wall with a crash. A gasp of air exploded from her along with her false teeth and a pretty substantial fart. *What was it with these locals and their teeth, I thought?*

I easily wrestled the gun from her grasp and scooped up the shells rolling around next to her prostrate body, I sincerely hoped she wasn't dead or dying as she was simply an unlikely pawn in Bos's game, but I couldn't wait to find out.

I'd noticed during the fracas someone lurking behind her in the shadows as she was furiously trying to reload and then quickly disappear deeper into the house when it had all gone to shit. That had to be Bos, typical of the cowardly bastard to be hiding behind a little old lady, who must have been in her eighties, possibly even older.

Springing to my feet and heading down the corridor further into the house, I saw the shadows once again move. Someone then burst from behind a sofa and out the door at the back of what turned out to be the old dear's living room, leaving lamps, ornamental plates and other precious keepsakes scattered throughout.

Giving chase and stumbling over several items of furniture, including an armchair with my friend the KP sitting in looking relaxed watching proceedings unfurl. And with more ornaments of all kinds taking a tumble and not winning the fight with the floor, I raced out the same door to the back of the property.

There up ahead and desperately trying to climb over a garden wall he had no chance of climbing over and struggling in just his socks, was Bos.

"Right, you bastard I've got you now!" I said to him as he looked feverishly over his shoulder, still desperately pulling at the wall for some kind of leverage.

Taking three long strides I reached up and dragged him down from the wall by his belt. Some of his fingernails tore out on the rough stone on the way down and Bos uttered a guttural scream.

"There is absolutely no point screaming dickhead, there's not another house for miles around here. But you know that, having just about taken up residence here for the two weeks that you should have been in the competition."

Blubbering almost incoherently and cradling his bleeding fingers, Bos squealed, "I've just come up here today, Jack, honestly. I just thought the rains were going to wash us out, so I thought I'd find somewhere to hold up for a bit, at least until the weather eased off."

"You're a total fucking disgrace, do you know that? You put a little old dear in front of you as a shield, why didn't *you* pull the trigger? I'll tell you why, Bos, because you're a pathetic filthy coward, that's why."

I booted him in the ribs a couple of times for good measure and for making me flatten an old lady who could be dead by now. Hearing the bones crack gave me so much pleasure and his howls of pain afterwards were even sweeter.

"That old woman could be dying in there and that's your fault and yours alone, but what I'm going to do to you is all down to me," I said quietly into his ear and his whimpering became even more pitiful than it already was.

On hearing this I kicked him once very hard into his face and he thankfully went silent. Crouching down to him I could see he was still breathing but was out cold, so I returned to the house to first check on the old dear. She was alive and breathing steadily but unconscious, tough old bugger indeed. When this was all over I'd get her an ambulance, but for now, I retrieved a cushion for her head and gently laid a blanket over her. Who said I couldn't be caring? I sincerely hoped she'd be OK.

Stepping over the old woman I headed outside through the destroyed door to see Schroder, his chest and arm were shredded and yet remarkably, he was still alive. It must have had something to do with the amount of drugs pumping through his system, but even with the pharmacy inside him I didn't think he had long to go. His breathing was increasingly shallow and under the torchlight his skin was a deathly white.

"Phillip, can you hear me mate?" I asked, nothing. "Phillip," I urged, "are you still with us? Come on, mate, all this way to get gunned down by an octogenarian, you can do better than that."

At this his eyelids fluttered open and through a mouthful of blood he muttered, "did you get the bastard, Jack?"

"I did, Phillip, he's in the garden unconscious and I'm going to make his last moments on this earth horrific, I can promise you that."

On hearing this he tentatively reached out a bloody hand to me and I clasped it in mine, he gave me the faintest of smiles, closed his eyes and died. Poor bastard, I thought and for the first time in a long time I felt a deep welling sadness I'd not felt since the loss of my parents. I do believe Schroder and I had become some sort of friends, companions, I would never have thought possible a mere two weeks ago. And with a renewed rage burning in me, I got to my feet and headed out to the garden hellbent on destruction.

Entering the garden and wiping my hands clean of Schroder's blood on my jacket, I looked to where I'd left Bos and unbelievably he'd gone. This fucker really was full of surprises. How on earth was that possible? I thought as I headed out through the garden gate that the fucking idiot should have seen in the first place instead of trying to get over an eight-foot wall.

Looking up the lane I could see no trace of anyone. Then glancing down and shining my torch across the ground I could see fresh footprints in the dirt heading around the side of the house from which we'd originally entered, so I followed at a run. Passing Schroder's body, again I felt a twist in my stomach that could have only been sadness.

I looked up at the doorstep and noticed Bos's boots had gone, the sneaky fucker! I could have sworn he'd been out cold. Running back down the way Schroder and I had come must have been Bos's way of thinking himself cunning. He'd presume I'd expect him to take the route further west in search of some other farm, not backtrack towards his cabin, so he must have thought he'd easily rid himself of me.

In the distance, albeit there being very little moonlight and the rain was still coming down hard, every now and then I felt the shadows up ahead shift and I knew that was him and I was rapidly gaining on him. After all, he must have several broken ribs and had taken a hefty boot to the face.

Once past the derelict outbuildings of the farm and onto the track, the going once again got tougher, so I could only imagine how much Bos was struggling. Negotiating the next bend I almost ran into him as he was stood, hands clasped to his knees panting furiously. I didn't try to slow my momentum but ploughed straight into him leaving him poleaxed on the ground clutching his ribs.

Taking my torch, I set about his head and body with fierce blows until this time he was most definitely out cold. I sat next to him in the grass, breathing hard, but relieved, I'd caught up with my quarry. The rain pelted my head and I realised at some point I'd lost my hat, probably in the farmhouse.

There would be plenty of evidence even without that, so no use in going back for it. I dragged Bos beneath a tree to offer us a little bit of shelter, stripped him naked, tied his hands and feet with some washing line I'd picked up from the farm and waited for him to come round. I was in no hurry now, I had bloody revenge to exact on behalf of Schroder and I was going to enjoy it.

***

Looking up I was startled to see my KP friend had appeared and was sitting opposite me with a look of obvious—how I knew this only I could tell—disapproval, so I raised my voice to hm and hollered.

"Look, if you're not happy with how things are progressing then why don't you just fuck off back to whatever limbo you conjured yourself up from, eh? Because I honestly don't give two fucks what you think of me, you're always skulking about in the shadows looking like someone has just pissed on your chips. Say what you came here to say or piss off, the damage is done now."

And with that suddenly he was gone, he just seemed to wink out of existence, poof! How long he'd be gone for I didn't know, hopefully not for good as at times he had become something of a comfort for me. And for someone who was a little short on the friend front—especially since the recently deceased Phillip Schroder—I instantly regretted my outburst.

"Come on, get back here. I'm sorry, I was just angry, you can't hold that little rush of blood to the head against me, for fuck's sake!" I screamed into the rain and the dark, but he didn't reappear.

There was just the sound of the storm and the ever-present rush of the river in the distance, was this it? After being my near constant companion for so long was he really gone for good? Upset by these thoughts and feeling another wave of intense loneliness, I pulled myself together and got to the task in hand dragging myself over to Bos's strewn clothes.

I searched through Bos's gear and in one of his trouser pockets I discovered a mobile phone. This guy was unbelievable! The cheeky little bastard had been secretly in touch with his family and friends since the very beginning. For this indignation and blatant disregard of the rules I gave him another kick to the ribs as he curled into a foetal position. It was made all the more difficult by his bonds and he moaned in some longful manner in his now semi-conscious state.

Slapping his face repeatedly until he regained more of his faculties, I sat down next to him and sighed, "you got Phillip killed, Bos. I bet you were hoping it was me who took both barrels from old *Ma Barker* back there, eh? Phillip also told me what you did to him at the hotel. And that you were blackmailing him along with the help of those other two idiots with photos you had of him in, shall we say a compromising position. You're a sick man, Bos, you need help."

The irony of this last statement wasn't lost on me but then again I didn't stick toilet brushes up people's arses.

"Phillip now, is it? Best buddies with Schroder now are we, Jack? Thought you didn't do friends," he muttered through gritted teeth, fearfully looking down at his naked and bound self and realising what a pickle he found himself in.

"In all honesty before this little sojourn into the woods I didn't partake in friends. Under normal circumstances that is but I find myself of late in progressively more and more difficult situations. Like I find myself in now, what am I going to do with you? Not only did you get my friend Phillip killed, but there's a little old lady up there in her farmhouse lying prostrate in a puddle of her own piss," I said.

"What have you done with Hilda, you sick bastard?" Bos screamed, suddenly full of vigour, "she was just trying to help me out. I really cared for her, she was kind and generous, we knew that once I'd stolen your precious deer you'd come after me."

"I did nothing to your precious Hilda, Bos, it was you who manipulated an old woman into doing your dirty work, did you not have the guts to pull the trigger yourself? You've also been living up there, haven't you?" I asked, also thinking I knew it was him who had stolen my deer.

"Maybe, I have," Bos said. He knew I had worked out his little scam. "Hilda just wanted some company, the first day I got to this hell hole I knew I had to find somewhere else to stay. Hilda took me in and I helped her out with chores around the farm."

"You're so full of shit, Bos, you're no better than a conman, a trickster trying to clear out her pension. You were supposed to live and survive in the wild, that's why we're here, you useless sack of shit and that's long before you had to create any dishes for the judges on the final day. That was the whole point of this damn competition and you fucking well know it," I shouted into his face.

"Come on, Jack, give me my clothes back, will you; what are you some kind of a fag? It's freezing with my arse up in the air, this weather will kill me," Bos yelled.

"It's not the elements you need to worry about, Bos and if anyone is a fag as you so nicely put it then I think we both know who that is. But just before we start I have a question for you. Please tell me, why the fuck did you settle on Bos? I know you must have given yourself the nickname."

He started to protest here but I shushed him impatiently.

"Yes, yes, of course I know the connection with Dickens but really? It's pathetic, you're such an absurdly pretentious cunt. Do you tell everyone that mummy and daddy called you it because of your love of Dickens from an early age? Absolute clowns, they must have hated you deep down or been so high in some crack den with your mum being fucked from some disease ridden junky for her next fix!"

Bos was understandably outraged by this and struggled furiously against his bonds.

"I'll kill you, Jack, you crazy bastard, I swear to God I will!" Then something suddenly dawned on him and he stopped struggling and through his pain and anguish said, "Anyway, what did you just mean, before we get started?"

At this I unsheathed my knife and brought the blade right up into his face, so he could see it gleaming in the sliver of pale moon light. As I did this the smell of hot urine hit me through the piercing cold and a puddle of warm piss formed between his legs. They were all the same in the face of absolute terror. Crying freely now he tried to plead with me and claim his supposed innocence in the demise of Schroder.

"Jack, please, I didn't think she'd shoot, Jack. I just thought she'd brandish it as a warning, a deterrent to get rid of you. We had seen someone sneaking up on the place, I didn't even know it was you guys, it could have been anyone. I was just as shocked as you when the gun exploded."

"Didn't know she'd pull the trigger," I screamed at him, "are you mad? She's an old farmer, they kill fucking everything that crosses their path, you complete tit! Please, don't try to insult my intelligence that you didn't know it was me, who else would it be out here in the middle of nowhere?

Schroder also told me about what you did to him in the hotel room with those other two wankers helping you. He also told me about the toilet brush, Bos, you sick fucker, that broke him. He was trying to get on the straight and narrow and you knocked him back months of recovery.

You even threatened him with the pictures, what kind of man does that, eh? I'm going to teach you a lesson, *Bos*. You've been using and coercing people into your personal slaves for years," I said his name with utter disgust and the contempt it demanded, then took my knife and drove it the full length into his arse.

His ear-splitting screams—if there were actually any farmhouses around—would have woken up any occupants, the blood gushed out of his arse and down the handle of my knife. I turned away in utter disgust, withdrew the knife and wiped the blood and shit from the blade onto his discarded clothes.

Whimpering and snivelling like a child now I think he finally and at long last realised that he wasn't going to walk away from this encounter. The fear in his eyes was what I'd been waiting to see as I plunged the knife once more into his arse and twisted slowly.

"That's for what you did to Schroder, I promised him as he lay dying that I'd return the favour."

He was howling from the pain and complete indignity now. I punched him a couple of times in the face smashing his nose and forcing his head into the dirt, then grabbing the handle of the knife and much more slowly this time I removed the knife once again.

I didn't bother to clean it this time and stuck the tip of the shit streaked, bloodied knife in his newly broken nose and ripped upwards, so the nostril split right up to the bridge. He screamed again.

"Ever seen Chinatown, Bos? Classic film noir, you look just like Jack Nicholson now," I said and laughed at the mess I'd made of his face. I wasn't sure I had anticipated feeling such joy and wonderment at the dismantling of someone's soul.

I sat down again and watched him for a while writhe in pure agony, because of the way he was bound he could hardly move and his shuddering movements made him look almost disjointed. I could only imagine the damage I'd done to his innards and the amount of blood coming from there meant I wouldn't have that much longer, but I still wanted him to suffer for what he had done.

His sobs were just starting to subside, so enjoying myself now, I pressed my knee down on the side of his head pinning it to the ground, took the knife and this time stuck it into his eye socket, pried it behind the eye—as Bos desperately fought against me with the last of his strength—and ripped it free of its membrane.

As his mouth opened in yet another howl, I shoved the offending eyeball into his mouth and held it closed with my hand. Now, coughing and spluttering while still fearfully trying to plead with me, I let him spit out the eye. With blood pouring from his nose and eye socket—not to mention his ruined arse—he suddenly seemed to sag, violently spasm and then pass out into what was to be an only too brief peaceful oblivion.

***

Looking at this broken, almost pitiful specimen I decided that that was it and we'd both had had enough. Taking longer to bring him back this time, I slapped him awake once again and between his soft mutterings and now feeble incoherent pleading for help, I took his not so pretty face anymore by the hair and shoved the knife as hard as I could through his ear.

His body jerked once then instantly went limp in my hands, for Bos it was over. I let his head fall to the floor then with the last of my strength stamped repeatedly upon his face until he was unrecognisable. When I finally stopped, sweating and out of breath, I had to wipe my shoes on the grass to get the bits of his face and teeth from out of the tread of my boots.

Satisfied with my endeavours I looked up into the heavens, but for what I knew not, some sort of pardon perhaps? Someone to understand and accept what I had done? Possibly redemption even? I knew it was a ridiculous thought, as there was a special place for people like me reserved in some lowly circle of hell.

Coming back to my senses I cleaned my knife once again on his clothes and sat looking at what was left of his body. I pondered whether to hide it in the trees or just to leave it on this track, one final humiliation for an altogether vile man. Some poor fucker walking his dog or some lost rambler would stumble across the body at some point. The rain might keep people away for a while, but he'd be found and I'd be caught soon enough, not just for this but for the debacle back at the farm and the efficient dispatching of two other contestants.

I decided I may as well head back to my cabin, drink some of my magic tea, finish my last bottle of whisky and wait for the appropriate authorities, it was getting late, or should I say early, as it would be dawn in a couple of hours.

16. A Surprise Encounter

I headed back down the trail towards the wooden bridge, which would get me over the river and back into the forest, it was still dark but there was a hint of light starting to appear from the east and that made it a little easier to see up ahead.

As I got ever closer to the bridge, I could make out a figure coming across it, running straight towards me. I leapt into the long grass and bushes at the side of the track and withdrew my knife. As the figure approached, I could see it was a man and then as it got even closer, I was surprised to see it was Orry. I had not seen Orry since the very start of the competition and I was taken aback to see the state he was in.

His whole appearance was dishevelled, unkempt, he looked like he'd been in the wild for months, not a mere fortnight. He was bearded and dirty, the boy obviously hadn't been brave enough to take a plunge in the freezing pools down by the river. When he was almost on top of me, I stepped out of the grass and onto the track.

Orry froze and then took a cautious step backwards as I was still brandishing my knife.

"Jesus, Chef, you scared the shit out of me, you expecting some big game to hunt?" he said gesturing to my knife.

"What are you doing out this way, Orry?" I asked suspiciously and put my knife away to try and ease the tensions a little.

"My cabin is just about half a mile that way," at this he pointed east. "I woke up when I heard screaming and came running to help, at first I thought I was dreaming but as it continued, I knew I'd have to get off my arse and help."

Just then he seemed to take in my appearance for the first time, I followed his eyes and looked down at myself. In the early morning light I could see that I was covered in blood, some of it I'm sure was Schroder's but most of it was

Bos's. I was a mess with it; feeling my face and hair, it was also sticky and wet with something other than the rain.

"Fuck me, Chef, what the hell's happened? Have you been attacked, are you OK?"

"I'm fine, Orry, simply fine. The screaming was down to me, but it wasn't *by* me, it was that spineless cunt Bos. I've put an end to his antics for good, I'm afraid it had to be done, mate," I said.

Looking like he was about to bolt or possibly throw up, I couldn't tell which he said, "Holy Shit, I know he was a wanker but what have you done, did he really deserve that?" Here he pointed to my jacket, "have you killed him? Are you sure?"

"I'm sure, Orry," I said a little dreamily, I was tired now, the come down was going to hit me hard and I seemed to be staring off into the distance as Orry spoke again.

"Where is he, Chef? I'll go and check on him in case he's still alive."

At this I started laughing, "Believe me when I say it, mate, but he's most definitely dead, I mean just look at the state of me."

I pointed to myself. Orry looked scared and uncertain but I must hand it to him he didn't run and persisted in his questions.

"So, how'd all this come about, I know you don't like him but—" Orry began.

At this I corrected him, "I didn't like him, he's dead, mate. I stuck my knife right through his head. Go up the track and find his body if you like, it's not the prettiest thing you'll see today, I'm afraid. Then you can do me a favour, some old dear is lying in her farmhouse about a mile west of here. Take this phone," at this I handed him Bos's mobile.

"And call her an ambulance, will you? I didn't hurt her intentionally, she killed Schroder with her shotgun and was trying to kill me, all because of that bastard Bos. He had been living there, cheating all of us, he didn't even wait to see if she was alright, he just took off like the coward he was.

"I tracked him down and killed him, it's that simple. And that phone was also his by the way, the cunt had it all the time. And by the way, have you seen that prick Cecil or the gamekeeper, have they been out this way?"

At this he shook his head wondering what was coming next.

"Better let you know then. Celestine is also dead, died from exposure when he wandered into the woods, not helped by the fact that he was pissed and didn't even bother to put a jacket on for fucks sake."

"Fuck me, Celestine and Schroder's dead as well?" he asked, looking utterly dumbfounded and petrified, he was wrestling with all kinds of emotions, after all he was just a kid really. Eventually, he pocketed the phone and started to move down the track, he turned back to me and said, "What are you going to do now, Jack?"

The use of my Christian name didn't go unnoticed, but I thought I would let the kid have this one and let it slide seeing as he was in shock and meant no disrespect.

"I'm off back to my cabin, where I intend to get stoned and pissed at the same time on what remains of Schroder's distinctly impressive stash. If or more to the point when they come for me, I'll be hopefully so fucked up I won't even notice. You take good care of yourself, Orry, and don't look so worried, you don't have anything to fear from me. I've done what I set out to do."

I turned away from Orry and started to wander down the track, he shouted after me, "Jack, are you going to be OK? You look like shit, man."

I thought, *That's rich coming from you, you scruffy looking cunt.* I tossed him a wave thinking he looked more relieved I was leaving than concerned about me, but I'd give the kid the benefit of the doubt as I continued on my way picking up the pace as I went.

I realised that I'd probably have a welcoming party when I got back to my cabin and unfortunately, that whisky of mine seemed a long way away. I went splashing over the bridge noticing that the level of water was already higher than it had been a mere couple of hours ago when Schroder and I had crossed. The rain was falling steadily and the river was as fierce as ever, at this rate the cabins such as my own would be lost even with the stilts lifting them above the ground.

Exhausted as I was now feeling, I hurriedly ploughed on. I figured that once the ambulance got to the old dear's place—Hilda as I now knew her to be—and saw the carnage then the police wouldn't be far behind. They may even beat the paramedics if Orry had explained the situation correctly. He'd have passed Bos's remains and I can't imagine he would have stayed there long, probably threw up then scuttled off to the farm.

I gave myself maybe an hour before they'd be heading in force to my cabin and knew that wouldn't be enough time for me to get there.

The only other thing I could think of was to curtail my hike to my cabin and wait at Subi's place and hope that Schroder had left plenty of his stolen produce for our return journey. I knew I was screwed, so I may as well enjoy some of his spoils. Battling through the woods and with the time always against me I reached Subi's cabin. Being careful as I approached from the trees and finding it in the same condition as we'd left it, I collapsed through the cabin door and onto the floor in a puddle of bloody rainwater.

My hair and face were washed clean, but my clothes resembled a very recent knife fight. I grabbed an open bottle of whisky, took the longest drink I could, coughed and spluttered once then drank deeply again. Stripping out of my soaked jacket and covering myself in a discarded blanket I propped my back up against the cabin wall with my feet outstretched and then reached for Schroder's bag of goodies.

Taking out a carefully rolled joint, I lit it and breathed deeply. God, that felt so good and looking around once more I saw to my utter bewilderment, stashed in the far corner which I hadn't noticed on our last flying visit, a box containing all kinds of provisions. A whole side of hot smoked salmon along with carpaccio of beef, a jar of horseradish cream, a jar of cornichons, along with other gourmet titbits.

Next to these was an array of cheeses, with packets of water biscuits, olives, tetra packs of oat milk and several chutneys. Unbelievable that Schroder had been *surviving* with all this decadence and we'd been living on rabbit, pasta and boiled rice. Laughing like a maniac—and feeling a little stoned—I ripped the salmon apart and shoved great handfuls into my mouth, washed down with the finest single malt and the odd tangy pickle.

With my hunger stemmed for the time being, I then turned back to his bag of illicit drugs, tipped a line of coke out from a small vial, snorted it and then returned to my joint. Within no time at all a feeling of pure drug fuelled contentment washed over me and with a beatific smile I let myself succumb to it and the welcome oblivion that beckoned.

17. Subi's Cabin

Once again, I was roused by enthusiastic shouting outside and the door almost being lifted from its hinges from the beating it was receiving. *What the holy fuck is happening now, I thought?* Looking down at my watch and seeing it was almost midday.

I'd had a couple of hours sleep but still felt utterly exhausted. Looking around I remembered that this wasn't my cabin and the previous night's exploits came rushing back to me with a bang. Groaning and raising myself up off the floor, back stiff and head fuzzy I shouted at the door.

"Alright I'm coming, what's with all the banging, what the actual fuck is going on?"

I thought I might as well play along and give myself a chance, until I see what's on the other side of the door. Once on my feet I risked a glance out of the window, on opening the shutters the first thing I noticed was that the sun was finally shining and the rain had ceased, at last the deluge had ended. Bloody typical when it was most definitely my last day here. The next thing I noticed was the small area outside of the cabin was awash with police cars.

"Oops, what have you done now, Jack?" I asked myself, giggling like the half-drunk maniac I knew I now was.

"Open the fucking door, Jack, we know you're in there, we could see you through the bastard shutters for God's sake. The only reason they haven't busted the door in is because I said I'd be able to talk to you and bring you out of there peacefully," Cecil shouted.

"Cecil? Fucking Cecil?" I said to the empty room.

I might have known it would be that prick! Who did this guy think he was, some kind of cowboy, was this High Noon? Un*bastard* believable!

"Yes, yes I'm coming, just give me a second," I hollered through the door. Desperately looking around the floor amongst my detritus of discarded breakfast and drugs. I found my knife and approached the door, also grabbing the whisky for one last swig.

Slowly opening the door and only by a fraction I peered through the gap and saw Cecil standing there with a smug—told you so—grin on his face and next to him one of the *faceless* producers.

"What the fuck is going on now, Cecil?" I asked.

"Enough of this charade, Jack, we know what you've done," said the producer whose name I had no idea of.

"He's right, Jack, Cohen's body turned up at the bottom of someone's garden about five miles further downstream, he'd got trapped in a fishing line. The fish had made quite a job of his face when they finally pulled the big fucker out.

It was also quite a shock for the old guy who had managed to reel him in. He thought he'd caught a whopper, but when Cohen's half eaten face came up out of the reeds he'd lost his supper into the river." Cecil affirmed.

"The police have also been to the farmhouse where Bos had been holed up for the past fortnight and they've also spoken to a visibly sick Orry, who then took them down the track to see Bos's body. A formal ID hasn't been made as you didn't leave much of his face to actually identify him with."

"Right, so you're telling me I'm blamed for fatty Cohen as well as that useless shite Bos. I tell you one thing, I most definitely wouldn't recommend eating the salmon out of the Coquet if some of fatty Cohen is now in the eco system," I joked.

I was still feeling exhausted, but this little exchange was giving me the first spark of adrenalin.

"Look, Jack, I don't know what's wrong with you, but this isn't funny anymore, just come on out and speak to the police, if you don't, they're just going to break this door down and drag your sorry ass out anyway," said the faceless man looking increasingly worried and edgy, as this wasn't going exactly to Cecil's plans.

Looking past Cecil and the producer, I could make out police crouched down behind their four-by-four vehicles, quite clearly armed and looking like they weren't going to wait much longer. I had to make a decision, so as deftly as I could, I grabbed Cecil by the collar at his throat and planted a well-aimed headbutt across the bridge of his nose. As he squealed out in pain I dragged him quickly inside as a panicked producer flung himself off the veranda and into the dirt.

Just as I was closing the door an explosion of pain ripped through my left shoulder and lifted me off my feet, it took me a split second to comprehend I'd actually been shot.

"Bastards!" I shouted.

Falling to the floor but hanging onto Cecil's collar and dragging him with me, I managed to get a foot to the door and kick it shut. Cecil was wailing about his nose and cupping a hand to his face to staunch the blood, the pain in my shattered shoulder was immense, nothing could have prepared me for the intensity of it.

I turned to a visibly shaken Cecil, grabbed his hand with my good arm and then manoeuvring myself and using my knee to prop his arm up against the cabin wall I drove my knife through his hand and pinned it to the wood beyond.

He screamed this time and immediately tried to pull the knife free from his punctured hand. Seeing this I quickly stood up, braced myself against the cabin wall from falling over as a dizzy spell threatened to topple me and rammed a knee into his already shattered nose.

His head jolted back and clattered into the wooden wall of the cabin and he slumped down unconscious. Stumbling back, I sat on the bed and risked a look at my destroyed shoulder, what a mess. The hole at the front was a round neat opening but at the back, it looked a complete disarray of blood, splintered bone and shredded muscle. The hole was a large, ragged gap where the bullet had burst out of, I could see into it and the broken collar bone and shoulder blade were clearly useless.

I thought to myself that my drumming days were surely over now (not that I had ever played the drums before in the first place) and again I could only laugh at the situation I found myself in, but quickly stopped as it worsened the pain. I grabbed the blanket and fashioned a makeshift sling then delved into Schroder's bag of goodies and found what looked to be—and I hoped—plain old pain killers, so I chugged a couple down with a sizeable slug of whisky. I desperately hoped this might take the edge off, but I wasn't convinced.

I pulled myself up to the window and risked a quick look outside, immediately a bullet whizzed just over my head as it smashed through the glass and into the cabin wall behind me.

"OK, I'll not do that again," I muttered and noticed Cecil was slowly starting to come around.

What must be intense pain in his hand was no doubt helping to bring him back to the light. Suddenly, there was a burst of static from some barely workable megaphone along with a string of curses.

"Fuck me, every bastard time it does that, can we not get some better fucking equipment!" Someone yelled, obviously the copper in charge or at least some kind of negotiator. Then he tried again, "Jack Cunningham, can you hear me, Jack? We need to talk, can you come outside so we can resolve this?"

"Do what? Are you mad? Some fucker on your team has just blown my window in and nearly put a hole in my head!" I shouted back. "I'm not coming out there while some trigger-happy moron wants to put a bullet through my skull. Why don't you all go home and me and Cecil here can have a nice little chat."

At this I booted Cecil in the face again, "what do you think about that, Cecil?"

Cecil groaned and I crouched down next to him.

"You had to try and be the big hero, didn't you *Survival Man*? Why didn't you just let them kick the door in and shoot the shit out of me, eh?"

"We wanted to give you a chance," Cecil slurred spitting out blood and a tooth into his hand. "We also thought you could help us find Pritchard, that might go well for you with all this other shit if you can help us. He's still missing and hasn't been seen for days."

At this I laughed out loud, "you haven't found him yet? I thought he would have washed up by now, he went into the river the night after Cohen, he's dead, Cecil. I carved the big bastard up then threw him in the water to be with his mate."

Cecil's rapidly swelling face sank, if for some stupid reason he hadn't already understood, now he knew exactly who he was dealing with. Bos and Pritchard had all died by my hand, Cohen I'd simply helped along. This prick if I was given the time, was next.

Another explosion of static outside and again the same copper spoke.

"Let Cecil go, Jack, what's the point in keeping him in there? We know you're hurt, come on out and we can get you the medical attention you need."

"Blah, blah, blah," I said looking at Cecil but gesturing to the party outside and then I said, "You do realise don't you, Cecil, that between you and the producers of this shit show, you are partly to blame for this slaughter."

At this he looked askance and spluttered, "what the fuck are you on about, Jack? That's utter bollocks and you know it."

172

"Come on think about it, if you muppets had actually put everyone through the correct vetting process and shown some sort of due diligence then none of this would have happened. You would have had competitors that would have actually wanted to compete instead of the dead beats that you enlisted."

I went on through gritted teeth as the pain in my shoulder was all encompassing, "All you have left are the real hopefuls, Alex and Orry. Obviously, if I hadn't gone and gotten carried away with my nightly pursuits then I would have won. Just think of the people you actually allowed to take part, Cecil.

Bos: absolute nitwit who's been living in a farm with a pensioner. A pensioner, no less for two weeks, because he didn't have the strength and attitude to give it a go himself.

Pritchard: Big ugly fucker who just wants to bully everyone and expected Cohen to help him out. Tell me, how'd that one work out for him?

Cohen: Fat, unfit and completely inept, should never have got past the initial process. When I found him he was talking to himself in the freezing cold, no fire, no food left and going out of his mind and that was after a week!

Celestine: And then we come to this guy, which by the way his death had fuck all to do with me. He was drunk the very day we were supposed to start and you still let him compete and you fucking idiots were even going to let him loose with a gun. You had a duty of care to these people and you failed them all, so when the fingers get pointed, point one at yourself, you self-satisfied prick!"

Exhausted after my rant I sat on the bed. All Cecil could do was whisper like a chastised child, "I said Celestine wasn't allowed to shoot."

At this I pulled myself up and gave him a toe in the ribs and then twisted the knife a little for good measure that still had him pinned to the wall.

There was still lots of talking outside directed at me, but I just didn't have the strength to listen to them. It was something again about doing the right thing and handing back Cecil, but I phased them out. Every now and then I'd kick him in the ribs or face just so they could hear him scream and knew he was still alive, therefore deterring them from simply kicking the door in.

Eventually, they'd come crashing through but for now, I felt I had the upper hand.

"Strictly speaking, not that you give a shit, but I didn't actually kill Cohen, the fat fucker fell down his steps and caved his head in on the outside grill. In all honesty that was the catalyst for this whole shit show," I said to Cecil in between his groans and mutterings.

"Yeah, right," Cecil said. "I suppose you're also going to tell me Schroder wasn't in on it and had nothing to do with your crazy night's carnage."

"Well, actually, Schroder had absolutely nothing to do with it, why do you think I'm sitting in his adopted cabin? Eating his fine food and drinking his expensive Scotch. Granted I didn't kill him, that was the old dear with her blunderbuss, I can't take credit for that one, but I had dragged him around half of Northumberland against his will, in the vain hope he would come in handy. And as it happened, he did.

He took the blast from both barrels of her shotgun that were clearly meant for me. Just because Schroder had worked you out and knew you are a useless shower of shit, doesn't mean you have to try to rubbish his name now that he's dead."

I thought it was probably best to keep Schroder's name out of it as in the end his life had turned to shit, there didn't seem any point creating an even worse legacy for him. I was fucked anyway, so what did it matter to me.

"You do realise that you're not in a position to make accusations about me or for that matter, Schroder. He may be dead, but I'm not so watch your fucking mouth."

And I kicked him in the balls for good measure.

The megaphone relayed its pre-determined spiel in between bouts of ear-splitting static and was that dogs I could hear? Jesus, the sneaky fuckers. But now, I had very little interest in it, my wrecked shoulder was a constant source of excruciating pain, the drugs had had no effect whatsoever.

Dizziness came in ever more frequent waves from the loss of blood and I wondered if eventually I'd just pass out and that would be it, game over. Pleasingly for me Cecil's face was a mess, his nose was shattered and pointing at a ridiculously impossible angle, his eyes were already swollen shut and blackening. His hand—where my knife was still sticking out of—was an awful shade of blue and the wound seemed to be lengthening as gravity and the weight of his arm slowly took effect and pulled the knife up through his palm towards his fingers.

I needed to make some decisions, do I let this piece of shit go and simply succumb to my fate or do I go out in a blaze of glory? I knew I would yield to my injuries soon, which would then make surrender impossible. I just didn't want this supposedly super tough *Survival Man* getting the better of me, I knew for a fact if I did pass out, he would take the credit for overcoming his assailant and make himself out the hero.

Cecil had passed out again, what a pussy, I thought. I've had my shoulder destroyed and yet here I was, in the words of Elton *still standing*, albeit metaphorically and only just. As I sat slouched against the wall of the cabin, remarkably the sun came through the window and bathed my face in warmth.

It seemed like forever since I'd felt the sun on my skin and I basked in this little piece of heaven. The police by now must be getting restless. I must do something. I struggled up to my feet and slapped Cecil hard once, then twice until finally he roused himself from his insensibility.

"What now, you fuckin psycho? What the hell do you want from me?" he pleaded with me.

"Honestly, Cecil? I want nothing from you, in a moment I'm going to rip that knife from the wall, if you're lucky I won't plunge it into your back as you vacate this fine property. On the other hand, I might just do it anyway for shits and giggles," I stated matter-of-factly. "So, what to do, what to do?" I pondered. "What would you do tough guy?"

"If it were me in your shoes, I would let you go; honestly, Jack, I would. I think that you've achieved enough, do you not?" he asked.

After a few moments thought I said. "Tell you what, *Cecil*, (I still got a kick out of calling him that.) I want you to shout as loud as you can that you're coming out and not to shoot. That is if he'll shut the fuck up for a minute with that pathetic speaker. How's that sound to you my little beaten up compatriot?"

"That's great, Jack, shall I open the door a touch, so they can get a better chance of hearing me?"

"Can do, but be careful, if they think it's me first—bang and you're fucked!" I replied with a snigger.

I was aware of what he was doing, he must have thought me in a worse state than I actually was, he was giving himself the best chance to get out without any further injury. Slowly and very deliberately I started to pull the knife from his hand, the scream he gave was like music to my ears, this twat was suffering. Just as I was about to free the knife from his hand, I plunged it back through the palm and Cecil all but passed out again.

Laughing in his face I shouted, "Do you think I'm fucking stupid, you're going to run out there and tell them to blow me into kingdom come, aren't you?"

"Jesus, Jack, come on," he slurred. And with a last attempt at defiance said, "either pull it out and let me go or you can go and fuck yourself!"

"OK, OK, sorry about that Cecil. I must have slipped, this time I'll pull it out and don't forget to shout before you make a run for it, we don't want any unnecessary accidents now, do we?"

Just as before I slowly pulled on the knife and with Cecil watching me feverishly, in case I rammed it back in, gradually the blade came free. Cecil cupped the hand to his breast and looked at me with utter hatred and for a split second he looked like he was going to lunge at me.

"Right then," I said as jovially as I possibly could, "off you go to your little buddies."

He staggered to his feet, keeping one partially closed and blackened eye on me and opened the door a fraction, keeping behind the side wall for cover.

"I'm coming out, it's me Cecil, please don't shoot, it's just me!" And after a moments pause he opened the door further and started to creep through the gap all the while trying to keep me in his line of sight. Just at the exact moment, when he turned his back fully to pass out through the door and blessed freedom, I buried the knife deep into his lower back and then ripped it straight out and pushed him through the door and into the glorious sunlight.

Cecil let out a stifled gasp of shock and amazement then dropped to his knees. I slammed the door as quickly as possible and just caught a glimpse of paramedics running up to the cabin. After a brief pause, just until the ambulance crew had dragged Cecil from the porch, the guns opened fire. Bullets rained in above my head and giggling like a child I grabbed for the whisky and waited for the door to crash in.

The megaphone started up again.

"Why, Jack? I thought we were making progress, we're going to be coming in now, I would like very much to be able to take you to hospital to get that shoulder treated. I can't imagine that's much fun at the moment but any wrong move and my officers have been given permission to put you down. Do you fully understand what I've said, Jack?"

Swigging whisky, I shouted as loud as I possibly could although I feared it was more of a whisper, "Yep that's all perfectly clear, boss, in you come."

Next second the door crashed in and a hefty boot to my hand despatched the knife that I had forgotten I still held.

"Don't fucking move!" one of the rozzers shouted, pressing a gun into my face while another grabbed my hands, discarded my makeshift sling, clasped them together and fastened them in front of me with some sort of cable tie.

I screamed out as my wounded shoulder was wrenched upwards and I all but collapsed at their feet. Desperately, I tried for one last chug of that fine scotch, but the bottle was kicked from my reach and I was hauled to my feet and dragged outside. I was in a state of almost dreamlike quality, coming into the blinding sun after the gloom of the cabin was like a jolt in the arm, but I soon reverted to my blissful reverie.

There were police everywhere, all of them with a mixture of bewilderment or accusatory looks. The dogs were going crazy, beautiful German Shepherds all straining at their leashes desperately trying to take a chunk out of my arse. The previously unseen megaphone voice was an older policeman, who just looked puzzled and asked why I'd try to kill Cecil.

"He's still alive?" I asked. "Shame, the guy's a total wanker."

And with that I was dragged away and pushed into a waiting four-by four cop car. Once inside, I leant against the cool of the glass, took a last look at the cabin bathed in the early afternoon sun—albeit an adopted cabin and thought— *what a beautiful day it's turned out to be*. We sped off through the trees with yet more wheel spinning and I sincerely hoped for my sake to a waiting hospital.

The competition for me was finally over.

18. Twelve Months Later

Once my shoulder had been put back together with pins and some kind of metal plate—according to the doctors it wasn't as bad as first assumed; well, that's easy for you to say—I had gone through the courts incredibly quickly considering the British judicial system.

It was helped by the fact that I had admitted to everything and refused representation. Along with the overwhelming evidence and statements they had, they'd also found my journal which documented the end of Cohen and the fact, I hadn't reported Celestines body. The only problem they had was proving whether I was *actually* bad and could face trial or quite simply mad?

Many an argument ensued about my sanity, whether I knew what I was doing, if it was premeditated, something else about lacking *mens rea,* whatever the hell that meant. For my part I knew exactly what I had been doing at every stage of my destruction. I readily admitted this but others saw it differently and I ended up in a 'hospital' for the criminally insane.

I always forget what the place is called, it's somewhere in Scotland I think and as I know I'll never get out, it therefore means nothing to me. In all honesty the place isn't so bad, I mean the warders—sorry orderlies—are some big ugly fuckers and what therefore would be the point of upsetting them. I am the model prisoner—sorry patient—so, no point getting my head cracked for no reason.

I have to say though most of the prisoners—sorry patients, I must endeavour to get that right—are absolutely off their tits. I mean these guys are completely wacko. One guy fully believes he is the second coming of Christ and was—amongst other lesser crimes such as animal sacrifice, can't remember that in the New Testament—convicted for grooming and molesting up to twenty-five kids, the most unbelievable part is that their mothers brought them willingly to procreate with the new *messiah!*

I spend most of my time here reading and I've also been writing a book on my experiences. I am only allowed the use of crayon or pastel, so it may take some time. I also have to see a lot of different doctors as they wish to study me and find out what made me crack and all that sort of bollocks. I get probed—no, not like that—from all kinds of psychotherapists and psychoanalysts but I don't mind.

Apparently, there are some patients in here who don't say a word and remain in complete silence, they don't want to discuss their crimes. But I find myself for the first time in my life really wanting to talk and explain—if I can—why I did what I did and what I got from it. I'd like to think that Schroder really helped me in that.

He was, I believe and in all sincerity and although it was fleeting, one of the closest friends and allies I have ever had. I do so miss him but thankfully, he came out of this OK and became another *victim* of the 'Competition Killer'! Yep that's what I became known as, quite catchy I find. I'll make sure I don't include this part in my book or Schroder will be rumbled.

The food is pretty good in here, most of the servers call me chef, which is nice, takes me back to the kitchen, which now that I think about it, was always my happy place. I try to offer my advice and help in the kitchen, but I'm not allowed anywhere near the knives, funnily enough. I have a PlayStation, a radio and a TV. Both my parents are dead and my younger brother has never forgiven me from when we were kids, so I have no visitors, although I have heard that he is writing his own book entitled "Living with the Competition Killer".

Well, if it makes him a few quid then why shouldn't he, good luck to him, I say. I did notice that many people from my past, colleagues and the like have come out of the woodwork to say and I quote, "yes, we always knew he'd turn out like this, mad bastard that he was."

Even the fat drunken slob of a landlord in Jersey who I barely said two words to confessed to a local Jersey rag that he had always, "suspected me of wrongdoing and thought I was responsible for the guy they found beaten and left for dead in the back alley". Well, they can say whatever they so wish if it makes them feel better about themselves, let's be honest, there's fuck all I can do about it stuck in here.

Another thing about being in here that I find quite bizarre is that there are a few incredibly strange women out there, who send me naked pictures of themselves in all kinds of poses and want to have sexual relations with me, one even proposed marriage! How the hell they're on the outside and I'm in here is beyond me, they're crazier than I'll ever be.

Fortunately, I also still get to run. I've kept up a decent regime and am probably in a better physical condition than I've ever been, even bettering the shape I was in before the competition. One thing I do miss is the alcohol, a fine scotch whisky or a glass of quality red wine is one of the greatest pleasures in life but alas, that will have to remain a distant memory.

The best thing to come out of the competition being cut short was that I didn't have to face my old chef and now judge, it was a blessed relief as I'm not sure I could have controlled myself. In the end, he was always going to score me down, no matter what I had been able to produce for the final day.

Our chequered history together along with his hatred of me would have ruined my chances. It wasn't my fault the guy was a sick pervert and liked to cheat on his wife with barely legal girls. With any luck I can alert this to the authorities—with the help of the orderlies—and maybe, it could ruin his career. Wanker.

Hilda, the old farmer made a full recovery, you'll be pleased to know and was devastated at the loss of her new friend Bos. That went down a storm in the papers and Bos was lauded as a saint to the elderly and not the conniving cheating cunt that he was. She was also racked with remorse for the killing of "that lovely presenter" Schroder and wished it had been that and again I quote; "awful Competition Killer who had been on the end of her shotgun."

I should have left the old bitch to rot, to think I tried to help her. I will know better for next time. *Ha!* If only.

They finally found Pritchard's body which had travelled further down river than Cohen's fat arse had managed. He was in a hell of a bloated mess as he'd been in the water for over a week with all kinds of creatures feeding on him before they got to him and dragged him out. Apparently, some religious ramblers had stumbled across him while out on a *'Jesus loves you'* money raising walk.

They found him caught up in the reeds, although I think even for those crazies it was a stretch for Pritchard to be a modern-day interpretation of Moses. I'd also heard from one of the orderlies that Pritchard's wife was relieved he'd been killed. Supposedly, for years he had tormented her with mental and physical abuse and that even when she finally left him, he had tracked her down and continued with doling out his misery upon her.

She'd also come out publicly and said while his death had been a shock for them, both kids were quite pleased daddy wouldn't be coming back. Why thank you, I am always happy to oblige in any way I can.

Unfortunately though, Cecil also survived. He had been rushed to the RVI hospital in Newcastle via air ambulance. He lost a kidney and they had to amputate two of his fingers as they were deemed beyond repair and he underwent several operations on his hand to repair certain nerve damage. He also had to have his shattered nose rebuilt.

Such a shame as I had hoped to kill the bastard, his super hard man survival image is surprisingly still intact though as he "*single-handedly*" brought me in and the police did the rest. What a total crock of shit but that's the romance of the tabloids, I suppose. Thankfully, his hunting days are over, at least until he learns how to shoot left-handed that is.

I have been assured I'll be in this institution for life, I will have no chance of parole or early release and therefore, I must come to terms with what I have done. I, at this present moment in time am most certainly comfortable with what I have achieved and therefore, see no use in penance or have to undertake any kind of atonement for the crimes I have committed.

The doctors are making—according to them—great strides with me and are learning a great deal from my variation of psychosis. Well, that's all fine with me Doc, as I've said it's quite pleasant in here. No unreasonable customers with their absurd demands to deal with, no restaurant owners with their unrealistic expectations and no hotel inspectors with their utter pretentious bullshit.

I also found out that the competition was wound up following the trail of carnage I'd left in Northumberland and as some sort of compensation the money was split between the two remaining competitors Alex and Orry. Good for them, I thought; twenty-five grand a piece was not to be sniffed at. Orry had put a down payment on a house and Alex and her wife had gone into partnership with a new venture of Anglo/Asian fusion food, whatever the hell that entailed.

I also kept as many clippings as possible from the papers the orderlies brought me—illicitly obtained for me as I was not supposed to add to any of my so-called visions of grandeur apparently—of the unravelling of the Northumberland competition.

It had originally been billed as the greatest food competition and deemed the future to end all other "*previous inferior imposters*," until it had become an unmitigated disaster. Obviously, the best articles for myself were of the detailed articles pertaining to the carnage I had wrought, the highlights of one such article were:

Death and Torture in Northumberland

What made an aspiring chef snap; is the industry to blame? (Article written by Ben Saubers)

What can we learn from the happenings in the beautiful county of Northumberland during a new format of cooking/survival competition? How could this have been allowed to escalate into the carnage that we can now reveal. Where was the protection for the contestants and what can we expect for future competitions based with a similar premise? With no apparent motive, three men brutally tortured and murdered, one dead from exposure, one gunned down in mistaken identity and thankfully, one cold-blooded killer behind bars.

The victims have been named as:

Charlie (Bos) Dickens—chef—32, tortured and murdered in cold blood.
Joseph Pritchard—chef—38, tortured and murdered in cold blood.
William Cohen—chef—37, tortured and murdered in cold blood.
Phillip Schroder—presenter—52, gunned down in mistaken identity.
Harry Celestine—chef—54, died from exposure.

An elderly lady named locally as Hilda Stephenson—82—who has been a farmer in these parts for over fifty years was also knocked unconscious in a callous attack, but thankfully made a full recovery. She had managed to scare off the attacker and killer known locally as 36-year-old Jack Cunningham, who was also a chef and fellow competitor.

Another victim of the Competition Killer's *brutal reign of terror who survived was Cecil O Connelly—42. A local survival expert and advisor to the competition, he had managed to talk the killer Jack Cunningham out of the cabin for the police to make the arrest. A true hero who sustained multiple life changing injuries and underwent emergency surgery, where he had to have a kidney removed. Our thoughts and prayers go out to the families of the deceased and also to Mrs Stephenson and Mr O Connelly for a speedy recovery.*

The thing that stood out at me the most from that article was Schroder was only fifty-two, I thought I had been kind when I believed him to be mid-fifties. Also "Cecil O Connelly"—wow, what a name, very apt for an utter twat. You'll notice I also got the blame for Cohen's death, even though I pleaded my innocence over that one.

Another article, this one a great deal smaller, showed a photograph of the two "Winners", Orry and Alex, with a heading of:

Last Guys Standing (Written by Alice Cotton)

Alex Simmons—30, of Blakey Ridge Yorkshire and Orry Jones—24, of Sutton Coldfield Midlands, were the last two and eventual winners of the disastrous Northumberland competition. Where the now notorious Jack Cunningham aka The Competition Killer brutally tortured and murdered three of the competitors. Two others also lost their lives, one to mistaken identity and the other to the severe weather that Northumberland can spring upon you at this time of year.

Jack Cunningham is now serving life in the Highlands Institute for the Criminally Insane *dubbed "The Scottish Broadmoor".*

Because the competition had been immediately cut short, they had both been declared winners and each received a cheque for twenty-five thousand pounds. Alex said of the money, "Yes, the money will come in handy I've no doubt, but can I just say that I'd much prefer none of this had happened and my heartfelt condolences go out to the families."

Orry declined to comment and for such a young man may I the author, say he had a terribly haunted look to him, a look that belied his years. Clearly, the experience of this competition has left its mark not only on the deceased but on the survivors also. Another survivor who had thankfully left the competition early was Subi Kahn—25, he also declined to comment.

***

One other conciliation to come out of the competition was that I'd finally gotten onto mainstream television. I was on round the clock for weeks, albeit the local and national news. During my trial I also came forward and admitted to the killing of the kitchen porter in Jersey, the court was in uproar at this point which gave me no end of humour.

The clerks and police scurried off and within a day—after a description of said KP—they came back with the cold case from St. Helier and a hatful of witnesses such as the bed and breakfast owner, who just *knew* I wasn't right. The

KP's name had been Carlos Rodriguez. He was 38, Portuguese and left a wife and two kids (bet she was relieved).

I had somehow completely forgotten his name and had always just thought of him as my creepy little KP friend. The best thing is that after the first week of the trial Carlos came back to me and has been with me ever since. Through the rest of the trial he sat with me in the dock, always keeping vigil, at times he would even wander over to the judge and sit by his side, this caused me no end of amusement.   -

His appearance now is, as you can imagine, almost skeletal, a little rotting green flesh still hangs from his jaw and skull and as always, he's not the greatest conversationalist, but nevertheless, it is companionship of a sort. The best thing is that because I'm ensconced in this nuthouse, I can talk to him until my heart's content and no one cares a jot or asks silly questions.

Although one doctor seemed extremely interested in my relationship with Carlos and wanted to know what he looked like and if I felt threatened by him and such like. Did I feel that Carlos had come back for me to shadow me in some kind of purgatory?

What the hell is the doctor on about? Carlos is really low maintenance, so why living with a good friend was supposed to be purgatory, I will never know. At one point though, the doctor did ask if I was sure it was Carlos and was I not in fact conversing with the Devil?

Jesus, what do they think I am in here? Crazy!

The End